BETWIXTERS

Once Upon A Time

Book One in the Betwixters Series By

LAURA C. CANTU

Winterwolf Press
Las Vegas, Nevada

ALSO BY LAURA C. CANTU

Ole Grum's Tales: One Barmy Beetle

Xandria Drake: Ancient Rising

Viktor LaFontaine: Beautiful Games

Laura's Official Website:

www.LauraCCantu.com

Please visit Laura's website for more information
about Laura, the Betwixters, and to download
The Betwixters Workbook for Parents and Teachers

Laura's social media handle:

@LauraCCantu

BETWIXTERS
Once Upon A Time

Book One in the Betwixters Series By
LAURA C. CANTU

First Edition

Library of Congress Control Number: 2017904004
ISBN: 978-0-9885851-9-5

Books may be purchased by contacting the publisher and author at:

Winterwolf Press
8635 West Sahara Avenue, #425
Las Vegas, NV 89117
www.WinterwolfPress.com

Info@WinterwolfPress.com

Chapter art and Cover art by Laura C. Cantu: LauraCCantu.com
Betwixters Logo font by Imagex Fonts: Imagex-fonts.com
Interior formatting by Clark Kenyon
Cover design © 2017 by Laura C. Cantu
Cover art and Chapter art © 2017 by Laura C. Cantu

Every story in The Vathylite Realms is dedicated to my nieces and nephews.

You are my inspiration, my hope, and my love.

This book is for Noah.

May you know your heart, live your truth, and have the courage to always be yourself.

Brody's
Human Tales

Brody's Collection of Human Tales

The Fledgling Faerie Archives
Scroll 25
Tale 7

Woe to the Fae who do not believe,
a warning from Ambrosius Merlyn,
Keeper of Scrolls and Holder of Keys.

There's a drifter among us,
to which we are bound;
a creature of fugue
and ambition profound.

He stalks in the shadows
and dons many faces.
His name is Man,
the destroyer of races.

In times long past,
before the distortion,
there did exist Merlydon,
a realm of proportion.

The kingdoms of Elves,
of Faeries, of Gnomes;
and magical creatures,
called Merlydon home.

They were known as the Lydon,
the just and the fair.
They nurtured the earth,
and purified the air.

Their magic was pure.
Their hearts were so kind.
Then the breaking of One
brought twisting of minds.

The Bellwethers too,
did suffer vile fates.
And these bearers of light,
were forced into hate.

From their seats in Haventhrone,
these angels did flee.
The Chondours were born,
and brought victims to knees.

And lastly the humans,
the prey of fear's pangs,
some grew hairy faces,
while others white fangs.

Pure species no longer
exist on this earth.
And terror runs rampant
from death to rebirth.

—Former High Seat of the Betwixter Council, Keeper of Scrolls and Holder
of Keys,

Ambrosius Merlyn

PROLOGUE
The Birth of a New Day

A menacing glare from wicked, miserable eyes pierced the depths of Neevya's soul. She squirmed uncomfortably under its weight; her wings involuntarily shuddered.

"I found ye," the stranger spoke in a gravelly and sinister voice. "Tell me yer name, lass."

No matter how much she tried to resist, she felt an irrepressible desire to say, "Neevya."

"Ye don't say?" Yellow, decaying teeth hid behind his crooked sneer. "Me chondour will be best pleased to meet ye."

"Chondour?" She gasped, imagining a horrific winged demon crafted from pure evil. She'd never perceived a chondour before, but she'd seen numerous depictions of them in her childhood human tale scrolls. Scenes showing wars between chondours and their counterparts, those angelic beings known as bellwethers, plagued her inner sight. It was only a matter of seconds, however, before an even more worrisome idea infected her awareness. In those same scrolls, she recalled seeing images of legendary creatures more dangerous than even the chondours. They were supposedly so wicked, they had created all that was corrupt in the world, *including* the chondours. She searched the elderly stranger's dry and sagging wrinkles as realization hit her like a swarm of plump bumble bees. *He* looked like one of those abysmal monsters. He looked like a *human*.

Neevya woke with a jerk. Discombobulated and confused, she looked around, taking in her surroundings.

A relieved sigh escaped her lips as she wiped the sweat from her brow. "It wasn't real. It was just a night phantasm, thank Good Mother." There she was, nestled safe and sound inside a beautiful pink lily in the magical forest of Ayin, her home in the kingdom of Faerie.

The flower she had chosen as her bed for the night opened as Father Sun peeked over the horizon, and a Wake-Up Faerie sprinkled rays of sunshine over its lustrous petals. Like the Wake-Up Faerie, Neevya harvested beams of sunlight, but was thankful she didn't work in the Day-Dawning Department. She couldn't fathom how anyone could enjoy waking up while it was still dark outside, even if it was to birth a new day.

As the lily's petals stretched to greet the morning, so did Neevya; first, her pale-yellow legs, each one in turn, then her arms together, and finally, her shimmering pink and yellow wings. While she loved sleeping snug and warm, enveloped in the luxurious embrace of the flowers, the thing she loved most was waking to a brand-new day, full of potential.

The lily's stem bowed to drop Neevya gently to the forest floor, where the young faerie scooped a handful of dew from a blade of grass and splashed it over her face. The water was much colder than she anticipated, and her yelp startled Ole Grum, a wandering gnome who'd ventured out of the gnome kingdom of Gwyndovia. The squat fellow had been staying in Ayin these last few months. He, like many other gnomes she'd encountered, seemed to think every kingdom in the enchanted realm of Faeyelwen was his for the napping, including the kingdom of Faerie. Neevya couldn't fathom being so bold. Sure, she hoped to visit each region someday, but she wouldn't dare venture into other lands without invitation. The idea seemed ridiculous, and she giggled as she imagined dropping in on a couple of elven friends in their kingdom of Etorevyth.

"Uh-hum. What're you gigglin' on about? Can't you see I'm busy here?

Thought I'd found a peaceful snoozing spot, and then here you come along, bumbling around and making all kinds of racket. Don't you know not to bother an ole gnome when he's napping?" Ole Grum complained. He'd arrived with a gnomestool slung over one shoulder and declared that wherever he laid it down was his home. And who was Neevya to argue? She, like the other faeries, was a custodian of the forest, not its owner. If he wanted to stay, then he could. Maybe—just maybe—he wouldn't be so grumpy when he left.

"You faerie-folk, always flying about with your magic this and enchanted that. Can't you take the time to sit down for once?" Ole Grum rubbed his eyes. "There's nothing to prepare an old gnome for the day ahead like a fine sit-down after a good night's sleep."

Neevya slung her enchanted pouch over her shoulder and rose into the air. She hovered above the squat gnome's head and bent forward to look him right in his small, beady eyes.

"We each have a unique purpose, Mr. Grum, and mine is to bring nourishment and life-force to the plant-dwellers. When might I find time to rest? Not when Father Sun is awake, I'll tell you that. Furthermore, there's grass to comb, shrubs to feed, pollen to scatter, and buds to hatch. Do you think a beautiful forest like this happens by magic alone?"

"Doesn't it?" said the gnome, spluttering into his white beard.

"No, a lot of hard work goes into keeping the enchanted forest… well…enchanting. It simply won't do, lying about in a flower bed all day like *some* I could mention, especially with spring upon us."

Ole Grum got to his feet and wrung the dew from his hat. It had been pointy when he'd first arrived, but nowadays it flopped over to one side. He pulled it down hard on his head so that his ears stuck out under its large, floppy brim. He did his best to prop up its peak, but it still looked like a wilted weed, no matter how hard he tried.

"Spring, you say? It's about time we had some change in these parts. Winter's too cold for my liking. Snow's all well and good. Pretty, if you like that sort of thing, but you can't beat a good bit of sunshine." He locked his thumbs into his weathered suspenders and tilted back on his heels as he sniffed the air. "Well, I'll be. The scent of spring *is* in the air."

The very thought of spring made Neevya's heart soar. Spring was a time for new growth and change, a time to let go of old ideas and to create new, beautiful visions that would form the foundations on which the forest would thrive. It was also the busiest time of year for Neevya and her workmates from the Sunbeam Sector. Gathering enough sunlight during a season prone to cloudy skies and spring showers was quite challenging when there was so much new life to assist into the world, and nurturing new seedlings and sprouts was a vital part of their jobs. Likewise, it was the Sunbeam Sector's responsibility to help awaken those plant-dwellers which lay dormant through the winter. The forest must wake up, and although winter had its own chilly charms, Neevya would take blossoms over icicles any day.

"You'll see, Mr. Grum, this will be the most splendid spring ever."

"Well, you'd better get a move on then, hadn't ya? No point flapping your wings in my face when I've got some good resting up to do. Just think, you could be out there talking to blackberries, or whatever you lot get up to."

With that, Ole Grum sat back against his gnomestool and yanked the brim of his hat over his eyes, leaving just enough of a gap for him to watch the faerie zigzag off through the pollen-laden air.

"Bah! Faeries."

By the time Father Sun reached his zenith, Neevya began to wonder if she'd overdone it. Her wings ached and spluttered like tattered, whirling maple seeds. If she didn't land soon, she just might crash, and that would be dreadful.

All faeries took pride in their work, but Neevya went above and beyond the call of duty. Today was no different. She'd taken it upon herself to go farther into the enchanted woodlands of Ayin than she'd ever been before. Sure, there were the traveling faeries who roamed far and wide in beetle-drawn caravans, spreading life wherever they went, but even they couldn't be everywhere *all* the time.

Neevya thought about how pleased Mother Nature, more commonly called *Good Mother* by the Fae, would be with all the work she would accomplish, and a sense of adventure filled her heart. She threw her arms wide and let Father Sun's radiance fill her to the brim. It was his life-giving energy Neevya would take with her into the darker parts of the wood. Yet, to bring cheer to that kind of gloom she would have to do more than simply absorb radiance; she would have to capture a few super-sunbeams. The trick was to catch them unawares.

Neevya quickly flitted over to a lush maple tree and landed on one of its many branches. Tucking behind a bundle of budding leaves, she watched and waited for a super-sunbeam to appear. To her satisfaction, it didn't take long for a brilliant blaze of light to flash through the sky and she couldn't help but smile. This super-sunbeam was fast, bright, and full of potential. It would make a wonderful gift for a seedling in need of some extra love and attention. As the sunbeam approached, a rush of excitement coursed through Neevya's veins, fueling her enthusiasm until it seemed she would explode.

Her wings twitched.

The sunbeam stopped mid-motion and cautiously dimmed its light until only a faint shimmer remained. It was a cloaking mechanism she knew all too well. If she didn't make her move soon, the super-sunbeam would escape.

Neevya pounced.

Lunging forward with her hands outstretched, she grabbed for the super-sunbeam, but unexpectedly missed. The world suddenly became a blur of blues and greens as she spiraled out of control and barreled toward the forest floor. Luckily, she regained her balance just in time to keep from slamming into the spiky tangles of a wild blackberry bush.

Taking a moment to let the dizziness wear off, Neevya tentatively reached out and traced her fingers along one of the blackberry bush's many sharp and foreboding thorns, which were large enough to spear a faerie her size. An involuntary shudder ran the length of her body. "So much for doing it the hard way. I think it's time to break out my suncatcher."

Much like her dreamcatcher, Neevya's suncatcher consisted of a hoop made from whistled willow branches and a net of intricately laced faerie silk. Unlike the taut net on her dreamcatcher, however, her suncatcher's net fell loosely away from its hoop, creating an undulating, iridescent, bubble-like pocket.

With the remaining strength in her weary wings, Neevya hoisted herself into the air. She flew toward the tree tops until she reached an open patch of sky where she could clearly see Father Sun without obstruction. The climb was more difficult than she had expected, and she hovered in the unusually thick and heavy air for a long while, struggling to stay aloft. She couldn't remember ever having to fight so hard just to fly, fatigued or not. Was Sister Sky moody and messing with her? Or had Neevya finally reached her limit? She started to conclude that perhaps she was not as fit as she'd supposed, but that didn't explain the nagging feeling that was suddenly swelling in the pit of her stomach. Something was dreadfully off in the forest today. Something was out of balance.

More determined than ever, Neevya began waving her suncatcher through the air. Beautiful tones and melodies emitted from the faerie-silk as the wind coursed through the lace-like net. The melodies were irresistible to super-sunbeams, and would attract them like gold attracts leprechauns. The downside was that the tunes could hoodwink faeries as well. If she paid too close attention to them, she might get caught in their spell and find herself bamboozled for up to three days. She knew from experience that that could be quite embarrassing.

The task was difficult, but she pulled it off. Her enchanted pouch was soon filled to the brim and popping at the seams, jam-packed with squirming super-sunbeams. Relieved to finally relax her wings, she descended to land on a gnarled root of an ancient oak. The uneasy feeling in her stomach unexpectedly dissipated. Pleased, she smiled, stretched her arms wide, and hugged the tree. "Good afternoon, Mr. Oak. You're in for a treat today. Just wait to see what I've brought you."

Careful not to let any escape, Neevya extracted two radiant sunbeams from her pouch and massaged them into the old tree's roots.

"Now, doesn't that feel delightful? I bet you didn't expect sunbeam delivery service today."

Neevya patted the oak's weathered trunk. "Ah well, it's the least I can do for a great oak like yourself. But you'll have to excuse me. I must be on my way. You have a wonderful day, you hear?"

Neevya didn't wait for a response. Most trees, especially old ones, could take a very long time to speak, and she didn't have a moment to spare if she hoped to be back in time for the evening feast. As Neevya walked away she happened to spot a fallen acorn, its hull dull and weathered.

She bent down, plucked it from between the old tree's roots, and began polishing its exterior. "Don't you worry, Mr. Oak. She may look a little worn, but she's unusually powerful. I'll be sure to find her the perfect home." Tucking the acorn into her pouch so it could marinate in sunbeams, she continued on her way.

Before long, Neevya arrived at a stream. Its brilliant blue water bubbled and churned down a twisted, narrow ravine. She considered crossing, but quickly thought better of it, content to walk along its banks and enjoy the playful melodies of some nearby water nymphs.

A few songs into her walk, she spotted a purple nymph basking in the sunlight on the stream's bank. "Excuse me, Miss Nymph, I want to let you know I think your singing is divine. If it's no trouble, might I make a request?"

The nymph hastily hopped into the water and fled without a single backward glance.

Neevya thought she must have scared the poor thing. In fact, she figured she must have scared the lot of them, because suddenly there was no more music to be heard.

She looked down and mumbled, "Oops. Sorry, friends."

At that moment, her gaze landed on the perfect spot to plant the acorn. She clapped her hands and jumped up and down with glee; just the thought of the little acorn blossoming into a great oak tree, living a vibrant life, and bringing shade to the creatures in the woodland made Neevya's heart burst with delight, causing her pale-yellow skin to glow. But there was one tiny problem. When she fluttered her wings and tried to lift herself from the ground, nothing happened. She tried again, and then four more times. It was no use. Her wings were too tired and sore for even the shortest flight.

Frowning, she looked at the acorn's prospective new home. It wasn't anyone's fault that the ideal spot for the seedling happened to be on the opposite side of the now-menacing stream. "Not so charming now, are you, Miss Stream?" she mumbled. "Funny how perspective changes things."

Neevya needed to think. How might she get across?

I wonder if there are any grasshoppers nearby.

She made the customary whistle to summon a possible hopper and waited for one of her oversized friends to show up and allow her onto its back, but none came. Neevya paced and deliberated. "What to do? What to do?"

Hopeful that a better spot to plant the seedling—or at least one just as good—might present itself, Neevya glanced around. She headed toward an area that looked suitable, and although it wasn't as inviting as the one on the other side of the stream, she figured it might do.

She bent to ask permission from Good Mother for the planting, but quickly straightened, chastising herself.

How could you, Neevya? You promised that old oak you would find the perfect home, and by the light of Father Sun, that's what you're going to do!

There was no way she could bring herself to settle for anything less than the sunny bank with plush grass and dark, rich-looking soil.

Neevya stepped up to the bank and examined her options as she gave herself a pep talk.

"I can do this. It's just a nice little stream."

She dipped her toe into the water and shivered.

"*Brr...*a nice little stream full of ice cold water. Not a problem. Nymphs do it all the time."

She found a crossing point that seemed promising and worked up her courage. "Hold on tight, little acorn. Here we go." She stepped into the frigid water.

Icy currents engulfed Neevya's ankles and swirled violently around her legs. The stream bed suddenly gave way under her feet, causing her to slip backward into the water with a splash. She furiously tried to bat her wings and instinctively grabbed onto a nearby vine, but it dislodged, leaving an intimidating pile of foliage to hang directly over her. She barely managed to wrap her wings around her body before the pile collapsed on top of her, plunging her underwater.

If fear existed within her heart, this would have been the moment for it to take hold. But like most young faeries, fear was as foreign to her as plastic spoons, jelly beans, and friendly trolls.

The only thing she could think of was the poor little acorn trapped in her pouch. She'd been so keen to give it a helping hand, and now here she was, completely helpless, being carried downstream. Her head popped above water and she gasped for air. Her wings were too wet to be useful, so she did her best to swim to shore. Like most creatures born to fly, she wasn't the greatest swimmer. She paddled as fiercely as she could, but the current was just too strong.

This stream must stop somewhere. It can't just go on forever.

The more she considered her predicament, the more she realized she had no idea where this stream went. Perhaps it was one of those lazy rivers Ole Grum had been reminiscing about a few weeks back. According to him, lazy rivers went 'round and 'round, with no beginning and no end.

That would be terrible!

In a burst of effort, Neevya fought against the current. Gradually, the shore came closer. Now all she had to do was latch onto an exposed root or a tuft of grass and she could pull herself to safety.

Downstream, Neevya spied a small tree growing along the bank.

She praised Good Mother. It was *exactly* what she needed. She lined herself up to float directly into the path of one of its roots. As chance would have it, that was the moment she noticed something peculiar. The landscape looked distorted, as though a transparent bubble overlapped the stream. The tree's roots that protruded from the bank were skewed, and they didn't quite match up with where they hit the surface of the water. Stranger still, a whole section of the stream and the bank appeared stretched.

What in the realm of Faeyelwen could that possibly be?

Neevya squinted, focusing on the area.

Her breath suddenly caught in her throat as she realized what she was seeing.

"Oh no! Not a Precarious Portal!" she gasped, choking down water.

Coughing, Neevya paddled furiously and reached for anything that might help her escape. She'd been warned about Precarious Portals. They could lead anywhere, and some of the nastier ones, known as Permutation Precarious Portals, had the power to strip all the joy from a faerie's heart and transform her into…

No! Anything but that!

Neevya reached out. Her fingers clamped around a small vine and she pulled as hard as she could.

Instead of towing Neevya to safety, the vine rushed at her, entangling her wrists.

Good Mother!

A giant wave suddenly hovered over her, like a great king cobra ready to strike. Neevya inhaled sharply. The wave crashed down on her, driving her into the stream's gloomy depths. She fought to free her hands and kicked with all her might, but it was no use. The icy water pressed on her with the weight of a dozen caravan beetles. The stream continued to sweep her along its rocky bottom toward the portal.

If she had the choice between going through the portal or dying at the bottom of the stream, Neevya would have preferred death. But the stream didn't ask.

A rush of bubbly water suddenly hit her, spinning her into a whirlpool and loosening the vine that entrapped her arms. The vine fell away as if it had never been there. A current of warm water plucked her out of the whirlpool's spiral and flung her upward. She soared through the air, and to her dismay, she landed right back in the turbulent stream.

Neevya paddled wildly, arms flailing and feet kicking.

Down the stream she went, eyes fixed on her unavoidable destiny.

Yielding to her misfortune, she figured there was one last thing she needed to do before leaving her home and all she knew.

With great sorrow, Neevya hastily pushed her farewells into the consciousness of every plant-dweller in the vicinity.

Goodbye, dear friends.

She sent the plants feelings of love mixed with grief that she would no longer be able to assist in their growth and development.

She was surprised to feel an ancient presence waft into her awareness. Its whisper was soft and kind.

As a tokken of myyy grattitttude, pleeaasse acccept myyy giiiiftt.

A strong sense of calm suddenly passed over Neevya. It was a peace like none she had ever experienced. For a moment, she felt as though everything was right in the world, exactly as it should be. She was grateful for the gift of serenity, but it didn't keep a question from tugging at her mind.

Before she got sucked away, she wished to know one last thing.

Who are you?

She reached out to the ancient and powerful presence with her mind.

A whisper as calm as a summer's breeze floated to her attention.

Thaankk yoouu for waatching oovveerr myyy seeedling.

Neevya whispered, "Mr. Oak?" right before she squeezed her eyes shut and hugged her pouch tightly to her chest.

The stream hurled Neevya through the portal.

CHAPTER ONE
The Promise

Little did Noah Walters know that his dilapidated stone house, which he supposed was quite possibly as old as the Giza pyramids, was once an outpost known as Evwin; a meeting place for faeries, humans, and bellwethers. He didn't even know what a bellwether was. Why should he? He didn't pay attention to silly stories about faeries or other magical creatures. That kind of nonsense was not for twelve-year-old boys like Noah. Aliens, on the other hand, seemed much more plausible. After all, Noah was a man of science, just like his father.

Noah glanced up from his computer screen and peered out the window. "Where are you, Dad?" Dark storm clouds enveloped the moon, causing ominous shadows to slither across the ground; his stomach sank. He glanced over his shoulder at Madison, a salt-and-pepper mini-schnauzer resting on his pillow. "Something must be wrong, girl. He never works this late."

She tilted her head and looked at him with seeming anticipation.

Intent on going downstairs, he glanced at the door and stood. If anyone could ease his worries, it was his mother, but there was one tiny problem—he was supposed to be asleep and might get in trouble for being awake this late on a school night. Sitting back down in his computer chair with a sigh, Noah balled his hands into nervous fists. "I just wish Dad would come home." He turned to Madison. "Do you think he's okay?" Just as he was about to throw caution to the wind and head downstairs—despite the possible consequences—a sinister laugh cackled from his computer speakers. He cringed at the noise and hastily pushed the mute button. Turning back to his monitor, his eyes settled on his digital enemy.

"Oh, no you don't!" Noah hissed as his fingers flew across the keyboard. He punched several key combinations, bombarding his opponent with magic spells and bottles of exploding potions. Just when he thought he might lose, he unleashed his secret weapon and hurled it across the battlegrounds, squarely striking his foe. "Gotcha!" His grin widened as his nemesis disappeared in a bright flash, leaving behind only a wisp of digital smoke.

"Who's laughing now?" Noah reveled in his victory, albeit at a whisper. "That'll teach you to mess with Noahmadeus the Great!"

He rubbed his eyes, not because he was tired, but because he had been staring at his computer screen for over four hours while playing his new game, *Empire of Elderealm,* and waiting for his dad to come home, or at least call. Just as he moved his character into the Caverns of Oblivion, the squeaking brakes of his father's car sounded in the driveway. His heart leapt as he quickly saved his game, put his computer to sleep, and hopped into bed.

Madison whimpered and darted from the room, her claws tapping on each step as she made her way downstairs to greet Mr. Walters.

Clatters of the front door opening and closing travelled up the stairwell. Relief that his dad was safely home spread through him, but was quickly followed by frustration. His mom's muffled, "What kept you so late?" and what sounded like a brief discussion, followed by his mom saying, "I'll let Madison out while you go up and talk to him," let Noah know his father would sneak in to say good night, even at this late hour. He peeked through his eyelashes, watching his father quietly approach his bed.

Mr. Walters knelt and gently nudged Noah's shoulder. "You awake, kiddo?"

Noah opened one eye and looked at the clock; it was well past midnight. He rolled over, turning his back to his father. "You missed my birthday, Dad."

"I know, and I'm sorry. I just…"

He waited for his father to say more, but an ocean of silence swelled between them, becoming more and more turbulent with each passing second. Surges of sadness swirled around Noah like a category four hurricane, and he felt as if he were a tiny sailboat being tossed in its waves; if he didn't say something soon, he'd be doomed to sink. Fighting back tears, he peeked over his shoulder. "You've never missed my birthday before."

His father let his hand slide from Noah's shoulder as he turned his head away and sighed. Droplets of rainwater hung suspended from a few strands of his dark, wavy hair. They glistened like tiny jewels in the dim light from the hallway.

Noah rolled over and faced him. "Did I do something wrong? Is that why you didn't come to my party?"

"No." His father's regretful expression did nothing to help Noah feel less disappointed.

"Don't ever think that. You're my boy. You could never do anything that would make me miss your birthday."

"Then why didn't you come home?"

His father slowly shook his head. A bead of water splashed onto Noah's face. "I wish I could tell you. Top secret stuff, you know?"

He ruffled Noah's straight black hair, trying to lighten the mood.

Noah pushed his hand away. He didn't care if his dad was assigned to some kind of top secret mission or not. "You said the whole reason we moved here was because you wouldn't have to work so much. This was my first birthday party in England, a birthday I'll remember for the rest of my life because it's my first one outside of the United States, and you couldn't even call."

Mr. Walters sighed. "I know, and I don't expect you to understand. This job is just different than I anticipated. It's important."

"More important than me, apparently." Noah said under his breath, too quiet for his father to hear. He knew his father's job had something to do with investigating unsolved cases for an international private security firm in Herogate, England. It sounded like deep, undercover spy stuff to Noah. Before reclaiming his civilian status a few years prior, Allen Walters had served in the United States Air Force, which meant the family moved every two years or so. He'd even worked for the National Security Agency for a while. When he quit his job at the NSA and relocated his family to Herogate, however, he promised they would not move again, even if it meant another change in careers. He also promised to be around more often. Noah had been excited about the prospect of staying put for once, but if it meant seeing even less of his dad, he didn't know if it was worth it.

He tried to imagine what it would be like to have his father around more, but when it came down to it, how could Noah blame him, really? From what little he could discern from the few comments his father had made, Mr. Walters had some pretty amazing technology at his fingertips. Noah had spent countless hours daydreaming about all the cool toys his dad got to play with. He reasoned that if *he* had the chance to mess around with supercomputers, the newest gadgets, high-powered workstations, and advanced alien technologies, he wouldn't come home, either.

A rumble of thunder rolled across the sky as gusts of wind caressed the eaves, producing low-pitched howls. Rain pelted against the old, flimsy windowpanes in his bedroom.

Noah looked up. "The clouds are weeping." It was a phrase his mom had used when he was little, before he knew what rain was, and now it was a family saying.

His father quickly glanced out the window. "This can't be. It followed me home."

Noah suddenly noticed the fear in his dad's eyes. Why hadn't he seen it before? He shuddered in spite of himself. "*What* followed you home?"

He wondered if his dad actually *did* have a good reason for missing his birthday. "Answer me, Dad. What's out there? Why are you so scared?"

His father took a moment to look him over, as if sizing him up. "My boy's no fool." He stood and prodded Noah. "Scooch over for your old man."

Noah scooted just enough to give his dad room to sit.

Mr. Walters sat on the edge of the bed and tried to smile, but his would-be grin didn't reach his eyes.

He was stalling; Noah knew it. "Tell me the truth; why did you miss my birthday, and why do you look like you've seen a ghost?"

"A ghost?" his dad scoffed and stared down at his twiddling thumbs. "A more appropriate term might be monster, I think." He spoke as if Noah wasn't even there. "What else could do something like that? I've never seen anything like it."

Noah sat upright. "A monster! *Seriously?*" All thoughts of his dad missing his birthday fell by the wayside.

Mr. Walters opened his mouth and started to speak, but quickly snapped his jaw shut.

Noah clenched his covers to his chest and waited for his father to say more, but he just sat there in silence. When he couldn't contain his apprehension any longer, Noah tentatively asked, "Monsters? Real live monsters? Here in Herogate?"

His father looked straight into his eyes, his gaze so intense Noah felt as if lasers might shoot from his dad's pupils at any second and fry his brain.

Noah looked away.

"Son, I wish I could tell you, but I can't. Just trust me when I say it's for your own good. There are some things no boy should know."

Noah spoke before he could stop himself, "What kind of lame answer is that?"

His father looked just as stunned as Noah felt.

Noah cleared his throat. "I mean, that doesn't make any sense. I'm not a kid anymore. I'm twelve now, remember? If there really are monsters out there, don't you think that's something I should definitely know?

What if I run across one? How do I defend myself? What are they, exactly? Can they fly? Are we safe here, in our house? How many are there? Are they just here in Yorkshire? Or are they all over England? Or maybe, the world!"

His dad abruptly stood and swept his hand across the sheets, wiping away stray raindrops. "That's enough. I've said too much already. I just came in to say goodnight. Now go to sleep."

"But, Dad!"

"I said, that's enough! No more questions."

Noah slammed his body into the bed and turned his back on his father with a huff. "Fine, who cares if I get eaten by monsters, anyway? Obviously not you. You can't even make it home for my birthday."

His dad walked to the door, but stopped just shy of its threshold. "Maybe you're right."

"What?" Noah turned around, utterly surprised.

"I said, you're right. You're not a child anymore. You're growing into a young man, and I suppose I can tell you this one thing."

Noah sat up, eager to hear the news.

His father held up a finger. "Mind you, I can't tell you much. It's top secret, and I don't want to lose my job or get in trouble with my bosses. So don't ask questions I can't answer."

"I understand." Noah nodded, eyes wide.

His father acknowledged Noah with a tilt of his head and then paced the room. "Promise me you won't go in that forest, the one near your school."

"You mean The Dark Wood? A few kids at school were talking about a man who was recently found with deep gashes all over his body right outside that forest. I thought they were just trying to scare us."

Mr. Walters seemed to mull Noah's comment over in his mind.

Waiting for his dad to say something, Noah slumped, deep in thought. Were the rumors true?

"Noah?" His father searched for his attention. "That forest is dangerous. Promise me right here and right now that you'll stay out of it."

"But, what about—"

"I said no questions; now give me your word!"

A flash of lightning bounced off the bedroom walls, directly followed by a deafening explosion of thunder. His dad whirled around, spreading his arms wide as if to protect Noah from whatever was about to crash through the window, but nothing came. He spun back around to face Noah, his eyes desperate. "Give me your word, now!"

"Okay! Okay! I promise!" Noah recoiled; an irrepressible shudder ran down his spine.

Stamping footsteps echoed through the hallway. "What's going on in here?" Noah's mother rushed into the room. Her Chinese accent was thick, and her almond-shaped eyes were full of concern.

At the sound of her voice, his father stiffened. Locking eyes with Noah, his dad gave him a look that told him to keep his mouth shut. "Nothing. Nothing's wrong."

She crossed her arms and lifted her chin high; her long black hair was draped over one shoulder. "That didn't sound like nothing."

His dad lightheartedly rubbed the top of Noah's head. "We were just trying to reach an understanding. Isn't that right, Son?"

Noah cleared his throat as he struggled to keep his chin from quivering. "Yeah, that's right. No big deal."

Noah's mom placed her delicate hand on her husband's shoulder as she stepped past him. Her eyes were tender when she bent down and gently cupped Noah's chin in her palm. In Mandarin, her native language, she asked, "Are you okay? Is there anything you wish to tell me?"

Noah chanced a quick glance at his dad. Even though his father could not speak the language, it didn't keep a moment of understanding from passing between them. Noah withdrew from his mother's touch and rested his head on his pillow. "*Wǒ hěn hǎo*," he said, which meant, "I am fine."

"Well, I'm always here if you need me," his mom continued to speak in her native tongue as she kissed his cheek. "I love you."

"I love you too, Mom." This time, Noah answered her in English.

She took Mr. Walters' hand in hers. "Come, he needs to sleep if he's going to wake in time for school tomorrow."

His father backed away.

Noah pulled the covers up to his chin. "'Night, Mom. Night, Dad."

"Sweet dreams." His mom smiled and stepped through the doorway.

"Good night, Son." His father turned to leave the room, but Mrs. Walters nudged his side and whispered something Noah couldn't hear.

His dad closed his eyes and clenched his jaw. Noah could barely make out his murmur, "Can't believe I almost forgot."

Slowly turning to meet Noah's eyes, he forced a smile. "Happy birthday, buddy."

Just as he was about to close the bedroom door, Madison dashed into the room, hopped onto the bed, and nestled into Noah's arms; he was glad to have her with him, especially on a stormy night like this.

The door closed, shrouding the room in darkness.

Noah scrubbed his fingers through the fur around Madison's snout. "At least *you* have time for me."

Madison growled playfully and nipped at his hands.

He rolled onto his back and stared at the ceiling, which was dotted with glow-in-the-dark stars. Madison climbed onto his chest and settled in. She nibbled on his fingers as he imagined how his new best friends, Skye and Ethan, would react when he told them what his dad had said.

Thunder rumbled overhead, echoing the storm brewing inside his mind.

A sudden screech, long and drawn out, erupted at his window. He yanked his covers over his head, sending Madison reeling to the floor. She landed on her feet and dashed to the window, barking wildly. He imagined a monster tracing sharp claws down the windowpanes. The howling wind confirmed his suspicion that there was in fact a huge and bloodthirsty beast right outside his window instead of just a weathered old tree.

Madison jumped back onto the bed and pressed her body to his.

Visions of werewolves, vampires, zombies, slimy beasts with tentacles and razor-sharp talons, and other terrible monsters plagued Noah's imagination. If his visions even remotely resembled what might be lurking in that forest, he definitely intended to keep his word to his father.

Years later, Noah would recall that promise and sigh; it was doomed from the start. When Fate steps in, everyone is at her mercy, promises or not.

CHAPTER TWO
The Outsiders

The old man's breath came out in puffs of white clouds as he raced through the frigid night air. Wind snaked through rustling branches and caused the forest canopy to sway as if the trees were made of rubber. His muscles burned, but that didn't slow him down. A portal had opened somewhere nearby, he could feel it in his bones. All he had to do was find it and kill whatever had traveled through it. He hoped it was that faerie he had met in his dreams. What was her name again? Neb? Neev? No, that wasn't it. He stopped running and plunged his hand into his pocket. "Neevya," he whispered. "That were her name." Somehow, he knew she was the cause of all the trouble he sensed coming his way. He had felt it approaching for months—a huge black, storm-like premonition that roiled with deception and danger. It was a storm he was set on thwarting, even if it meant unleashing the chondour he had trapped in his dungeon. He pulled his hand out of his pocket and inspected a small iron trap. "If she comes through these here parts, this ought take care of 'er." He stooped, placed the trap on the ground, and covered it with a dry, dead leaf.

An eerie howl echoed in the distance. It was a cry that made him cringe. He'd heard it before, about eight years ago, and he knew death was sure to follow. As much as he had tried, he'd never figured out where it came from or what manner of creature had made it. But there was one thing he did know for sure; a common wolf didn't make that kind of sound. He started to run toward the howl to investigate, but abruptly stopped to cast a faerie attracting spell over his snare and to make sure his trap was set just right.

The howl came again, this time louder. He glanced over his shoulder and rushed toward it.

Noah's alarm sounded.

Shocked it was already time for school, he bolted from his computer chair. Throughout most of the night, he had found it difficult to sleep; the storm was way too loud, and every time he closed his eyes he was plunged into a nightmare. So instead of laying anxiously in bed, fretting about which monster might cast the next shadow over his window, he'd decided to get up and distract himself by playing his new video game. Thankfully, the diversion worked; he got so caught up in trying to figure out a particularly tricky magic spell, he hadn't even noticed it was getting light outside.

Stretching and yawning, Noah looked over to see Madison curled up on his pillow. It was a typical sight that made him feel silly about fixating on monsters that probably didn't even exist, regardless of what his father had said. He figured his dad must've been working too many long hours, and the lack of sleep was getting to his head.

"Morning, girl." Noah said, surprised at how awake and upbeat he felt.

The schnauzer's ears twitched, and she acknowledged him with a tilt of her head.

"Go outside? Go potty?" He asked in a way that was special to only him and his bestie.

Madison darted off the bed and stood by his feet, her tail wagging so violently it shook her entire body.

Noah chuckled as he opened his door and headed downstairs. "You're such a good girl, Miss Madison. Let's go out and then I'll get you some food."

Madison made a trilling sound that reminded Noah of a bird as she hopped from stair to stair.

"Thanks for singing for me, Madi-girl. You know I love your songs almost as much as I love you." He walked into the kitchen and paused at the back door. Madison placed her front paws on his thighs. He bent forward, kissed her forehead, and opened the back door.

Madison darted past him. Noah thought he couldn't ask for a better companion, even as he stepped outside to make sure she did her business.

Just as he turned to go back into the kitchen, Mrs. Walters entered the room, making Noah jump.

"You scared me." He stepped through the doorway.

She studied him with a calm demeanor. "Oh, sorry. Did you sleep well?"

"Yeah." Noah gave her a hug, hoping she wouldn't ask about what happened the night before; that was the last thing he wanted to talk about. "How about you?"

She hugged him back, fetched a bowl, and scooped rice from a pot she'd been heating on the stove. "That was quite the storm last night."

Noah shrugged. "Yeah, it reminded me of the tornadoes back in Missouri."

His mom smiled, set the bowl on the table, and handed him a spoon. Noah blew on the rice to cool it down. He reminisced as he ate his breakfast.

Besides Madison, Mimi Walters was the only constant in his life. With his dad always darting off on one military mission or another and the family moving from one city to the next, she'd spent countless hours helping him with his science projects, taking him to museums and concerts, and playing with him in the backyard when he had yet to make any friends in whatever new city they found themselves.

He had fond memories of sitting by her side as she told him about their relatives in China. She had spent countless hours teaching him to speak Mandarin, which they took advantage of when they wanted a bit of privacy. They'd spent so much time together he'd gotten to the point where he could read her like a book. He figured he could tell *exactly* what she was thinking at any given moment as long as he could see her face.

Madison pawed at the door, pulling him out of his daydream. He pushed himself away from the table and let her inside.

Reaching into a jar on the counter, Noah winked and pulled out a treat.

Madison barked excitedly, stood on her hind legs, and performed a twirling trick he'd taught her when she was a pup.

That's when he remembered. "Oh no, Skye's dance video!"

Skye's foot slipped off the edge of a stone, causing her to tumble off the uneven rubble left by the ruins of a sheep shed. She was glad for the thin mattress she'd placed on the ground before attempting her latest dance routine. It was the third time she'd found herself sprawled across the cushion, but she wasn't about to let a little thing like that discourage her. She was determined to perform her choreography just right, and if that meant a few injuries along the way, so be it.

"Daft things are slippery," Skye mumbled.

Ethan, one of her two best friends, gestured to the clouds. "At least it stopped rainin'." He reached into his pocket and unwrapped a piece of taffy. Popping it into his mouth, he chewed and said, "I'd 'ate t' fink o' missin' a good torm justta 'elp you 'ith 'is 'aft ideo."

"What'd you say?" Ethan's cockney accent was difficult enough to understand, but with him chomping on a piece of candy, Skye considered herself lucky if she heard one word right.

Ethan's jaw worked hard for several moments as he chewed and swallowed. "I *said*, I'd hate t' think of missing a good storm just to help you with this *daft* video."

"It's pronounced *think*; T-h-i-n-k. Not *fink*." Teasing Ethan about his accent got him every time. Skye smirked, but the tiny triumph wasn't terribly satisfying.

He scowled. "Hey, we agreed. Making fun of the way I talk is off limits. That's below the belt."

She shrugged him off, figuring he deserved it. Even though she was used to Ethan's jests, each time he made a joke about her video, it was like a small jab to her heart. She *needed* this. She needed to win back her father's love and make him proud. If only she could become a superstar, she was sure he would return and they would be a family again. *Everybody loved celebrities*, she reasoned.

Skye climbed onto the wet pile of rubble and combed her fingers through her disheveled hair, separating her pink braids from her long black mane. Unwavering, she said, "You'd better be filming all of this. I don't want to break a leg only to find out you didn't press record."

Grinning, Ethan joked, "*What*? You never said anything about filming it!"

Skye raised one eyebrow and shot him a withering look. "Don't mess with me, Ethan Castleton. This is serious business. The casting agents for *Britain's ExtravaDance* are going to love me. I'll get my audition. You'll see."

"Whatever, Skye Williams. Why would you want to be on a stupid show like that, anyway?" Ethan shot back.

"It's number one right now. How stupid can it be?"

Ethan picked up a small stone and chucked it into a nearby puddle of water. "Anyone with half a brain knows it's next to impossible to get on that show. We're wastin' our time."

"Nothing's impossible." Skye pointed to the ground and stomped. "And I don't care what anyone thinks or how long it takes."

"Well, at this rate it's gonna take forever." Ethan searched for another stone.

"Oh, that reminds me, have you heard from Noah?" Skye looked toward the road, hoping to see his bobbing head appear just over the next hill. "He should've been here by now."

Ethan picked up a pebble. "I got a text from him late last night, something about that game I gave him for his birthday. I wouldn't count on him showin' up." He tossed the stone onto the pile of rubble.

Skye crossed her arms and struck a pose, her leg extended to the side. "Fine, his loss."

Ethan raised his smart phone and framed Skye in his digital display. "Don't know how you're gonna get an audition if you can't even get to the end of the song. Do you really have to dance on these stones? It looks *chet*, but not chet enough for a broken arm."

Chet was a word Ethan used to express any sort of emotion he wanted to emphasize. Originally, he'd claimed to have invented it because he got tired of getting in trouble for accidentally cursing in front of his parents and teachers. But nowadays, he used it for just about anything, including when he thought something was cool. It had even caught on in his family, and although she never said so, Skye thought he said it way too often.

"Ethan, Ethan, Ethan." She clicked her tongue with exaggerated weariness. "It's a cutthroat world out there, and the only way I'm going to stand out is if I have a gimmick. I need something with a twist. Any old nutter can dance in front of a camera, but who else has a location like this?" Skye gestured to the demolished sheep shed.

Ethan glanced around. "That's barmy, that is. One of these times, you're gonna miss the mattress, and I'll be the one hauling your body to the chettin' morgue." He bent forward, stretching his back. "I don't think me spine can handle that kind of stress today."

Skye placed her hand on her hip. "So you think it's ridiculous, do you? Stand up straight when I'm talking to you!"

Ethan reluctantly stopped stretching.

Satisfied that she had his full attention, she said, "Tell me, when have you ever seen a beautiful black girl busting some fabulous moves in a magnificent setting like this?"

Ethan shook his head and raised his phone for yet another take. "Never," he lowered his voice, "and at this rate I don't think I ever will."

"I heard that." Skye started the music and moved into position, waiting for her cue. "Now, be sure you make me look good."

"I can't make miracles happen, love."

Skye pretended not to hear him.

"You do realize that we have school in like…" Ethan looked at his phone, "half an hour, right?"

"And you do realize that if you say one more word, I'm going to come over there and introduce you to my fists? Now, get filming. This is the one." Skye bit her lip to keep from smiling at the look of exasperation on Ethan's face. Then she danced her heart out.

Ethan trembled at the sight of Herogate High School. It wasn't so much the lessons that bothered him. It was the bullies, and the school was full of them.

Tyrants patrolled the hallways, lunchrooms, and toilets; it seemed they had special abilities to seek out and intimidate anyone who was *different*. Ethan didn't think he looked any different from the others; if anything, he was the most normal looking kid in the school. Well, perhaps he *was* a bit good-looking, *thank you very much*. Even a few older girls occasionally flirted with him, but they quickly lost interest. He and his friends were only in Year Seven, after all. Noah kept calling it sixth grade, which Ethan teased him about. If he saw signs that Noah was getting too frustrated by the taunts, however, he would quickly turn the attention back to himself and joke about how his stylish blond hair, athletic build, and keen fashion sense were wasted on kids his own age. Skye often joined in, sarcastically comparing him to one celebrity or another. Ethan feigned modesty, but inside, he loved the attention. After all, it took work to look this good.

Nothin' to see here folks, move along.

The Outsiders

Waiting near the iron gate at the back of their school, Skye leaned against the school's stone wall. "Noah really should've been here by now. He was supposed to meet us ages ago. Do you see him anywhere?" She gestured to Stillwater Street, the inconspicuous road that served as the city's eastern border. It was the longest, curviest, and most dangerous road in town. It snaked around hills and along the edges of a vast, thick forest as if it were an invisible winding fence, separating the town from the woodlands. The school sat on the street's southern rim, while Noah's house was nestled among its hilly coils beyond the far side of the forest and at the town's north-eastern border.

"I'm sure he's fine. He'll be here soon," Ethan said, although he wasn't entirely certain.

Skye pushed herself from the wall and walked through the gate, squinting as she searched the school's entrance. "Maybe he's gone inside without us."

"Well, maybe if we hadn't spent all morning trying to make you the next chettin' *Britain's ExtravaDance* star, we wouldn't have missed him." Ethan adjusted the tie of his dark blue school uniform.

"I'm going to get on that show. Mark my words. When people check out my mad skills, they'll be like 'Ouch! Move over! New girl's in town.'"

"Right. Nothin' says mad skills like a girl fallin' on a mattress."

Skye looked over her shoulder, ignoring him. She had a habit of doing that.

Ethan spotted a small figure darting toward them on Stillwater Street. There was no mistaking the scrawny, half-Chinese kid with an oversized school uniform and a huge backpack that made him sway back and forth as he ran.

Ethan smiled and pointed. "Here's the chet now."

Panting and huffing, Noah came to a quick stop, clinging to Ethan for support.

"Where were you this morning?" Skye crossed her arms firmly over her chest.

Noah spoke haltingly between gulps of air, "Sorry. Lost track of time. Couldn't sleep. Stayed up all night. Got my character to level 90."

Ethan patted Noah's back. "Aww, poor baby couldn't sleep? Scared of a li'l storm?"

Noah straightened and scowled at Ethan. Then he focused on Skye. "Sorry, Skye. Really. I didn't mean to miss your video. My dad got home late." He paused. "And he was acting all freaked out. Made me promise never to go in *there*." He gestured to the forest with his thumb. "I think there's all kinds of monsters and stuff in those woods."

Skye frowned. "Really Noah, monsters? What are you, like five years old? Get off it."

"But what about that storm? Tell me you didn't think *that* was normal."

Skye shrugged. "Define normal."

"Blimey! That storm was amazing! Did you hear the thunder?" Ethan couldn't contain his enthusiasm.

Noah threw up his hands. "Amazing? Are you kidding? That thing had a life of its own. Besides, every time I see a cumulonimbus cloud I get nervous." He rubbed his arms as if trying to thwart an attack of oncoming goose bumps.

Skye nudged Noah. "A cumulo-what? You're such a geek. Until I met you, I thought Americans were cool."

Noah nudged her back. "I didn't mean to burst your bubble. Imagine my surprise when I found out you Brits weren't all geniuses. And to think I was afraid I might not measure up in the brains department. Boy, was I wrong."

Unable to resist, Ethan stepped up. "Isn't your dad American, Skye? And your mum English? I guess that explains why you're not cool *or* smart."

Ethan had been reliably informed that looks couldn't kill, but if they could, Skye's dagger-spitting stare could have finished both him and Noah off in a heartbeat.

"Are you coming inside now?" she said with the kind of calm that only made her more menacing. "Because if I hang around with you two idiots one more second, I may just snap." She snapped her fingers with loud emphasis.

Ethan flinched and quickly looked to see if Noah had noticed. Noah's snigger said it all.

Ethan frowned and tried to think of something witty to say that would get under Skye's skin. There were few things he really loved in the world, and winding up Skye was one of them.

"You know I would pay good money to see you snap—snap like a twig." He mimicked her snapping gesture and added some dramatic flair of his own.

"Oh, you won't have to spend a penny. You're getting this one for free." Skye chased the two boys through the gate and into the main school building, neither of them running slow enough to be caught, nor fast enough to escape.

One thing Noah loved was science, and the opposite of science had to be PE. It wasn't that he didn't like to be active, but being one of the smallest boys in his class had its disadvantages. Having to participate in rugby, hockey, and other group activities with boys who towered over him wasn't exactly appealing. Heck, it wasn't even slightly appealing.

The putrid smells of sweat and mildew assaulted his nose the moment he stepped into the changing room. The stench reminded him how much he despised changing clothes in front of the other boys. Noah kept his head down and darted past the others, avoiding eye contact. They were a rowdy bunch and liked to snap their towels at people once they got a shot at bare skin. When he arrived at his usual spot, Noah turned his back to the other boys and began to undress. After removing his vest and tie, he pulled off his shirt and tossed it onto a wall hook. His pants were the next to go. He slowly stepped out of them, peering out of the corner of his eyes to make sure no one was watching, and threw them on the bench. When the rest of his school uniform was wadded in a bundle on the bench, he hastily stepped into his gym outfit and sighed.

Done.

In less than two minutes, he was jogging through the gymnasium and beyond the double doors to join his classmates outside on the field.

Mr. Cordell, the PE teacher, stepped up and enthusiastically announced, "Right lads, who's up fer a game of footy?"

Most of the class whooped in excitement.

"Brilliant! Nuttin's better than a football match t' make yeh feel like a man!" A boy shouted.

Yeah, right, there's nothing like getting tackled by a bunch of brutes twice my size.

Mr. Cordell proceeded to assign team captains. "Grucker. Chris Grucker. Take the pitch." He pointed to a spot on the field.

Noah sighed.

This is just not my day.

Grucker was an oversized, dark-haired bully who had it in for Noah. Perhaps his size was due to the fact that, even though he was in Year Eight—seventh grade to Noah—Grucker was fourteen years old. Apparently, when his mom died, he had gone a bit mad and had been held back at least a year. But that didn't explain why he was larger than many of the older boys in the school. Noah imagined Grucker was half human and half sasquatch. It was the most likely explanation he could think of—and the most amusing. It's also why Noah enjoyed calling the bully a 'great oaf,' something he'd recently heard on a British sitcom. Incorporating British words and slang into his American vocabulary was something Noah found quite entertaining. He fancied—a word he picked up from a game show—that he would fit right in, accent and all, in about a year. If it weren't for Grucker constantly picking on him and making him stand out, he might be able to accomplish his full assimilation even earlier.

Grucker and Noah shared a brief and disturbing history, one filled with harsh words, threatening looks, and stolen books. As the school's self-appointed bully, Grucker had made Noah's life a nightmare. Ethan often joked that Noah did him a major favor by becoming Grucker's new favorite target, which allowed Ethan to finally use the toilets in peace. What was it about Noah that made Grucker hate him so much?

Nerves churned a hard knot into the pit of Noah's stomach. Grucker as a team captain pretty much guaranteed Noah would be tackled more than any other person in the class. If he ended up on Grucker's team, he would assign him to the most dangerous position on the field. If Noah went with the other team, Grucker would order his lackeys to target him. It was a lose-lose situation. Noah was going home with at least one broken bone, whether he liked it or not.

"Dawson. Finley Dawson," Mr. Cordell called out.

An athletic boy with auburn hair stepped forward. He was tall, with wide shoulders, but he wasn't massive like Grucker.

"Dawson." Mr. Cordell pointed. "Go over yonder."

Lineups were picked, and to Noah's relief, he landed on Dawson's team. If he played his cards right, he could hide behind his teammates.

Mr. Cordell reached into a black duffle bag and withdrew a soccer ball. It was then that Noah realized his mistake.

"Soccer, not football. I should've known," Noah mumbled to himself, shaking his head. Maybe, just maybe, he could escape with only cuts and bruises, and no broken bones at all.

Dawson gave out assignments. Looking at Noah, he said, "Winger."

Noah nodded and pretended to understand.

He wasn't overly interested in sports. Heck, he wasn't even *underly* interested in them. In fact, sports were so completely off Noah's radar that he had never watched a full soccer game, let alone played one. All he knew was to kick the ball, not use his hands, and to aim for the goal—that was about it. His logical mind reasoned a winger would probably be positioned somewhere near the outside of the field. Just where, he had no clue.

As the boys took the field, Noah was relieved when Dawson nudged him into the proper position. Throughout most of the game, Noah ran up and down the field and tried to stay out of everyone's way.

Near the end of the match, the score was tied and Grucker had the ball.

The anxiety that had plagued Noah throughout the first half of the match had finally worn off as he easily trotted up and down the field. He and his teammates had established an unspoken understanding. He stayed out of their way, and they never passed him the ball, which was perfectly fine by him.

When Grucker barreled down Noah's side of the field, however, everything changed.

"Outta me way, Kamikaze!" Grucker yelled as he kicked the ball.

Seeing Grucker charge toward him, Noah panicked and forgot which direction he should go to get out of the great oaf's way. Instead of running away from the goal, he ran straight for it.

Grucker closed the distance; Noah could practically smell his sweat.

"I said, outta me way!"

Noah twisted to dash in the opposite direction, but as he did, his feet became tangled and he tripped, right into Grucker.

The ball bounced off Noah's face just before his eye smashed into Grucker's knee.

Grucker yelled, "I'm gonna kill you!" as he tumbled over Noah.

They landed in a sprawled heap on the field.

The great oaf was much heavier than he looked—which was saying a lot, and the impact had driven all the air from Noah's lungs; he struggled to breathe under Grucker's weight.

Someone kicked the ball, and yet again, it bounced off Noah's head.

Dawson recovered the ball and sprinted down the field.

Grucker pushed himself to his feet and snarled, "Yer a dead man," before darting after Dawson.

Dawson kicked.

Score!

CHAPTER THREE
Little Big Man

Worse than PE class was the obligation to take a shower afterward.

Noah didn't understand how the kids could be so comfortable showering next to each other. But what choice did they have? At the beginning of the term, Mr. Cordell made it clear that anyone who didn't shower would get poor marks. Then he muttered something about complaining teachers. His logic didn't make sense to Noah because this was the last class of the day.

After the game, Noah skirted around Grucker, who was wrestling with his band of bullies next to the water fountain. He thought he could enter the changing room without attracting attention, but Dawson swiftly spotted him and slapped him on the back. He practically yelled, "Nice play, Walters, stoppin' Grucker and all. I knew you'd be a good winger! We would have lost if it weren't for you."

Noah gave him a sickly smile and hastily glanced back at Grucker and his crew, who were thankfully too busy to pay any attention to him. Relief flooded through his chest and Noah let himself enjoy the moment. It felt good to be complimented by someone, especially a peer.

Noahmadeus the Great strikes again! By accident, sure. But who cares? We won!

A pleasant warmth engulfed him. It was the kind of feeling he got when his dad patted him on the back for a job well done. Noah breathed in that feeling. His smile grew as he walked through the dingy hallway that joined the changing room with the showers. He still had his gym shorts on because he didn't want to remove them until he absolutely had to. The tiles felt cold on his bare feet, despite the steam-filled air.

Noah paused when he heard a boy's voice echo through the hallway, "Did yeh see how that kid got smashed? He took a proper poundin'. What's his name? Waters or somethin'?"

Someone answered, but the reply was less than pleasant. Noah tried to block out the subsequent chuckles and snarky comments. The warmth that had brought a smile to his face disappeared and was replaced by a cold stone that formed in his throat. He tried to swallow it down, but it was lodged too deep. He looked at the ceiling and blinked rapidly.

Will I ever be good enough?

He had just made himself the number one target of the school bully, and for what? Noah was really beginning to have serious doubts about staying in England. He wiped his eyes as he tiptoed back into the changing room and skulked in the most discreet corner he could find.

A small group of wet boys exited the showers, dried themselves, and dressed. As they left the changing room to wait in the gymnasium for the end-of-day bell, Dawson spotted Noah in the corner and pointed. "The showers are all yours, Walters."

Another boy trumped in, "Yeah, runt, you better get in there. I don't want to smell your pits."

Dawson grimaced, but then shook his head and walked away.

Noah heard someone near the doorway say, "The runt hasn't showered yet, Mr. Cordell."

Mr. Cordell walked into the changing room, looked at Noah, and nodded. He didn't need to say a word.

Noah wrapped his towel carefully around his waist, removed his gym shorts, and tossed them on the bench. Then he meandered down the dank, slippery hallway.

When he reached a suitable shower stall, he looked over his shoulder at the few remaining boys in the shower room.

This is so embarrassing.

At least none of the boys were paying attention to him.

He looked down at his towel, and then up at the showerhead. He reached for the faucet, turned it on without removing his towel, and shivered when cold water hit his skin. Ten seconds of that was enough. Noah turned off the water and rushed to the changing room. His feet slapped the floor, and he almost slipped a few times as he headed straight for his clothes, his towel dripping wet around his waist.

"Well, if it ain't the Kamikaze Kid."

Noah skidded to a slippery stop. "Grucker," he whispered and glanced at the clock.

Grucker followed his gaze. Then he ground his fist into his palm and focused all his attention on Noah. "Not time yet, is it? Bell's not gonna save yeh."

Noah looked for anything that could protect him as he inched closer to his clothes.

Where was Mr. Cordell when you needed him?

A small group of boys gathered.

An Irish boy named Tomas O'Heaphy strode up from behind. "Leave 'im alone, Grucker. Can't yeh see the poor thing's scared outta his wits?"

Grucker slowly turned to glare at the boy.

Noah glanced at his shirt, which was hanging on a hook, barely out of reach. Using the distraction, he sidestepped to the shirt and yanked it down.

"You'll be gettin' outta here, O'Heaphy, if you know what's good fer yeh," Grucker glowered.

Tomas's face turned as red as his hair, and then he scampered out of the changing room.

Grucker turned back to Noah. "What's the matter, Kamikaze? Scared?" A menacing sneer crept from one ear to the other on Grucker's distorted face. The bully advanced, a brutish swagger to his walk. He had a thick

Yorkshire accent that Noah sometimes had trouble understanding, but he didn't need to catch every word. The message was completely clear.

"Yer quite the li'l big man, winnin' and all."

Noah knew there was nothing he could say that would save him from the situation, but he tried anyway. "It…it was just a game."

"Just a game, eh? How about me and thee play a li'l game?" Grucker pounded his fist into his palm. "Let's play smashfest."

Noah imagined his skin turning chalky white from the fear that gripped his heart and squeezed every drop of blood from it. The cold water from the wet towel traced down his legs, causing goosebumps to erupt all over his body.

Grucker smirked and eyed his gang; all of them were now standing behind him. Turning his attention back to Noah, he reached down and ripped the towel from Noah's waist.

Tell me that didn't just happen.

"Look, boys. Look at the baby without his diaper." Grucker dropped the towel to the floor.

Noah quickly tried to cover himself with his shirt.

The gang sniggered.

Leaning in, hot breath blasting Noah's cheek, the great oaf said, "Yer stupid face makes me so angry, I just want to smash it. Seems to me yer face is a magnet fer smashin'. Jus' look at how me knee gave yeh that black eye."

Noah hadn't seen himself in the mirror yet, but he had to assume he bore a few battle scars from the game. Keeping his gaze on Grucker, Noah slowly inched closer to the rest of his clothes, which were lying in a messy pile on the bench.

Noah flinched when a gust of wind whizzed by his left ear, followed by a thud. He looked over his shoulder and saw Grucker's fist planted firmly on the wall behind his head. He clenched his eyes shut.

By the time he dared to open them, Grucker had pulled his fist back and was swinging it from side to side as if it were a live snake. The more it swayed, the more erratic Grucker's actions became.

"I can't control it, Kamikaze. It's—it's yer face. It's a magnet fer smashin'. I can't be held responsible if anythin' bad happens to yeh."

Noah was driven backward until the bench buckled his knees, but he refused to sit. He pressed his back against the wall.

How on Earth could he escape?

Without taking his eyes off Grucker, Noah slowly reached toward the bench and grasped what he hoped was the entire bundle of his school uniform.

Grucker's fist struck the wall to the right of Noah's head, near the shirt hook.

Noah hastily ducked under Grucker's arm and hightailed it out of the changing room, stark naked.

He charged through the gymnasium, which was full of boys pointing and sniggering, and into the school's main corridor, all the while clutching his bundled clothes.

Where could he possibly hide?

He darted toward the school's main entrance, but thought better of it. Then he raced back the way he'd come and tripped, landing hard on his side. He picked himself up just as the end-of-day bell rang, loud as a fire alarm.

Noah watched in mute horror as every classroom door flew open in unison. At the same time, Grucker exited the gymnasium.

The great oaf cupped his hands around his mouth.

The world slowed down as Noah screamed, "No!"

Too late.

Grucker's voice boomed off the walls, too loud—*way* too loud. It was as if he had magically produced a bullhorn. "Look at the naked Chinese kid. Naked as the day he were born!"

Maggie Melbourne, a girl from Noah's art class, was the first to see Noah. Their eyes met.

Maggie dropped her schoolbooks.

Noah couldn't move, he just stood there, his feet glued to the spot.

Other kids bumped into Maggie's back. Shouts and laughter erupted up and down the hallway. Deafening roars came from every direction and slammed into Noah like a sandblaster peeling paint off a house, leaving him raw and wounded. Mortified, he felt more vulnerable than he'd ever been in his entire life.

"What're yeh cryin' fer, loser? Can't take the heat?" Grucker teased.

Noah was living one of his worst nightmares, and all he wanted to do was wake up. But this was no dream. He would have to live with the humiliation of this terrible moment for the rest of his life. Oh, how he wished a spacecraft would suddenly appear and rescue him by beaming him onto its holodeck. It was his only hope.

Or was it? Maybe there *was* another way.

He had spotted his escape—a large brown door labeled, "Toilets."

Noah ran, jumped and literally dove into the restroom, landing flat on his belly. Cold tiles pressed against his bare skin. Two girls were sitting on the sinks. A girl with brown hair looked shocked as she lost her balance and fell. She picked herself up while her friend, an older blonde, eyed Noah appreciatively, slowly looking him up and down and taking in every inch of him.

"Hey there, fitty," the blonde girl said with a twinkle in her eye. She gestured to an empty stall. "Are you just gonna lie there? Or would you like to get dressed?"

Noah followed her gesture with his gaze and realized she was offering him a bit of privacy.

"Of course, we don't mind a good show either." She smiled and twirled her vanilla curls around her finger.

Noah carefully stood and sidestepped into the bathroom stall, where he gently closed the door and cried.

He thought about Skye and Ethan, all the good times they'd had, and how the three of them had become inseparable. Never before had he made such good friends so quickly, but never before had he felt so humiliated and shamed. How could he face them now? How could he look into their eyes, ever again? Regret and sadness pooled in his heart just thinking about how much he would miss them when he ran away.

CHAPTER FOUR
Backfire

Noah buried his face in his hands. "He's such a jerk."

"He was lying. Your eye looks okay to me. I don't think it'll bruise," Skye said.

Noah rubbed his eye, testing it for tenderness. It didn't hurt too bad. Maybe Skye was right.

"You shouldn't worry about that dreadful brute." Skye bent down and ripped up a clump of weeds. "I'll bet a tenner he leaves school early and becomes a caretaker."

She shredded the stems. "Grucker won't have the social skills to cope in the real world, and he'll end up living with his granny in her two-bedroom flat because he won't even be able to afford rent."

Without taking a breath, she threw the weeds down and picked another bunch. "He'll be eating beans on toast for the rest of his life because that's the only thing he'll know how to cook. And he'll eat it alone in front of the telly watching old VHS tapes because that's all he can find in the bins he cleans."

More decimated stems cascaded to the ground around her feet. Noah bet she didn't even hear the whispers or notice the glances from their classmates, who were pointing at him and sniggering. She simply continued to pulverize the weeds.

"Yeah," her voice grew louder, "and he's got one of those old video players, not only because he can't afford to buy something more modern, but he also thinks the new remotes are too complicated. You know, because he can't read. Oh, and he has a stuffed animal that's a cat, but it only has one eye and no back legs. He thinks it's real and calls it Stumpy."

It always amazed Noah just how long Skye could talk without taking a single breath. He was also pleased to note that her tactics of distraction were working; he already felt much better.

Ethan nudged her. "Your mind is a strange place, Skye Williams."

Skye blinked at him. "What do you mean?"

Noah and Ethan looked at each other and grinned.

Ethan shrugged. "Nothing. We just love you."

Noah scanned the area for Grucker before stepping from the sidewalk at the rear of the school and heading for the iron gate.

He was nowhere in sight.

"Thanks for trying to cheer me up, you two. But, I understand if you don't want to be seen with me." Noah halfheartedly kicked at a rock. "I'll be okay by myself."

"As if." Skye put her arm around Noah's shoulder and squeezed.

Ethan slapped his back. "If we don't look out for each other, no one else will, mate." He pushed Skye out of the way and gave Noah a noogie.

Noah tried to squirm out of Ethan's grip.

"Stop it, man. That hurts."

Ethan stopped rubbing his knuckles against the top of Noah's head and readjusted his arm around Noah's shoulders. "Ya' know I'm only your friend for purely selfish reasons. I need a bit o' lookin' after, too." Ethan winked. "And you might not believe it to look at her, but so does Skye."

"Beg pardon?" said Skye with an exaggerated double take.

Noah smiled. He envied Ethan's ability to take everything in stride.

"Selfish reasons, huh?" Noah ran his fingers through his hair and gingerly patted the top of his head, testing it for possible noogie damage.

Thankfully, his earlier humiliation was beginning to feel like a dream, which made it almost bearable that his most embarrassing moment would become a legend in their school for generations to come. *Almost.*

"'Course it's for selfish reasons. You don't think I hang out with you two clowns out of friendship, do you?" Ethan forced a chuckle. "I'm hangin' out with Miss Personality over here and the smallest kid I've ever seen that doesn't need a chettin' pacifier. You're like me support group. A support group that I'm forced to put up with 'cause I'm so pathetic no one else'll have me."

The key to Ethan's sense of humor, Noah had learned, was never knowing whether he was being serious or not. Ethan's sarcasm was so natural that Noah doubted if even Ethan knew.

Skye placed her hands on her hips and held her chin high. She looked Ethan straight in the eyes. "Hey, Noah, shall we ditch this guy? What do you think? Is he worthy of our company?"

"Ditch me? You wouldn't make it a day without me expertise, good looks, and keen sense of humor. Besides, who else would wake up at the crack of dawn on a school day to film your 'Most Memorable Mattress Face Plants'? Trust me, love, you're better off with me."

Noah shook his head and smiled, appreciating the show they were putting on for his benefit.

Skye jabbed a finger into Ethan's ribs, something she claimed would drive him crazy. She was right; he flinched and pushed her hand away. It was all she needed to start jabbing him again. Ethan ran away, waving his hands in the air and swearing he would leave Skye out of his will if she continued. They ran rings around Noah, who just laughed.

Right before they reached the gate, Noah froze and pointed. "Guys, stop. Look over there."

"I'll stop when she chettin' stops assaultin' me. I'll report you!"

"No, seriously, guys, I need you to stop."

"I'm having too much fun making this nutter run." Skye started to push her weight into the iron gate to budge it open.

"Guys!"

Like a couple of cartoon characters, Ethan plowed into Skye's back and they both crashed through the gate.

"Now look what you made me do!" Skye picked at the remnants of a broken fingernail.

Ethan quickly scanned her hand and then turned to Noah with a puzzled expression. "What is it, already?"

"Look over there." Noah gestured to the school's primary entrance. The main walkway that funneled students to and from the school sat between two stone walls that were just high enough to tempt the taller students to sit on their ledges. The southern wall, which cut into the side of a hill and was therefore somewhat lofty from the back side, sprouted a wrought iron fence that served as a safety measure to keep students from toppling over and plunging to certain death.

From where he stood, Noah could see his schoolmates going home at the end of the day, their heads and torsos bobbing above the top of the wall. He had spotted one particular head he knew all too well; it was large, bulbous, and had a haircut that looked as if it had been done in the dark by a one-armed barber.

"Grucker," Noah said with a tinge of what he hoped sounded like disdain instead of abject fear.

Ethan and Skye spotted him immediately. Grucker stood out like a sore thumb—a sore thumb with a bad attitude. His braying, distressed-donkey laugh made Noah cringe.

"Not much of a looker, is he?" Skye tossed her hair over one shoulder.

Grucker stopped and glanced around. He shoved a small boy out of his way. Tossing his backpack on top of the wall, Grucker leaned against the stone with his back to Noah, Skye, and Ethan. His gang followed suit.

Skye narrowed her eyes and spoke through her teeth. "Seems he needs to be taught some manners."

Ethan rubbed his palms together eagerly. "So what's the plan?"

Noah started to say that *his* plan was to run far, far away, but a little voice inside argued. *Don't let that hater get away with humiliating you in front of the entire school. Grucker should pay for what he's done.*

Noah shrugged, trying to shake an imaginary demon off his shoulder.

If you don't do something to stop Grucker now, things will only get worse. He'll think he's won.

With a shudder, Noah relived the shame of being caught naked in front of the entire school. His hands balled into fists and heat rushed to his cheeks.

The demon's right, Grucker needs to be taught a lesson.

Noah pointed to Grucker's bag, which was propped up against the iron railing. The straps hung enticingly through the bars.

Ethan, Skye, and Noah exchanged glances, already on the same page.

"I'm all over it like a bad rash." Ethan grinned.

"Let's do this." Noah nodded.

"I'll keep a lookout," Skye said.

Noah began to jog toward Grucker with Ethan in tow.

Skye whispered loudly, "You got this."

Ethan and Noah snuck up to the wall and flattened their bodies against its southern edge, directly beneath their target. Ethan laced his fingers together to make a saddle step. Noah placed his foot in Ethan's hands and was hoisted toward the seeming innocuous backpack.

I can't believe I'm doing this.

Noah felt as if he were floating outside of his body, observing himself and the scene—a new and improved Noah had taken over.

He heard Grucker bragging about a girl he claimed was in love with him. Had Grucker not been preoccupied with letting everyone know how cool he was, he might have noticed Noah poking over the top of the wall and tying his bag to the metal bars.

Ethan lost his grip. Noah instinctively grabbed the iron railing to keep from falling. His forearms scraped against the stone. Just when he was about to slip, Ethan grabbed Noah's feet. The boys wobbled and recovered. The blood pumping through Noah's veins made him feel giddy, and his pulse pounded in his ears. The thudding distracted him, and prevented him from hearing what was being said. He wondered if one of Grucker's cronies had spotted him, and forced his shaky hands to rush as he pulled the straps tight and secured them firmly to the railing. In a final flash of inspiration, Noah carefully and quietly unzipped his tormentor's bag.

This is going to be good.

Noah hit the ground running, Ethan scrambling behind him. Skye was at the gate and had it propped open for them. All three plowed through it, and Skye shut it behind them.

"Don't worry," she said. "I've got this part."

Noah grinned. "I knew you would."

Noah and Ethan peered over Skye's shoulders, their eyes trained on Grucker.

"Hey, potato head," Skye hollered through the iron bars with an extra helping of sass. "Did you make that wig out of your gran's chest hair? I tried texting you this morning but my phone kept auto-correcting your name to 'Yorkshire's biggest idiot.'"

Grucker turned around and glared, but that didn't stop Skye.

"You know that time you set your potato head on fire? Shouldn't have tried putting it out with a hammer. Just sayin'."

Noah prodded her in the back. "That's enough, Skye."

"I don't think so; I'm just getting started."

"We need to start running." Ethan tugged at her sleeve.

Just as Skye started to shout another insult, Noah placed his hand over her mouth. If it were possible, Grucker would have steam bursting out of his ears. He certainly looked mad enough. His face had gone bright red.

Grucker grabbed for his bag, and when it didn't move he gave it an extra strong tug.

Noah watched with delight as Grucker's bag split open. Grucker jumped back. Pens, half-eaten sandwiches, and the usual schoolbag clutter flew into the air and landed on the ground behind the wall. Noah wished he had x-ray vision to peer through the stones near Grucker's feet; he was sure it had created quite the mess. Grucker inspected the torn bag as if it might tell him what had just happened.

"This is priceless," Skye said, hopping up and down and clapping. "Just look at his face! It's all scrunched up like a shriveled raisin. How adorable!" She cleared her throat when she saw Ethan and Noah eying her disconcertedly. "I mean, in a, 'so ugly it's cute kind of way.' Ya know?"

Ethan couldn't contain his laughter. He dropped to the ground and rolled from side to side.

Grucker eyed his gang, each member nodding in understanding.

Dawning comprehension crept over Noah. He pulled Ethan to his feet and at the same time reached for Skye. "Guys, we really didn't think this through. We need to run. Now!"

"I second that suggestion," Ethan said.

Skye nodded. "Running sounds good."

Grucker shouted, "Get 'em!"

CHAPTER FIVE
The Dark Wood

The old man went to check on the trap he had set the previous night, hoping to find that yellow faerie's body lying limp and lifeless in its clutches. He figured all faeries deserved to die, along with the elves, gnomes and every despicable creature living in that forsaken realm. Sure, some of them looked innocent enough, but he knew better. They were devious tricksters, determined to fool and enslave men with their magic.

He spotted the dead leaf he had laid over the trap, peeked under it, and sighed. Disappointment flooded through him. The trap was just as he'd left it. If there were a faerie in the woods, it wouldn't have been able to resist his spell. He straightened and sniffed the air. Perhaps he was wrong, perhaps a portal hadn't opened last night. Maybe that strange sense of magic he had felt was merely a premonition and not a portal at all. He often got warnings when something bad was about to happen. He turned back and walked toward his lodge. When he was halfway there a chill ran down his spine so strongly it caused him to stop. There was that feeling again, but this time it was more intense. It was as if the world shifted and the universe took a breath. There was definitely a portal somewhere in his woods and unless he was the one to conjure it, it was unacceptable. He began his search; he had to find it.

The Dark Wood

Skye knew they'd better find somewhere to hide before Grucker and his gang caught up with them, or they'd all be mincemeat.

She bolted toward Stillwater Street.

Stillwater Street was perhaps the most famous street in Herogate. It was rumored to be dangerous, yet also the last safe place to travel before entering the Forest of Shadowen, nicknamed The Dark Wood by the townsfolk.

Ethan called from behind, "We can't go in there!"

"We have no choice. Follow me if you want to live." Skye paused dramatically before crossing the street and plunging into the forest. Finding a place to hide wouldn't be a problem. Finding a place that wasn't too far from the forest's edge might be a different story. But Skye had more pressing things to think about, like the advancing brute who didn't have enough brains to count to two.

Ethan grabbed her arm. "That's far enough!"

Noah scrambled up beside them. "You guys? I'm uhh, not sure we..."

Skye slipped as she tried to make her way up a small hill.

"Let go of me!" She yanked her elbow from Ethan's grasp and continued to climb deeper into the forest. She would take her chances with The Dark Wood over Grucker and his gang any day.

When she thought they were a safe distance in, she abruptly stopped. Ethan plowed into her.

"Watch it!" Her whisper was loud and breathy.

"You watch it!" Ethan hissed.

She thought Ethan must be really scared, because his retort wasn't particularly witty.

Skye frantically looked for a place to hide, and when she found it, she climbed over a moss-covered log and ducked behind it.

"You two, get over here, fast!"

Ethan and Noah joined her.

Tortured trees loomed overhead, creating a canopy that shrouded the forest in shadows, despite the time of day. Twisted undergrowth covered the ground like a nest of writhing snakes, just waiting to slither around their ankles and yank them into the underworld.

Skye shook her head. *No more horror movies for me.*

Even though she usually kept her imagination in check, she had to admit that traveling this far into the forest made her nervous. She hadn't expected to feel afraid. Now she understood why absolutely nobody went into these woods, not even Grucker.

She flinched when Grucker yelled, "You can't stay in there forever!" Then she heard him say, "Spread out."

The sounds of running footsteps echoed as the gang stomped off down the road. One of Grucker's henchmen warned, "Yeh'd better come out soon or the forest will rip yeh to shreds. There'll be nuttin' left of yeh's."

Ethan glanced around wildly. He muttered under his breath, "Claws for branches and…" He pointed to a gnarly knot on a nearby tree trunk. "The chettin' trees have eyes!"

Grucker yelled at them again.

Ethan looked at Skye. "I hate to agree with anythin' that plank says, but he's right. This is the worst place we could be."

"Okay, okay, just be quiet." Skye gestured for silence.

Ethan closed his mouth and stared straight at her, as if waiting for her to rescue them.

How was she going to get them out of this mess?

She shifted under the weight of his gaze. "Don't look at me like that. I can't think."

It didn't help when Noah leaned in and whispered, "I promised my dad I would never come in here. He said there were monsters in this place."

Skye's stomach sank.

"I don't like this any more than you do, but I'm not so sure we have a choice."

Noah flinched at a nearby noise and shot a glance over his shoulder.

Skye looked too, afraid something might be sneaking up on them.

The Dark Wood

This is ridiculous. I can't let a few stupid rumors wipe out all my common sense.

Determined to overcome her fears, Skye stubbornly settled into her spot. "Looks like we'll be here for a while. Might as well make ourselves comfortable."

Noah and Ethan looked at her as if she were crazy, but they settled in beside her anyway.

The longer they waited, the more Skye convinced herself there was nothing to worry about.

Why do people make such a big deal about The Dark Wood, anyway? It's just a silly old forest.

She'd lived in Herogate for the past two years and had never known anyone who was killed, maimed, or even hurt in the forest. All the rumors that circulated through the school were about strangers passing by, not the townsfolk. That was probably because the rumors were just that—rumors. The scariest thing she had ever seen near the forest was an old man in overalls, and he hadn't seemed all that bad.

Grucker's taunts of "I'm goin' t' get yeh's" and "don't make me come in there" slowly faded away.

After a while Ethan stood, cupped his hands over his mouth, and shouted, "That's right, Grucker, run along and find your dad at the bookie's!"

Skye stood, craning her neck to see if the coast was clear.

Noah, still sitting, whispered, "Are they gone?"

Ethan shivered and rubbed his arms. "I don't know, but I feel like we're being watched, and not by Grucker." His eyes darted from one tree to the next. "Let's get the chet out of here."

He started toward the street, but Skye stopped him.

"We can't go that way." She pointed. "Look, Grucker's hiding behind that bush on the other side of the street."

Ethan's shoulders slumped. "Then what do you suggest? We can't stay in here forever."

Noah stood. "The air feels so..." He seemed to be searching for the right words as he looked at the canopy overhead, "…sad." His eyes reminded her of a lost puppy, and he practically whimpered when he said, "Something happened here; something terrible."

Skye felt it too, but she wasn't about to admit it, so she attempted to give him her best crazy-eyed glare. "Rubbish! Did you hit your head or something?"

Ethan huddled next to Noah. "No, Skye, he's right. Don't you feel it?"

Yes, but I'm not about to tell you that.

Skye sighed in mock exasperation. "You two are letting your imaginations get away with you. Come back down to Earth and help a girl out. We need to find a way outta here that doesn't include running into Grucker or his gang." She glanced around, hoping a solution would present itself. Then she had a thought. "Noah, your house is north of us, right?"

"Yeah, why?"

Skye pointed. "So that means we need to go that way."

"To my house?" Noah asked, surprised.

"Yeppers." Skye nodded.

Ethan planted himself between Skye and the thick of the forest, jabbing his thumb over his shoulder. "I know you're not suggesting we go straight through the heart of that chettin' mess. Trust me, it's a bad idea."

Noah walked up behind her. "You *have* been to my house, right?"

Skye turned to face him. "Are you kidding? Have I been to your house? Seriously Noah, I was at your birthday party. Give me a break!" She crossed her arms over her chest indignantly.

"It was a rhetorical question," Ethan chimed in.

Noah and Ethan exchanged knowing glances. Noah's cheeks flushed. "Yeah, it was rhetorical."

Skye knew better than to believe him.

Ethan must've known she hadn't bought it, because he puffed up his chest and said, "Who cares if he forgot? Give the boy a break. Can't you see he's scared out of his wits? We'll be lucky if he remembers his own name by the time we get out of this." He shuffled around nervously. *"If we get out of this."*

Noah thrust his hands into his pockets. "I'm not scared."

Skye studied him and thought he looked more worried than she'd ever seen him.

He licked his lips. "Did you pay attention to how you got to my house? It's too far away. I don't know if you remember, but it's completely on the opposite side of these woods, where Stillwater Street bends around Hollow Hills on the outskirts of town. We'll never make it."

Hollow Hills was a cluster of hills that were rumored to have loads of caves with only a few secret entrances, but Skye didn't get to that side of town much, so she couldn't confirm or deny if the caves existed.

She threw her hands up, exasperated. "Do either of you have a better idea?"

Ethan gestured down the hill. "Yeah, I say we skirt along the edge of the forest for a while."

Skye shook her head. "Grucker will see us. He'll follow us, and we'll be in the same mess we're in right now. We don't have a choice. We have to sneak out of here. We can't let Grucker or his brutes see us. When we think it's safe, we can make our way back to Stillwater Street."

Ethan started to say, "That's the worst id—" but just then they heard Grucker yell.

"You can't stay in there forever! We've got the road covered, so when yeh show yer faces, we'll be waitin'!"

All three jumped at the sound of his voice.

"See? We can't let them see us. What choice do we have?" Skye started slipping deeper into the forest, careful to be as quiet as possible and hoping Noah and Ethan would follow. She sighed with relief when she heard their footsteps behind her.

A span of time that seemed like forever passed without a single word as Skye led the way through the forest. The sounds of crunching leaves, twigs brushing against their clothes, and crickets rhythmically chirping became monotonous enough to make Skye feel as if she were in a daydream. She didn't stop to wonder why there weren't any birds singing.

Ethan broke the silence. He jogged up to Skye and planted himself on a small mound of earth, blocking her way and gesturing for her to stop. "It's been long enough. Time to leave."

Noah glanced around nervously. "Does anyone know where we are? How do we get out of here?"

Ethan gestured with a flick of his head. "She's the genius who wanted to come this way; ask her."

Skye and Ethan were the same height, but since he was standing on a mound, she had to tilt her head back to meet his eyes. "Don't mess with me Ethan. It's not my fault Grucker's an arrogant nutter intent on destroying our lives. We didn't have any other choice. We had to avoid him at all costs."

Noah unzipped his school bag and pulled out his water bottle. He twisted off the cap and took a sip. "She's right, this is the only way we could've escaped."

Noah offered the bottle to Skye; she took a swig before securing the top back on and tossing the bottle to Ethan.

Ethan caught it, but didn't drink. "Great, two against one." He directed his gaze at Noah as he gestured with the bottle to the deepest, darkest part of the forest. "Your house is that way, and I'm in no mood to play Hansel and bloomin' Gretel in woods like these. They'll swallow a man whole."

Skye glanced at Noah and saw him gulp.

She gestured to a fog-covered hill looming in the distance. "I think I spotted a house up that way." A chittering squirrel in a nearby bush startled her. As she turned to look, her gaze fell on an inconspicuous trail. It was the last thing she expected to see. She pointed. "I bet that path will lead us right to it."

Ethan's face drained of all color as he slowly turned to look at the path.

He dropped the water bottle. "Blimey, I've heard rumors about this place. I didn't think it actually existed. We need to get out of here *now*."

Noah picked up the water bottle and stuffed it into his backpack. "What rumors? You mean about this trail?"

Ethan nodded. "Yes, and rumors of creatures that can tear you limb from limb."

Skye rolled her eyes. "Rubbish! Do you see anything big enough to rip us apart?"

Ethan didn't say anything, he just stared at the path, his back pressed against a tree.

She huffed. "I didn't think so. Who told you those rumors, anyway? Grucker?"

Ethan picked a piece of bark from the tree and threw it at her feet. "I've lived here for five years now. Plus, I stayed here with me grandparents when some bad things happened in these woods. Me grandma swore blind that eight years ago, there was a man ripped apart here, and then kids started goin' missin'. The whole town went on lockdown. It isn't called The Dark Wood because it's full of chettin' daisies, you know." Irritated, Ethan stomped. "Grandma reckoned it all started on a path. Maybe this path. The man probably got ripped apart right where we're standin'."

Noah looked down at the trail and cringed.

Skye threw up her hands. "If a creature ripped a man limb from limb, how would anyone hear about it? He'd be dead, and dead people don't talk. Right?" She paused. "Think about it."

Ethan opened his mouth, but then closed it. He couldn't seem to find a flaw in her logic.

Skye headed toward the path.

Ethan grabbed her shoulder. "Fine, you've made your point. But just what are we supposed to do when we get to this mysterious house? Sit on our bums and make a cuppa tea?"

Skye yanked her shoulder from his grasp. "It's not the house I'm interested in. If there's a house, then that means there's got to be a driveway. And at the end of that driveway is a road. And if there are roads, then we can get home."

"She's got a point." Noah shivered as a cold wind blew through the rustling trees.

A feeling of dread suddenly crept over Skye and made her long to be in the safety of her home. "We need to move." Stepping up to the trail, she marched forward without opposition.

CHAPTER SIX
Beautiful Blackberries

Noah wasn't the best at keeping track of time, but he supposed they must have been walking for at least an hour. There was still no sign of the house Skye had spotted; he wondered if it had disappeared completely, this being some kind of haunted forest and all. By the time the path ended, their tensions had eased, and they were talking and walking through the forest as though they did it all the time. They hadn't even noticed when the path disappeared under a thick carpet of moss and vines, forcing them to create their own route through fallen tree trunks and loops of brambles that spilled from between the trees like nets lying in wait for their next victims. It wasn't the creepy twisted network of vines and plant life that slowed their progress, nor was it the uneven and treacherous ground. Their pace slowed because of something way more complicated—Ethan's sudden obsession with blackberries.

It seemed harmless enough when Ethan found the first ripe berry. He picked it and held it up. "Look at this beaut. It's chettin' *huge*."

Skye tried to snatch it from him, but missed. "I wouldn't eat that if I were you. Might be poisonous."

"Don't you know a blackberry when you see one?" Ethan popped it in his mouth. Juice squirted from the berry and coated his lips, staining them purple.

Skye walked away, shaking her head and saying, "Yes, and I know an idiot when I see one, too."

Noah jogged up to Ethan and tugged on his shirt. "Maybe she's right. There's something strange about this place." He studied one of the bushes. "And those berries don't seem right, either."

The polished drupelets were too beautiful, too perfect somehow.

Ethan plucked another berry from a nearby bush and looked at it appreciatively. "Rubbish! These are the best blackberries I've ever tasted, mate." He offered it to Noah. "Here, try one."

Noah surprised himself when he hesitated. "Uh, no thanks." Why hadn't he immediately refused? Never a fan of blackberries, he shouldn't have felt an overwhelming desire to take Ethan up on his offer, but the air was scented with sweet and enticing aromas; they were enough to make almost anyone want to stay there forever and chow down on the beautiful black clusters. Noah squeezed his eyes shut and shook his head. Turning down the berry was way more difficult than it should've been, and he was beginning to feel a little discombobulated. He would have to make a special effort to keep his wits about him in this patch of pleasurable perfumes.

"Your loss, mate." Ethan shrugged and tossed the berry into the air so he could catch it in his mouth. He missed; it landed between his eyes and bounced to the ground. "That's a chettin' waste." He nudged Noah out of his way and bumbled to another bush. "I won't be makin' that mistake twice."

Ethan proceeded to eat every blackberry he could find. The more he ate, the more he seemed to lose his ability to think clearly. What was worse, the longer they stayed in the intoxicating fragrances, the giddier Noah felt, which should've thrown up huge warning flags. It got so bad, Noah wondered if they both might be getting tipsy—Ethan even slurred his words and walked all wobbly.

"Seriously, Noah, you've got to taste this! These berries are lovely-jubbly!" Ethan practically sang the last two words.

"Keep it down," Noah said, working hard to keep the dreamy quality out of his voice. "We're in The Dark Wood, remember? This isn't some park where you can just have a picnic."

Completely ignoring Noah, Ethan grabbed another berry and popped it in his mouth. "Life is beau'iful, you know?"

He ate another one and sang to the tune of "Beautiful Dreamer." "Beau'iful blackberries, come here to me, me teeth an' me mouth are waitin' for thee…"

Noah watched, bewildered.

Ethan continued to sing, "These lovely beau'ies live in the shade, come here me berries, please don't go away."

He licked his lips and scampered to another bush, cramming his mouth full before moving on to the next. "Can you believe it? They're sooo big and juicccy." His face and hands now stained dark purple, he tilted back on his heels and lost his balance.

Noah lunged to catch him. "I think you've had enough."

Ethan leaned his back against Noah's chest and allowed his weight to drop into Noah's arms. Noah stumbled as he fought to keep his balance; he caught a whiff of the robust fruit on Ethan's breath when Ethan looked up and said, "I love you, mate. You know that? You're me bestest friend in the wholest, biggest world."

Noah couldn't keep from chuckling. He glanced at Skye, now several yards ahead of them, and teased, "Don't let Skye hear you say that."

Ethan tried to stand. "I bloomin' love her too and all. She's me other bestest friend."

Noah inhaled deeply, appreciating the sweet aromas that permeated the blackberry patch as he felt himself slip into some sort of mesmerizing trance. He realized what was happening and shook his head as if he could shake off the spell that was being cast over him. "I think those berries have gone to your head." He pushed Ethan to his feet.

What kind of berries make a person tipsy, anyway?

Noah picked one and examined it closely.

It looked like a blackberry. He held it to his nose. It smelled like a blackberry—a big, juicy, tantalizing blackberry that begged to be eaten.

Suddenly, Noah couldn't remember why he refused to taste the deep purple clusters of lusciousness in the first place, and it was becoming abundantly clear that resistance was not only futile, but silly. This small ball of succulence was exactly what he wanted—what he *needed*.

Noah opened his mouth, and just when he was about to place the blackberry on the tip of his tongue, Ethan plucked it from between his fingertips. "I think that belongs to me."

He shoved it in his mouth and stumbled toward a bush that had yet to be picked clean. "I'm gonna put a load in me bag and sell them, mate. Quid a piece, I reckon." He started to eat another berry.

Noah regarded him blankly, but then came to his senses and forcefully bumped Ethan's elbow, knocking the berry out of his hand. He grabbed Ethan from behind. "Oh no, you don't. You've had enough."

Ethan struggled against Noah, but he was no match in his altered state.

"But I need 'em. I gotta have 'em. I can't live without 'em. Just one more. Pleeaasseee?"

Noah strengthened his grip along with his resolve and pulled. "No. We're getting out of here."

It took quite a bit of time and effort to guide Ethan through the blackberry patch. It was a journey of slapped hands, ripped clothing, and even pulled hair, but Noah managed to get the two of them through the thorny obstacle course in one piece.

When they were well away from the barbed bushes, he sat Ethan down on a fallen log.

"Now, sit here and sober up." Noah was already starting to feel more like himself.

Ethan screwed his face up and scratched his head. "What d'ya mean? I'm all here."

Noah chuckled. "You could've fooled me. Look at yourself. Your shirt's ripped, you've got purple stains all over your face, and you've even lost a shoe."

Ethan looked down at his right foot and wiggled his toes. His smallest toe poked through a hole in his dark blue sock.

Noah reached into his backpack and withdrew Ethan's missing shoe. He tossed it to him. "Good thing I picked this up when I did."

Ethan worked to stuff his foot into the shoe, but became agitated and tossed it aside.

What could Noah do? How could he help Ethan regain his senses?

Searching for anything that might help, Noah peered into his backpack and withdrew his water bottle. It was almost full—minus a few gulps. He tossed it to Ethan. "Here. Drink this."

Ethan ignored him, letting the bottle hit his shoulder and fall to the ground.

Noah snapped his fingers in front of Ethan's nose. "Snap out of it." Noah picked up the bottle, removed its top, and shoved it against Ethan's lips. "I said, drink."

Ethan indignantly snagged it from his hand, but Noah didn't mind. As long as he drank, Noah could feel somewhat useful; if he were lucky, the water would dilute the berries enough to sober up Ethan.

Using two fingers, Noah tilted the water bottle up, forcing Ethan to drink.

Ethan gulped down three swigs, and then stopped to breathe.

"Keep drinking," Noah ordered.

Ethan shot him a defiant look.

Noah glared back at him.

Ethan stubbornly tilted the bottle and chugged the water.

A short while later, he looked at the bottle as if he didn't know how it had found its way into his hands. "What happened?" He wiggled his toes. "And where's me shoe?"

Noah took the bottle and jammed it back into his bag. "You really don't remember?" He was surprised his strategy to help Ethan had actually worked.

Ethan stood and examined a hole in his school uniform. "Bloomin' Nora! Me mum's gonna kill me."

"It's not so bad." Noah brushed Ethan's fingers away from the hole to keep him from making it even larger. "Besides, don't you have two extra uniforms tucked away in the top of your closet? I thought you won that bet with O'Heaphy a couple months ago."

"Oh yeah, I forgot."

Noah eyed his own school uniform. "I might need to borrow a vest so my parents don't suspect anything." Then he glanced around and found Ethan's shoe a few feet away. He went to fetch it.

Ethan eyed him warily. "You never answered me question. What happened?"

Noah handed Ethan his shoe for a second time. "Those blackberries were more than you bargained for." He started to make a joke at Ethan's expense as his friend thrust his foot into the shoe, but then noticed something that was both pleasing and disturbing at the same time.

We're closer to that house now.

Noah took a moment to examine it. Although they were still too far away to really see it clearly, there was one thing he could tell for sure—it was much larger than he had originally estimated.

"Ethan, what do you think that is? Is that really a house or some kind of barn or something?" Noah pointed.

Ethan didn't answer.

"Skye, what do you th…" Noah turned and looked around for her, and suddenly felt as if he'd been punched in the stomach, like all the air was knocked out of him.

A wave of confusion and dizziness washed over Noah as he tried to recall the last time he'd seen her. The memory eluded him. He remembered feeling giddy and disoriented, but how could he have been so befuddled that he had forgotten all about Skye? Sure, he was caught up in Ethan's escapade, but that wasn't enough to make him lose *all* his reason. Were the aromas from the blackberries really that intoxicating? His teeth began to chatter and his palms grew sweaty.

Fear seized his chest so tightly he could barely breathe. His voice was weak and breathy when he asked, "Ethan, where's Skye?"

"She was just…" Ethan started to point, but then let his arms fall to his sides. "I…I don' know."

Ethan's reaction did nothing to calm the terror gripping Noah's heart. He stood there, frozen, unable to move. The promise he'd made to his father the night before replayed in his mind.

Don't go near that forest.

Ethan pulled his mobile phone from his pocket. "Chet! No signal. What about you?"

Noah hastily checked. "Nothing."

Ethan looked around frantically. "I knew coming in here was a bad idea!"

Before he knew what he was saying, Noah voiced his deepest fear, "The monster's got her. I know it—I just know it."

Ethan nodded; he looked crazed. "She's probably ripped to pieces by now."

A vivid picture of Skye's shredded body strewn over the forest floor came to mind and Noah fought hard to push it away. He could not lose control. He would not lose control.

Repeating over and over, "Monsters aren't real. Monsters aren't real," Noah pinched himself, slapped his own face, and shook his head.

Ethan jumped up, seized Noah's shoulders and proceeded to shake him. "Keep it down! We don't want the monster comin' after us too!"

Noah was glad for the intervention. It connected him back to reality—a reality where science ruled and ideas of creatures that could rip a person apart were total nonsense. He held up his hand. "All right, all right. I'll be quiet."

Ethan let go of Noah's shoulders and said, "Skye's gotta be back at the blackberry patch. Maybe she changed her mind and decided to try a few. You have to admit, they *were* tempting. We just have to retrace our steps and we'll find her."

Ethan was right, Noah didn't even like blackberries, and he almost took a taste of one. How could Skye have resisted? At this very moment she was probably hobbling around the forest, popping berries in her mouth, not knowing up from down. The more he thought about it, the more Noah was glad he hadn't eaten a single one. What might have happened had all three of them lost their senses?

He figured those berries must have been genetically modified to produce a chemical that loosened screws in people's heads.

Noah and Ethan clambered over rocks and logs, and trudged through gullies. Noah didn't care if branches tore at his clothes. He didn't even pay attention to the occasional root that tripped him up. All he cared about was finding Skye. He wondered where she could possibly be. All the while, he forced himself to push aside thoughts of monsters.

They repeatedly cupped their hands around their mouths and shouted for Skye. Ethan even made a few threats. Noah's favorite was, "If you don't show your chettin' face this chettin' instant, I'm gonna break into your chettin' house, steal your chettin' laptop, and delete all your chettin' social media accounts!"

Even that didn't work.

They reached the edge of the blackberry patch and Noah held up his hand. "Breathe through your mouth. Maybe that will keep us from becoming intoxicated by the fumes again." Noah pinched his nose shut for good measure.

Ethan nodded his understanding and mimicked Noah.

They retraced their steps to the spot where Noah now remembered seeing Skye—the place Ethan had proclaimed his love for his bestest friends—but there was no trace she had ever been there.

Ethan paced back and forth, smacking his forehead with one hand while pinching his nose with the other. He sounded like he had a cold when he asked, "How stupid are we? How can we lose a whole person?" He pointed to a spot on the ground. "She was right there."

Noah walked to where Ethan pointed, bent down and inspected the ground. The nasal quality in his voice didn't sound any better than Ethan's when he said, "Check for footprints."

Ethan joined him. They searched for only a minute before Ethan stood up and sighed. "It's useless. There's too many vines." He reached down and picked up a chunk of flora. "And this moss doesn't help, either. Have a look at this; you squash it and it pops right back up, good as new."

Noah sighed. "We're wasting our time. She probably headed back. Come on."

They walked back some ways before Noah let go of his nose and sniffed the air. To his relief, there was no scent of blackberries to be smelled. He looked around. "Do you know where we are?"

Ethan pointed. "There's the path Skye found."

"I never thought I'd say this, but I'm glad to see it." Noah made his way to the path.

Ethan joined him, "Me too, mate."

Just when Noah was about to yell for Skye again, he stopped and listened intently.

Ethan started to shout, but Noah held his arm out to stop him. "Wait, I think I hear her."

"Where?"

Noah pointed. "Over there."

In the distance, shrubbery parted and a figure emerged from the gloomy shadows. The boys watched, their anticipation turning to horror as a tall man dressed in filthy, torn overalls stepped into view. "Well, well, well, what have we got 'ere?"

His crooked sneer and yellow teeth said it all.

They were in trouble.

CHAPTER SEVEN
Human Tales

Neevya landed in a puddle of mud. A squeaky hiccup escaped her lips and she placed her hand over her mouth out of pure habit.

The small glimmer of peace Mr. Oak had granted her carried over even into this new realm. She closed her eyes and drew in a deep breath, letting her consciousness spread within.

Yep, still there.

Her joy had not been stripped away. Her heart leapt.

It wasn't a Permutation Precarious Portal after all!

She spread her arms wide as relief flooded through her, but it was quickly replaced by a bitter coldness that crept into her skin. Neevya sat up and tried to flap the chill from her wings. They were still soaking wet and achy.

She cleaned the mud from her legs and feet. "Faerie dust! You put one foot wrong, and off you go. I could be anywhere. It wouldn't surprise me if the blasted thing sent me all the way to Etorevyth."

She looked around at her new location and was surprised to see she was sitting at the bottom of a ravine. It looked like the same ravine the stream had occupied, except the raging water had been replaced by only a trickle of murky water and mud. Colorful gnomestools decorated the ground in sparse patches near the ravine's edge. Something else had changed as well, and this something was not quite right. The colors of the forest were faded.

What kind of magic drained the trees of their deep browns and rich greens? And what about the soil? Why was it so dull?

Neevya continued to glance around.

"Where in the realm of Faeyelwen am I?" she muttered.

She stood to get a better look. Then she clambered to the top of a nearby embankment and felt something bounce against her side.

How could I have forgotten?

She cooed when she looked down at her pouch, "Hey there, little acorn. Are you still with me? I hope I haven't lost you." Neevya carefully opened her pouch to check on the seedling. She sighed with relief. "*Gratimas*, Good Mother." Gratimas was the Fae word for a very special kind of thanks. It was the kind of gratitude that was born from the depths of one's soul and could only be said from a place of truth and reverence.

The sight of the seedling nestled safe and sound among the super-sunbeams made her smile. She counted the beams and felt a glimmer of pride that she hadn't lost a single one. When she was satisfied that all was well and good with the acorn, she decided to turn her attention to more pressing matters. Many things around her seemed familiar. The trees all seemed to be in the right places, and the terrain matched what she remembered of where she had just been. But something simply wasn't right.

Why is the forest being so rude?

The shrubs didn't greet her, and the insects fluttered past without a single word. Even the vines were unusually tight-lipped. More than that, she didn't feel any connection with her environment. Well, that wasn't quite true. If she concentrated hard enough, she could feel the inner life of the plant-dwellers, but it was hushed, almost as if her ears had been stuffed with flower petals.

She pressed herself against a tree trunk. *Why can't I talk to you? What's wrong with me?* She squeezed her eyes shut, trying to hold back tears.

Was it possible that she had been transported to Izathra, the dark side of Faeyelwen? If so, she was in real trouble. But she couldn't let herself believe her situation was that dire.

She pushed herself away from the tree. With luck, she would be able to detect the portal nearby.

Neevya bent down and buried her hands in the dirt. "Good Mother, show me the way."

Currents of undulating energy usually coursed through the soil, but on this occasion, only a few breezy wisps were detectable.

She glanced at the ravine. All sensible faeries would say the portal should be right where she was standing, but Precarious Portals were... well...precarious.

Too bad I didn't pay closer attention when King Kearoth taught me about them. I should've gone portal hunting with him and Zarian when they invited me. What was it they said to look for when tracking one down?

Neevya couldn't remember, but she did recall that Precarious Portals had been created by the fracturing of the Vathylite Crystal, the most powerful and magical vessel in all the world.

Centuries before Neevya was born, a great war among all the realms had erupted. Numerous accounts of the battles made their way down through history, but the story repeated by Neevya's tribe told of vile mortals known as *humans* destroying the Vathylite Crystal and leaving the Earth in turmoil. Supposedly, it was then that the realm of Izathra was created; born along with it were goblins, bogies, trolls, and all sorts of other dark and frightening creatures. Although Neevya never truly believed in humans, the mere thought of Izathra's dark creatures made the hairs on the back of her neck stand up.

She shook her head, shaking off her uneasiness, and began searching for the portal. She examined every tree, mound, and rock. As Father Sun drifted across the sky, Neevya wandered farther and farther away from the ravine, questioning if she was wasting her time. She took a break, stopping at the edge of a vast, hilly meadow.

Human Tales

Have I really traveled such a long way that the trees just—end? How is that possible?

Peering out from the tree line, Neevya saw a great expanse of grass covering several hillsides. It seemed odd that there would be no trees. "What's the point of growing nothing but grass?" she blurted out and quickly apologized to the nearest blades of grass for her insensitivity.

In the distance, she saw large, dull gray blocks popping over the horizon. They looked like huge, angular slabs of stone with rectangular holes carved into them. She'd never seen anything like them before, except perhaps in the Shimmers.

At the height of summer and when Grandmother Moon was her brightest, the Shimmers could be seen best. Neevya and her young friends often sat on tree branches and told human tales while they watched the glistening images. The Shimmers were rumored to be echoes of human villages superimposed into the kingdom of Faerie, but Neevya believed those stories were simply myths. As far as she knew, the tales were told to keep young faeries from wandering off.

What happens when you don't mean to wander off and end up astray?

As she looked around, the coldness she had felt earlier returned, this time accompanied by nervousness and dread. The intensity of her emotions drove her to her knees, and for the first time ever, she thought she might be wrong about humans being mere tales. The shapes in front of her were definitely not echoes of a distant and extinct realm.

They were *real*.

The air suddenly became stale, heavy, and unbreathable, and Neevya found herself gasping for breath.

"Oh no. Ohno-ohno-ohno. This can't be."

A dark, foreboding sensation pierced her heart and oozed into her arteries, poisoning her blood with notions of desperation.

Why do I feel so cold? Neevya hugged herself. *And my heart is pounding faster than a grasshopper on lightning juice!*

Her body quivered uncontrollably. Something terrible was happening within her—something she had never experienced before.

Maybe I went through a Permutation Precarious Portal after all! Maybe I'm transforming.

It felt as if blackness was rooting inside her and scattering its tiny, barbed seeds. Even when she plunged through the portal, she had not experienced such…such…she searched for the right word.

Anxiety? Regret? No.

Neevya tried to identify what she was feeling, as though naming it would give her control over it. Her mind searched for any hint of what it might be, and when she was just about to give up, she found it.

Fear! This must be fear!

She hunched and rubbed her arms, not believing that she, Neevya Brightwings Merrygold Suncatcher, could actually experience such a terrible emotion. No faerie since the breaking of the Vathylite Crystal had experienced fear—none that she knew of, anyway.

Neevya took a deep breath and shook her hands wildly, as if she could shake off that horrible plague.

What was it Kearoth used to tell me?

Looking down, Neevya paced and repeatedly patted her forehead. "Fear is like…fear is like…"

She stopped and looked up. "Got it! Fear is like a slithering creeper, if it's allowed to grow, it will kill its keeper."

She bent down and touched a vine under her feet, pushing her consciousness into it. *Please don't kill me.*

Silence.

"Trollspawn! Get a hold of yourself, Neevya." She stood. "That vine's *not* a slithering creeper."

Neevya sucked in a deep breath, held it, counted to ten, and let it out.

She reasoned that even though Precarious Portals were unpredictable, it was extremely rare for them to deliver someone outside of the enchanted realm of Faeyelwen. Besides, if the legends *were* true, the human realm was said to be located far away from any realm of magic. So, she should be fairly safe, unless she was in Izathra. She looked around. The trees in Izathra were supposed to be dead and malformed. The trees here might be drained of color, but at least they were alive. Where else might she possibly be?

Neevya went over a list in her head, *Alabastoria, Gwyndovia, Etorevyth. Dra*—"That's it! I must be in Dravolin!"

Dravolin was the kingdom of dwarves. She'd heard dwarves lived in stone structures, but she'd never seen one of their abodes. Nor had she seen a full-sized dwarf before. They'd always been shrunken down when they visited Ayin because they travelled through Perpetual Portals, which were nothing at all like Precarious Portals. Perpetual Portals were permanent fixtures that existed between the kingdoms of Faeyelwen. They had daily maintenance schedules and options for size-adjustment factored into them.

Her confidence grew with each new thought as her fear started to fade.

Except, there could be some vile dwarves out there. Not all of them were nice, and some clans were rumored to have eaten a faerie or two.

Along the edge of the field were wooden posts going all the way to the bottom of the hill and extending into the forest. Wrapped along these posts were terrible metal snakes with bristling points.

Neevya stood and looked up, suddenly realizing where she was kneeling. There, hanging over her head, was a coiled and glinting metal serpent.

Some of her friends were snakes, and she even donated a bit of her spare time to the Serpent Orphan Egg Club, but she had no desire to tangle with these gruesome looking creatures.

She noticed a splinter of dark metal driven into a nearby post. "Iron," Neevya whispered.

She slowly turned and tiptoed away from the iron splinter *and* the snakes, hoping not to catch the serpents' attention. Once she thought she might have a fighting chance of escaping, she ran right back the way she'd come. She dashed through the forest, nimbly hopping over bushes, skirting around trees, and plowing through grasses and other plant-dwellers. She ran as fast and as far away as she could.

Her feet raced almost as fast as her thoughts as she plunged deeper into the forest as though guided by some mysterious and unknown force.

Why would the dwarves use iron splinters?

Dwarves were just as susceptible to iron as faeries.

When Neevya finally made it all the way back to the ravine, she was running so fast she lost control and couldn't stop. With a yelp and a splat, she tumbled head over feet and landed face first in the mud.

"Great," she said sarcastically. "I must've slept in the wrong lily last night; it's been a horrible day." She spat out the mud she'd accidentally eaten when she'd bit the dirt.

Pushing herself to her knees, Neevya sat on her heels as the gravity of her situation hit home. There she was, utterly alone and stranded in a strange land with no idea how to get home. The plant-dwellers were not speaking with her, the insects were just as oblivious, and the little acorn would never find its perfect home. Tears welled in her eyes and tumbled uncontrollably down her mud-streaked cheeks.

"That's what I get for trying too hard." Her eyes were stinging. "Why didn't I leave well enough alone?"

Neevya slowly climbed to her feet and tried to brush the dirt and mud from her dress—the one she had made from a few colorful leaves she'd found three days prior. "Someone, please help me."

She peeked inside her pouch to make sure the acorn was still safe and sound. When her gaze landed on the seedling, she realized it had a faint glow. Something in her mind clicked into place, and she realized the acorn could be her key home! Seedlings were always full of enchantment—of life—and they resonated with other magical objects.

It can lead me straight back to the portal!

She excitedly plunged her hands into her pouch, but before she had a chance to withdraw the acorn, movement caught her attention. She quickly closed her pouch and squinted through the caked mud drying on her eyelashes; it did nothing to sharpen her vision. She rubbed her eyes and looked again, but a single, blinding ray from Father Sun found her, and all she could make out was the silhouette of a figure stomping toward her. Neevya's first thought was that it could be a Rescue Faerie. Surely her friends had noticed she'd gone missing and sent someone to save her. Or maybe it was one of the Watcher Faeries. She hoped it was the cute one. Better yet, maybe it was Zarian, the head of the King's guard. She looked down at her mud-covered body. On second thought, she hoped it was anyone but him.

It soon became clear the figure was not a faerie at all, but something much larger. Gnomes were slightly larger than faeries, and goblins a bit bigger than that. Pixies were bigger still, but most were not any taller than a shrub. By all accounts, even Dwarves weren't known to be too terribly tall. The biggest things she'd seen in her neck of the woods were deer, but this thing looked to be even taller than they were. Perhaps the Dwarves were larger in their own kingdom than she had assumed they would be.

The figure lumbered straight to Neevya, and the closer it came, the more she could see it was a great awkward thing garbed in dark blue cloth. Neon pink streaks—dull compared to the pink of the flower she had slept in the previous night—sprouted from the creature's head. Long black hair fell under the pink streaks and framed a brown face.

Their eyes met.

Neevya instinctively jumped to her feet and ran in the opposite direction. She didn't get far, however, because she tripped and suddenly felt a stab of sharp pain in her left calf. She tried to wriggle away frantically, but her leg was trapped inside something cold and constricting. She looked down and screamed, "Iron!"

She didn't even notice when her pouch containing the super-sunbeams and the acorn slid from her shoulder.

"Wow!" The figure cried out as its shadow fell over Neevya, who squirmed on her stomach and fought desperately to dislodge her leg from the iron object.

"I don't believe my eyes!" The figure bent over Neevya, but also kept its distance.

Neevya huffed and puffed, unable to stop tears from flowing down her cheeks almost as forcefully as the stream that had swept her away. She yelped when another stab of pain shot through her leg.

The figure hesitantly came closer. "Am I going crazy? Are you for real?" It knelt and gasped, "Oh, you poor thing, you're trapped!"

Neevya continued to squirm, but took a quick moment to peek over her shoulder and have a look at the creature. It was shorter than she originally thought, and a bit stocky, too. Discovering this brought a small sense of relief, and confirmed she was indeed in Dravolin.

But she didn't let her guard down. Besides eating a faerie or two, dwarves were also known for being shrewd, which meant they were exceptionally good at pretending to be other than they actually were.

"It'll be okay, little thing. Please don't cry. I may be able to help."

"I'm not crying." Neevya wiped away her tears. Her wings had become soggy and muddy again, and her neck was cramping as she strained to look over her shoulder to keep an eye on the dwarf. She made another effort to kick the object from her leg and flinched. The iron burned her skin, and a wave of weariness suddenly washed over her.

"Don't be afraid."

Neevya wasn't about to admit she was frightened, especially not to a cunning and perhaps hungry dwarf. "I'm not afraid. I'm lost—and I'm stuck." She pointed to the iron object. "See?"

The dwarf inspected it. "Looks like a tiny trap. How peculiar." Tentatively reaching for the contraption, the dwarf stopped just shy of grabbing it. "Promise you won't bite?"

Neevya searched its eyes, utterly confused.

She said the first thing that came to mind. "Me? Bite? I'm not the one who goes around eating flesh like your lot." As soon as she said it, she realized her mistake, and quickly tried to correct it by saying, "Sorry. I didn't mean to be impolite. It's just so painful, I can't think clearly."

The dwarf looked down thoughtfully, then slowly reached toward Neevya with trembling hands.

Was the dwarf afraid? Maybe it was just nervous. She supposed being around iron could make even the most daring Fae edgy.

Carefully prying the device from Neevya's leg, the dwarf said, "Tricky little thing, isn't it?"

Neevya winced as the object's teeth-like edges pressed deeper into her skin, but she didn't make a peep.

"One last twist," the dwarf said under its breath as it fidgeted a bit longer. The trap suddenly sprang open, releasing Neevya's leg. The dwarf held it up. "There, got it. Much better now."

A weak sigh escaped Neevya's quivering lips as a spell of dizziness hit her. She collapsed to the ground, her cheek resting on Good Mother's surface. The cool soil felt good against her skin and brought a sense of calm to the whirlwind that was spinning inside her head. She lay there motionless, waiting for the world to right itself once more. When the spinning stopped, Neevya took a moment to catch her breath and gather her strength—or what remained of it—to flip over and face the dwarf, but her aching leg and exhausted muscles refused to cooperate. She tried again. This time, her arms trembled as she buried her fingers into the dirt of Good Mother and summoned currents of energy to fuel her movements. She slowly rolled onto her back, and several moments later, sat upright. When her breathing normalized, and when the pain subsided a little, she surprised herself by saying, "Gratimas."

Neevya impulsively covered her mouth as if she had just said something inappropriate. How could she have been so careless? Gratimas was not a word to be used lightly, and especially not in front of a strange dwarf. But then again, it would have been impossible for Neevya to say it if she wasn't genuinely and profoundly grateful. The dwarf had saved her life, after all. If the iron had remained next to her skin much longer, it might have sucked away every bit of her life essence.

The dwarf's lips curved into something Neevya thought might be a smile. Its white teeth were incredibly large, large enough to eat a faerie in one gulp. "Gratimas?" it asked. "What's that?"

"It means I am deeply grateful." Neevya was surprised she had to explain, but maybe dwarves didn't say it all that often.

"You're most welcome," the dwarf said and then looked around as if surveying the area. After several moments, it turned its attention back to Neevya and peered straight into her eyes. "Not to be rude or anything, but what are you?"

First, Gratimas, and now this? Has this dwarf never seen a faerie?

Uneasy and apprehensive, Neevya did the first thing she could think of—she introduced herself. "I'm Neevya, a Sunbeam Faerie." She wanted to be as friendly as possible. It was the best she could do; what she was really thinking was, *please don't eat me.*

The dwarf unexpectedly clapped its hands and bellowed, "A real live faerie? I can't believe it! This is amazing! Wait till I tell the guys!" It beamed at her. "Oh, where are my manners? It's so nice to meet you, Neevya. I'm Skye!"

Neevya nodded in bewilderment. "You're the sky?" In all her years, she had never heard of anyone meeting Sister Sky before.

The dwarf giggled, "No, silly. I'm not *the* sky. That's just my name. It's spelled S-k-y-e."

As with most things in this strange place, Neevya was having trouble understanding exactly what was going on. The fact that she could understand Skye at all was remarkable. Most dwarves had to use translator spells when visiting Faerie. Either Skye and Neevya shared the same language or, more likely, the remaining energy from the portal that brought her here was somehow translating the words between them like one of Goblin Bob's chatter spells. Goblin Bob was the only goblin faeries could trust.

Skye reached down to pick Neevya up in her gigantic hands. She paused when Neevya flinched. Her eyes softened, and Neevya dismissed any thoughts that this creature could possibly be shrewd or deceptive. Her eyes were too kind to harbor ill intent.

"Don't be afraid, Neevya. I know you're lost and probably scared. I'd like to try and help you," Skye's voice was soft and encouraging.

Neevya examined the quality of the air around Skye's shoulders and saw what she had previously missed. Her aura was bright and clear, and was made of flowing currents of pinks, golds, purples and blues. Neevya interpreted the colors and emanations of the aura to mean that Skye was indeed trustworthy. Perhaps, with any luck, Skye might be able to take her to a Perpetual Portal. Neevya crawled into the dwarf's cupped hands.

"Let's go find the boys. Maybe they'll know what to do." Skye walked much farther than Neevya could have walked on her own, especially in her weakened state.

Neevya took the opportunity to inspect her calf where the iron trap had seized it. "Oh no!" she gasped. There was a small, dark blemish. Had the iron pierced her skin? She couldn't see it well enough to tell.

Skye stopped and looked at her curiously. "What's wrong?"

The world started to spin again. Neevya needed to feel the currents of Good Mother. She needed to touch the earth. Between hysterical pants Neevya managed to say, "I need rest. I need to touch the soil."

Skye's eyebrows raised. "All right, let's find a safe place to hide you." Skye searched for only a moment before saying, "Perfect." She placed Neevya among a pile of leaves near the side of a small hill. "You stay right here. I'll be back in a jiffy with some help and we'll get you to safety."

With a hurt leg and feeling as tired as Ole Grum, Neevya had no intention of moving.

Skye went back the way she had come, leaving Neevya alone. Neevya never dreamed she could feel so comfortable with a dwarf. It was truly an odd sensation. All she could do was hope Skye would return, and soon.

CHAPTER EIGHT
Scaretaker

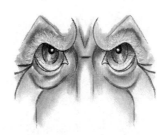

"This here's private property, lads."

Noah gawked at the spindly man with torn overalls, scraggly grayish hair, and a scruffy goatee. He thought the man looked an awful lot like one of those deranged, wicked sorcerers he'd been battling in his new video game.

"Know what happens t' bairns like ye in these woods?" The man spoke with a broad Yorkshire accent—short, hard a's, long o's and never pronouncing the t's. The heavy accent made it difficult for Noah to understand what the man was saying, and forced him to concentrate twice as hard. He'd never thought a time would come when he would have to translate English into English.

Noah gave Ethan a look that said, "What should we do?"

Ethan shrugged back an, "I don't know."

Noah stuttered when he said, "W-w-we're just on our way home."

"Well, ye can't come through these here parts, ye see?" He held up a wooden sign by way of explanation. "No trespassers allowed," he rasped, pointing to the sign. His voice was menacing, cracking at the end of each drawn-out word. He spread his arms wide, which made him look even more intimidating. "Look 'round, lads. Not a safe place fer young'uns like yerselves."

Noah looked sideways at Ethan, but he dared not turn his head or move a single muscle.

The man waved his hands in front of him as if swatting away a crow. "You'll be off now, I reckon. Go on. Run back the way ye came before the shadows wake up."

Noah started to turn, following the man's instructions.

Ethan grabbed Noah's elbow and whispered into his ear, "Not yet." He turned to the man. "Sir? I'm sorry to bother you, but you see, we're looking for our friend. She's lost. Maybe you've seen her?"

The man sniffed the air. "The only trespassers I see are ye two. Now be off with yeh's. Once they're awake, there's only so much I can do t' distract 'em."

Only understanding the first sentence the man spoke, Noah held up a shaky hand and amazed even himself when he said, "But we're not trespassing, really. Have you ever heard of the Right of Way law? It says we're allowed to cross here." He pointed to the ground. "Look, there's a public footpath. You can't legally impede us." Noah puffed up his chest and held his chin high, knowing he was pushing his luck. He locked eyes with the man, daring him to blink.

Both Ethan and the man looked at Noah with slack jaws.

Ethan whispered from the side of his mouth, "How'd you come up with that?"

Noah whispered back, "I've used it before."

The old man chuckled and spat to one side. "Well, ye've got a clever li'l noggin' on yer shoulders, ain't ye, lad?" He took two steps toward the boys and leaned forward. "You should know th' Dern didn't get its nickname fer nowt. There are things in these woods that'll gobble up fresh young'uns like yerselves."

Noah gulped. "The Dern?"

The man's crooked index finger came so close to Noah's nose that he could see the dirt under his cracked fingernails. "Th' woods lad!"

Ethan asked, "Don't you mean *The Dark Wood*?"

The man eyed Ethan, and then spoke to Noah as if he were the one who had asked the question. "I mean th' Dern. Townsfolk may call it Th' Dark Wood. But that name dun't even begin t' describe what's goin' on in here. It's th' Dern if I say it's th' Dern."

Noah heard what sounded like twigs snapping to his right.

The man looked in the direction of the noise and sniffed the air again. A strange expression crossed his face and he appeared to be straining to see something. After a few moments of silence, he turned back to the boys. "Even the smart ones get eaten in here. Brains don' matter in a place like this."

Noah worked up his courage to say, "She might be at that house way over there. Maybe she's waiting for us."

The man jerked his head in the direction of the building. "That's no house. That's a lodge. Ye've no bus'ness up yonder. If ye go snoopin' about, lads, I tell ye what, there'll be some—"

"But we need to find our friend! We can't leave her out here all alone," Noah pleaded.

The man sneered, "Oh, she's not alone, lad. That much I can guarantee." He looked around thoughtfully, as if considering all the things that could be keeping her company. Tapping his finger on his chin, he turned back to Noah. "I'll tell ye what; let's make a deal."

Noah and Ethan stared up at him, eager to hear his proposal.

"Ye come wit' me and I'll deliver ye outta these woods, then I'll look fer this lass of yers."

"No," Ethan blurted out. "We're not leaving here without her!"

The man shook his fist at them. "There's no way I'm lettin' ye stay in me forest! Like I said, th' Dern got a mind of its own, it has. I'm the caretaker, so I should know. Now if ye say yer friend's gone missin', that's a right shame. She may be alive, and well," he glanced around, "she may not. This wouldn't be th' first time some bairns bit off more than they could chew. But I won't be having it of ye two. *I'll* be the one to look fer the lass, just as soon as I get ye to the road."

Skye peeked through some bushes and observed her two best friends. They were speaking with a scraggly old codger who was clearly frightening them.

The git must think he's some kind of big shot.

She observed them for a few moments and then plowed through the bushes, waving her hands. "Hey, guys!"

Noah looked up with wide eyes. When she met his gaze, he let out a relieved sigh and tension visibly drained from his shoulders.

His respite didn't last long however, because he stiffened when she shouted, "I'm gone for a minute and you've already replaced me?"

Anxiety grew on his face as he made a frantic silencing gesture by cutting his hand back and forth across his throat. If she didn't know any better, she'd almost believe he didn't trust what she would say.

Skye quickly weighed her options and decided her best course of action. She stepped between the boys and the stranger. "Excuse me, sir, but it seems my mates here are lost. Good thing I came when I did." She tapped her foot on the ground the way her mother did when impatient. "Well, boys, what are you standing around for? Are we leaving or what? We can't hang out in the middle of this dingy forest all day, now can we? I don't know about you, but I've got places to be, people to see."

The old man seemed to be at a loss for words, which was exactly what Skye had hoped for. It wasn't the first time her brash approach had left someone dumbstruck. When he did find something to say, his voice was soft.

"Is this th' lass ye were lookin' fer, lads?"

"Aww, cute. You were looking for me? I just knew you two would fall apart if I didn't hold your hands the entire time."

"She's the one, all right." Ethan shot her a look.

Doesn't he realize I'm saving him? He should be down on his knees thanking me for rescuing him from this creep. Giving me dirty looks; the cheek!

The old codger regained some of his composure and grumpiness. His beady eyes narrowed. "All right then. Let's get movin'. Folla me."

Skye hastily wrapped her arms around the boys' shoulders and pulled them close. "No need to bother. We'll just head back the way we came." She flashed him her brightest smile.

The old man blinked several times and shook his head.

"Sorry to have been any trouble, sir." She winked and walked away, the boys in tow.

The man scratched his head as if completely stumped, then sniffed the air; a look of concern passed over his face and he headed toward the creepy lodge.

Like a force of nature, Skye swept the boys along, steering them as far away from the old man as she could, not knowing if she was heading back toward town or not.

When she was sure they were well out of earshot, she released her hostages and turned to face them.

"Is it just me, or does that guy have a few marbles missing? Who does he think he is, anyway?"

"He's the caretaker," Noah said.

Ethan chuckled. "*Scaretaker* is more like it."

"Scaretaker," Skye drew out the word and rolled it around her mind. It seemed fitting, and it had a certain ring to it. "That's what we can call him when we cross him again."

"Again? What do you mean, *again*?" Noah eyed her incredulously. "We're getting out of here and never coming back!"

Skye couldn't keep from smiling. "You'll never guess where I've been."

Ethan frowned indignantly. "Yeah, where the bloomin' heck did you get off to, anyway? You can't just leave us like that!"

"I didn't *just* leave you; I had a really good reason. There's something totally amazing I need to show you guys! It's so *chet*!"

Ethan looked surprised.

"What? I can't say *chet*?" Skye shrugged. Then she searched the forest and pointed. "We need to go that way."

Noah backed away. "Oh, heck no. I might not know where I am, but I do know one thing—that way leads us deeper into the forest."

Ethan began pacing and pulling his hair. "Have you lost the chettin' plot? We need to leave! Or are you turning into a nutcase like Scaretaker back there?"

Skye shook her head. "I'm going to pretend I didn't just hear you compare me to that creep."

Ethan looked at her as if to say, "Duh," and she responded with her best, "Whatever," look. He let out an exasperated sigh.

Skye could see he was about to lose it. "I tell you what; follow me and I promise you won't be disappointed."

"Why would we do that? It's Friday, which means it's sausages and mash for dinner. And I don't miss me mum's sausages and mash for nothin'," Ethan said with a seriousness that made the other two look at him sideways.

Somehow, she needed to convince them to follow her. Should she tell them about the faerie? Or should she lead them to the creature and let them discover the truth for themselves? She considered how best to break the news. It had to be done delicately, or they might think she'd gone off the deep end. Choosing her words carefully, she took a deep breath and asked, "Do you believe in faeries?"

The forest was still a nightmare to walk through. Noah kept snagging his school uniform on thorns and fallen branches. If Ethan didn't let him borrow an extra vest and maybe a shirt, he would have to come up with a good excuse as to why he needed an extensive repair job.

Mum is not going to be pleased.

Mum? Noah grinned. He was actually starting to think like a Brit.

"There are two things I want to ask you," Ethan said, jogging after Skye as she plowed through the undergrowth. "Well, actually I've got a thousand questions, but I'll start with two. First—faeries? And second— why am I following you through the chettin' darkest, dampest forest I've ever had the misfortune to be in, just so you can lead us to our certain doom, while there's still a scary-lookin' guy, who—whilst he was kinda helpful—won't be pleased if he finds us still here? Also, sausages and mash. Think about it."

Skye didn't stop to answer, or even to look back. She just kept beating a path through the trees. When she got an idea in her head there was nothing anyone could do to stop her, no matter how crazy it seemed. Noah and Ethan were swept along by the sheer force of her will. It happened a lot more often than Noah cared to admit.

"Trust me," Skye said. "I need your help with this. And when we get there I need you to be quiet. No sudden moves, no screaming."

Noah tugged the back of her shirt. "Screaming? Why would there be screaming?"

"Just remember, she's probably more afraid of you than you are of her."

She?

Something brushed against Noah's arm and he let out a yelp.

He swatted away the offending branch.

"Will you please be quiet?" Skye was being serious, which was rare for her. "I promised I would help her, but I didn't know what to do, so I came to get you guys."

Noah asked, "What are you talking about? You promised who?"

"Didn't you hear her earlier? She sounded scared, so I came over here to see what the problem was."

"You heard something in an eerie dark wood and just decided to go off and have a look?" Ethan hopped over a fallen log. "You've got a death wish, love."

"You're not taking this seriously. But you'll see. You'll both see."

Nothing Skye said made any sense, nor was it reassuring, but Noah had to believe that his friend wasn't reckless enough to get them seriously injured.

She stopped and pointed down a steep incline. "There she is."

Noah bent forward, but he didn't see anything unusual.

Ethan held his hand over his brow. "Looks like a chettin' hill to me." He turned to Skye. "What am I missing?"

Skye traipsed down the side of the hill and made her way to a clump of weeds. She knelt and mumbled something too quiet to be understood. The next thing Noah knew, she bent forward and picked something up.

Ethan started to speak, but Noah held out his hand. "Wait."

Noah suddenly felt apprehensive. It was the same feeling he had when he rode rollercoasters and was about to plummet over that first big hill.

Skye stood and turned to face them. Noah could see the edge of a wing—like a colorful, shimmering butterfly wing, only bigger. And then something spectacular came into view.

"Am I seein' what I think I'm seein'?" Ethan whispered.

Noah's eyes widened. "I...I don't know. What do you think you're seeing?"

"I'm not sayin' till you tell me. I'm not going to be the first one to say faerie." Ethan snapped his fingers. "Drat, I said it."

Noah was too stupefied to react. Nothing could have prepared him for what he saw. He stumbled down the hillside, barely catching himself in time to avoid tumbling to the ground. Ethan followed suit, but wasn't as lucky. Noah helped him to his feet and stared. In Skye's cupped palms, curled up in a ball with its knees tucked tightly to its chest, was, unmistakably, a faerie.

"Didn't I tell you?" Skye asked.

Before he realized what he was doing, Noah stretched his hand toward the creature, his mind desperate to confirm what his eyes were seeing. The faerie shrank away and shivered. He quickly withdrew his hand and looked at Skye. "I think I scared it—I mean her."

Skye looked at him with unshed tears in her eyes and smiled. "Isn't she amazing?"

In that moment, Noah saw something in Skye he'd never seen before. It seemed he could see straight into her soul, and it was radiant.

He smiled as his eyes, too, became damp.

Ethan knelt, which put him on the same eye level as the faerie, who was now pressing her back into Skye's belly. He motioned for Noah to join him.

Noah blinked back tears. The biggest scientific discovery in history had just fallen into his lap, and all he could do was get emotional? What kind of scientist would he make if he cried at every discovery?

He quickly knelt beside Ethan and began his analysis. By his estimation, if the faerie were standing, he'd guess she was roughly the height of two apples stacked atop one another.

How many centimeters would that be? His mind had a hard time thinking in precise terms at the moment, no matter how hard he tried.

He looked closer at the faerie. Her skin was pale yellow, and her wings looked like delicate, pink flower petals with bright, yellow veins. Around her eyes was an intricate decoration that resembled her wings. He leaned in for a closer look. That's when he noticed she was quivering. He wanted to find a way to comfort her, but was afraid anything he might do would only scare her more.

It would be just like me to mess things up.

Ethan cleared his throat loud enough to command Noah's attention.

Noah looked at him and shrugged, silently asking, "What?"

Ethan nodded and eyed him as if to say, "Well?"

Noah shrugged even higher and eyed him right back, continuing their silent conversation, "What do you expect me to do?"

Ethan shook his head before he turned back to the faerie. Resigned, he asked, "Wh-what's your name?"

Noah unexpectedly felt the reply as a sensation; the soft syllables were carried on the wind and spoken directly to his mind rather than to his ears. It was a soothing, tiny voice that said, "Neevya."

Chapter Nine
Faerie Tales

eading the way through the forest, Ethan hoped to see something that would tell him which way to go. Even though he wasn't familiar with his surroundings, glimpses of the setting sun revealed the general direction he thought they should travel.

Skye followed closely behind. "Anybody got a torch? It's getting darker."

Noah trailed her. "You mean a flashlight?"

"Yeah, that's what we call them on this side of the pond," Ethan answered. "Oh, and no. Somehow I forgot to pack a torch when I was getting ready for school this mornin'. Must've slipped me mind."

"I still can't believe it. It's been at least an hour and I'm still in shock," Noah's voice trailed off, as if he were daydreaming.

"I know, right? A real, live faerie!" Ethan glanced back at Skye, who cuddled Neevya protectively against her belly.

"Do you know what this means?" Noah's voice held wonder and excitement. "We can never look at our world the same way, ever again!"

"You two keep your voices down," Skye warned. "Scaretaker could be lurking around here somewhere."

As if he hadn't heard her, Noah continued to speak, "If faeries exist, then maybe unicorns do too, and what about elves? I'd love to meet an elf!"

Ethan imagined what it might be like to ride on the back of a unicorn, or better yet, a Pegasus. "Do you think the legends Mr. Bell keeps mentioning in history class are true? Do you think Achilles, Zeus, the Cyclops, and all those things actually existed?"

"I'll tell you what I think could exist," Skye said softly, "vampires, werewolves, and goblins. If there are faeries, that means there's gotta be bad guys, too."

Ethan shivered and hastened his pace.

A while later, they were still not out of the woods. Ethan knew he must have taken a few wrong turns, but he didn't want to tip off the others, so he started a small argument with Skye to keep her distracted.

"Don't get your bloomin' knickers in a twist."

"I still think she should stay at my house," Skye insisted.

Ethan sighed. "But your mum's way too nosy. Why do you think I let you keep your diary at me house?"

"Maybe because you know I write a lot of bad stuff about you in it. I'm sure you don't want my mum knowing half the trouble you get into."

She had a point. "Why do you keep a chettin' diary, anyway? All it can do is cause trouble." He turned and swiped at a tree branch. "Actually, now that I think on it, how 'bout let's have a diary burning party when we get back?"

"Don't even think about it! I'll just create a new one and fill it with nothing but Ethan Castleton factoids, and not the good kind. Then I'll leave it right on top of my bed for anyone to read."

Distracted by the thought of Skye's mum reading all about his mischief-making, Ethan accidentally bumped into a tree, scraping his elbow. "How's that for helpin' a friend out? If you had your way, I'd be grounded for life!" Before now, he had respected Skye enough to resist the temptation to read her diary. But if she kept this up, he just might have a go at it.

Skye placed her hand on his back, shoving him forward and steadying him at the same time. "That still doesn't settle the matter of where Neevya will stay tonight."

Noah chimed in, "Ethan's right, Neevya wouldn't be safe at your house, just like she wouldn't be safe at mine. Madison would probably eat her."

"But what about Olivia? Ethan's house is just as dangerous as ours. Can you imagine what his little sister would do if she found a faerie in her house? She'd probably—"

Ethan spun around. "Oi! Me sister's all right!"

Skye started to speak, but Ethan got in her face. "I mean it, Skye. You are one of me best mates, but I'll not hear a bad word about Livvy." It was okay if Ethan teased his younger sister, or even if he insulted her, but he wouldn't allow it from anyone else, not even a friend.

Skye defiantly stepped past Ethan and turned to face him. "I wasn't going to say anything bad about Olivia. How could you think that? Seriously, Ethan, sometimes I wonder what's rolling around in that pebble-sized brain of yours."

From the look on Skye's face, Ethan realized he'd misinterpreted the situation and felt a little guilty for snapping at her. But he wasn't about to apologize.

Thunder rumbled in the distance.

Noah skirted around Skye and Ethan to take the lead. "Cut it out, you two. We have to get out of here." He looked around and shivered, rubbing his arms. "Didn't you hear that? A storm is coming. This is the last place I want to be when it hits."

Ethan grimaced. How could he have forgotten he was lost in a haunted forest? How had he become a sucker in his own game? More importantly, why did Skye suddenly peer over his shoulder with a terrified expression?

Ethan's stomach sank. "What? What's wrong?"

Bright flashes of lightning suddenly reflected off the surrounding trees.

Ethan recoiled and waited for thunder to follow; only silence ensued.

He started to make a sarcastic remark to break the tension, but Skye slowly raised her hand and motioned for him to be quiet. Her words were barely audible when she whispered, "Shh, don't move. Don't make a sound."

Ethan froze and listened intently.

Her head jerked to the right. "There it is again. Did you hear it?" She squinted as if struggling to see something.

Ethan wanted to deny that he had heard anything, but couldn't. "Tell me that was only thunder."

All the color drained from Noah's face as his gaze settled on the same spot where Skye was looking.

Ethan struggled against his instinct to turn around for a peek, but maybe Skye was right—maybe if he stood completely still, everything would be okay.

He searched the others' faces for any sign of consolation, but found none. He looked at Neevya, who was now standing on her tiptoes. She had her hand up to her ear, listening intently.

Lightning flashed again, quickly followed by a loud clap and deep, rolling grumbles.

"Seriously guys. Tell me that was thunder and not some terrifying growl."

Noah shook his head and backed away, his hands thrust in front of him as if he were about to stop some unseen force from plowing him over. "Run!"

Neevya curled into a ball as Skye swiftly cocooned her hands around her.

Skye didn't have to be told twice. Neither did Ethan.

They ran, hopping over fallen trees, ducking under low-lying branches, and picking up their feet enough to avoid tripping over vines. Raindrops began pelting through the forest canopy. Ethan, now in the rear, fought the urge to constantly look over his shoulder, despite the feeling that something terrifying was right on his heels.

He spotted a familiar, crooked tree with gnarled roots and knots for eyes. Relief flooded through him as he realized they were close to Stillwater Street.

The feral growl came again, accompanied by a foul stench that took Ethan's breath away.

Stillwater Street came into view. He sprinted past Skye and Noah, not daring to turn around until his feet hit the pavement.

Skye was next to arrive, despite the fact that she was holding Neevya. Ethan had known Skye was fast, but he had always thought he could beat her in a race if he were serious about winning. Now, he wasn't so sure.

Noah kept running even after he reached the pavement; his feet slapped the semi-wet cement.

The rain stopped almost as quickly as it had started. The fading rumble of thunder retreated into the trees.

Ethan took a quick moment to catch his breath before realizing Noah was still running. He didn't have to work too hard to catch up with him and grab the back of his shirt. "Slow down there, mate. We're safe now. See?" Ethan gestured to the street.

Noah stared at him blankly, as if not understanding his logic.

"Besides what happened eight years ago, nobody's ever been reported to go missin' once they've made it this far," Ethan explained.

Skye jogged up to them. "We may be safe from the forest, but if we wait too much longer, it'll be completely dark, and vampires come out after dark." She shifted Neevya on her hands. "Even worse, if we don't get home soon, my mum's going to sit all three of us down and give us a what for."

As they walked, Ethan watched his feet, lost in his thoughts. He felt a little childish for panicking in the woods. If vampires and werewolves actually existed, *and* if they lived in his hometown, surely he would know it by now. His mum knew everything about the locals.

"Town gossip" didn't even begin to describe the talents his mum possessed in digging up the dirt.

Ethan suddenly realized that Noah and Skye were farther behind than he thought, and he adjusted his pace. When they caught up to him, he nudged Skye. "Can you move any slower?"

"Hey, watch it. I've got a delicate package here."

"Oops," Ethan chuckled. "Blimey! That forest was intense. I nearly lost it when I heard that growl."

"You can say that again," Skye agreed.

Noah giggled. "You should've seen your faces. You looked like you'd just swallowed some of my mum's spicy tofu."

They all laughed, and even though their laughter seemed forced, it made Ethan feel better.

"Sorry for being so hard on you back there, Skye. I know you wouldn't say anythin' bad about Livvy."

She elbowed him. "Aww, is the great Mr. Castleton going soft?"

Ethan felt his face flush, but it wasn't out of anger.

Skye uncupped her hands and held them so that Neevya was no longer hidden. "Look, Neevya, isn't he cute when he's embarrassed?"

Ethan was happy to see Skye smiling again, even if it was at his expense. He threw one arm around Skye and the other around Noah. "So, speakin' of Neevya, I think she should stay at—"

Skye threw him a doubtful glance, lifting one eyebrow. "Yeah?"

"Well, I guess the choice is yours, Skye. If you want to keep Neevya at your house, that's fine with me, and I'm sure Noah here will agree." Ethan squeezed Noah's shoulder, signaling for him to go along. Noah didn't protest. Ethan squeezed Skye's shoulder as well. "But just remember what your mum did the last time you brought home a stray."

Skye suddenly looked frustrated and handed Neevya to Ethan. "You take her."

CHAPTER TEN
Mark of Merlyn

Neevya traced her fingertips around the sore spot left by the iron trap, hoping it hadn't pierced her skin. She cowered at the thought of iron poisoning, especially since Ethan claimed he had no clue where a Perpetual Portal might be. He didn't even seem to know what a Perpetual Portal was. Her finger traced over a small divot in her calf, bringing her attention back to her injury. She twisted her leg and leaned over, trying to get a closer look, but couldn't see much in the darkness. *Oh well, I'll just keep an eye on it. It's probably okay.*

She was lying inside an odd hollow object that Ethan called a shoebox. That name didn't mean much to Neevya because she didn't know what a shoebox was. The lid was light enough to lift, but it was also heavy enough to make her feel protected. Feeling safe didn't keep her from tossing and turning, however, because her bedding—something called a flannel—was not nearly as soft as even the firmest flower in Ayin. How she longed to be back in her kingdom of Faerie. Nothing could beat being nestled inside a giant lily with its sweet perfume, caressing petals, and the welcoming essence that sometimes hummed lullabies to help a faerie drift into the realm of dreams.

As she lay there, thoughts racing, she suddenly felt a peculiar presence

- 93 -

nearby. It was faint, like a fleeting tickle in her mind. A shuffling noise seemed to be getting closer.

She had become accustomed to the sounds of Ethan's breathing, which contained the occasional snore; and she had to admit, the steady tempo of his inhalations and exhalations were quite comforting. This new noise was anything but. Neevya sat up and listened intently. Why had she refused Ethan's offer to poke holes in the sides of the box? Right now, she would have appreciated the ability to see what was out there.

Neevya released the remaining air from her lungs, closed her eyes, and concentrated on listening. She wasn't about to reach out with her mind, not until she knew what was coming for her. A tap, barely audible, sounded as if it were right outside her shelter. Neevya stood and pressed her ear to the cardboard wall. The lid of the box began to lift.

Hoppin' hobgoblins!

Neevya gasped and scampered away, pressing her back against the far side of the box.

A dark, shadowy form rose over the top of the box the way a merserpent rises from the sea.

Neevya pressed her hands firmly against the cardboard and pushed her knees together to keep them from shaking as two large eyes came into view.

The creature lifted the lid higher.

Neevya's legs went weak, and she crashed to her knees.

At first, she didn't understand what she was seeing, but light from a nearby window illuminated the creature's face, revealing what she believed to be a dwarf child; most likely a female.

Neevya sighed with relief. *I'm glad it's not a troll.*

Dwarves were sometimes known to associate with riffraff like that. Running into one of their lot might have meant her life. At least now she reckoned she was safe.

But why did she suddenly feel the urge to be near this Dwarf? Why did she unexpectedly feel that this was perhaps the most pure and innocent soul she had ever encountered?

And those eyes. They were green and vivid, like dazzling emeralds. Neevya craned her neck for a better look.

She caught a glimpse of a sparkle in the dwarf's left iris, but quickly lost it. She searched for it again and suddenly found herself feeling as if it were unimportant.

Without fully realizing what she was doing, Neevya pushed herself to her feet and took a step closer to those brilliant eyes. The young dwarf smiled and held out her hand. Neevya's first instinct should have been to withdraw or even run from the large palm, but something moved her forward, and she climbed aboard the soft, slightly sweaty chariot.

The next thing Neevya knew, she was in a different room, sitting among large strange animals covered in soft, velvety fur.

The young dwarf sat on her knees opposite Neevya. "I hope I didn't scare you." She brushed the hair from her face. "If I did, I'm really sorry. I didn't mean to."

Neevya reached out to the velvety animals with her mind but received no response.

The dwarf asked, "Is there anything I can do to make you more comfortable?"

Neevya shook her head, not knowing how to answer. Could anyone possibly be comfortable in the kingdom of dwarves? Comfort and Dravolin seemed as incompatible as faeries and leprechauns.

The young dwarf pointed to the two animals on either side of Neevya. "That's Henrietta Hoot and Todd the Turtle. They're me favorites. Ethan won them for me at a fair when I was little."

Neevya turned to the puffy purple owl. "Nice to meet you."

The young dwarf giggled. "No, they're not alive. See?"

She grabbed the lime-green turtle and held it up, squeezing its legs and head. Then she set it back down. "So, what's your name?"

Neevya cleared her throat. "I'm Neevya."

The Dwarf smiled. "Nice to meet you, Neevya. I'm Olivia, Ethan's sister. He's three years older than me, but I don't mind. I like having an older brother."

"You're the one he calls Livvy." Neevya was glad she had been paying attention.

"Yep, and I call him Eek-man when I think he deserves a good bit of teasing," Olivia giggled. "He makes a fuss about it, pretending to be upset and all, but it's just for show. It's kinda our thing."

A soft glow from a nearby nightlight cast just enough light for Neevya to see that the room the young dwarf had brought her to was covered in various shades of delicate pink stripes. This made Neevya feel more relaxed than the muted colors in Ethan's room. She gestured to the wall. "Lovely, the pink."

Olivia's smile grew wide. "It's me favorite color. It makes me happy, especially when I've had a hard day at school. School's not so easy for someone like me." She looked at the walls appreciatively. "There's just something about pink, you know?"

Neevya missed most of what she had said. She was too busy paying attention to Olivia's aura, a vivid luminosity around her body that she had never seen so intensely around anyone else before; it was brilliant as it sparkled and shimmered.

"Why are you looking at me like that?" Olivia asked.

Neevya fluttered into the air so she could inspect the radiant colors that glistened around Olivia's shoulders the way moonbeams danced on the water.

Olivia grasped a small crystal encased within an intricate silver wire-wrapping that dangled around her neck. Her gesture seemed instinctual, like she had done it a thousand times.

Neevya leaned forward to inspect the crystal.

Olivia held it up. "Do you like it? Me grandma gave it to me."

Neevya reached for the crystal, but Olivia quickly tucked it into the front of her shirt. "Me grandma said never to let anyone touch it."

Neevya, still dazed, whispered, "How unique," and turned her attention to Olivia's eyes, mesmerized by their innate wisdom and depth.

"Intriguing," was the next word to escape her lips.

A flicker in Olivia's left iris suddenly caught her attention, and once again she felt as if she were being hypnotized.

Neevya shook her head, and with great effort forced herself to focus. She fluttered even closer, searching for the source of the flicker.

Olivia simply looked at her, unblinking, as if it were quite normal to have a faerie inspect her eye.

Neevya's gaze settled on the flickering spot and her breath suddenly caught in her chest.

It can't be!

She zeroed in on the twinkle, confirming her worst nightmare. There, in Olivia's left iris, was the unmistakable Mark of Merlyn.

Rest my toad!

Neevya was so shocked her wings froze up and she tumbled onto Henrietta Hoot.

Olivia reached out to her. "Are you okay?"

Neevya sat up.

How is this possible?

"Neevya?" Olivia drew out her name as if searching for her in the dark.

Neevya shook her head and looked up. "Huh?"

Olivia bent forward. "Are you hurt?"

"Oh, no. I'm fine" Neevya pushed herself to her feet and forced a smile as she thought, *I need to figure out what's going on here.*

She flew into the air, determined not to miss a single detail that might give her possible clues as to who Olivia really was. The child's long, blonde hair fell loosely around her face. Innocent green eyes, flawless skin, and her ethereal aura made her look like one of the bellwethers she'd seen in picture scrolls back home in Ayin. The likeness was so uncanny that Neevya doubted this creature was a dwarf at all. Maybe she was one of those heavenly beings made flesh.

But where are her wings?

Neevya considered the possibilities and concluded that her idea was impossible; Faeries couldn't see bellwethers without the aid of Betwixters, those fabled humans who served as messengers between the bellwethers and her kind, the Fae.

Neevya blinked, a bit dazed. "Tell me something."

Olivia nodded, eager to please. "Sure, anything."

Neevya looked down and pressed her fingertips together in contemplation. *Don't jump to conclusions. I may be mistaken.* She paced back and forth over Olivia's plush comforter.

Olivia smoothed the wrinkles from the bedspread. "We wouldn't want you to trip or anything."

Neevya stopped pacing and looked up. "Do you know what I am?"

Olivia giggled. "Of course I do. You're a faerie."

"And, how did you know I was here? How did you know to find me inside that shoebox thingy?"

Olivia pursed her lips and seemed to think about it. "I'm not sure. I just woke up and...I knew."

Neevya took some time to form her next question. "Have you ever been to the kingdom of Faerie before?"

Olivia shook her head.

Neevya sighed, relieved.

But then Olivia added, "Unless dreams count. I've seen loads of faeries in me dreams. They come in different colors and sizes, and I've seen where they live, too. There's a castle with twisting spires, and a king with yellow skin like yours."

Neevya dropped to the bed and didn't even try to pick herself up. She was too stunned.

Have I found the fabled Betwixter from The Prophecy? I hope not. That would be terrible.

The Prophecy is about a human...not a dwarf!

Scaretaker didn't typically set foot in the forest once the sun had disappeared below the horizon, but his mission was important. He had to prevent any creatures from penetrating the magical barriers between the realms. He thought of Neevya as he knelt and examined his trap. He had checked it several times since he set it, but it still had not been triggered. "Curious," he whispered. Somehow, it had moved. Had the wind gotten a hold of it?

He shrugged and covered it with another dead leaf. As he stood, a wave of dizziness overcame him and a few words from an ancient prediction wafted into his mind. He found himself rhythmically chanting, "Those rare few who possess the gift shall save all souls beyond the rift."

How did the entire thing go? He could remember that one phrase, but knew there was much more to it than that. It had spoken of a time of destruction and darkness—a time when humans would battle a great evil. For no other reason than a nagging feeling in the pit of his stomach, Scaretaker figured that finding out *exactly* what it said seemed particularly important and relevant right now.

He headed back to his lodge to search his ancient scrolls for The Prophecy.

Chapter Eleven
Suntamor

kye woke early the following morning, even though it was Saturday. She had barely slept, unable to contain her excitement. Had she really found an actual faerie? Or was she having one of those dreams that seemed real but was actually her subconscious mind trying to mess with her? Perhaps it was telling her she needed to join the school play. Or maybe she was supposed to pay more attention to her history lessons. Whichever way she looked at it, Skye knew one thing for sure—if all this *was* real, nothing would be the same, ever again.

That night while lying in bed, Skye had re-played that first encounter with Neevya over and over in her mind. She vividly recalled Ethan eating blackberries, goop all over his face and dripping down the front of his shirt. Skye started to make an offhand comment about how she thought Ethan should wear makeup more often, but she hesitated when she felt a tugging sensation in the back of her mind. It was a strange cry that called to her. The compulsion to follow the call became so strong she didn't even bother taking her shot at Ethan. Skye dropped the blackberry she had just picked and found herself walking down a winding path that took her over a hill and through a tunnel of tightly packed vines that opened to an old dried-out stream bed.

Skye swung her legs over the side of her bed and slipped straight into her pink hippo slippers. Stretching, she lumbered to her wardrobe and put on her dressing gown. It was still very early, and even though the sun was up, the house was quiet.

She went through her normal morning routine, but flinched when her mum suddenly opened her bathroom door. The fact that Skye was brushing her teeth did not keep her mum from trying to start a conversation. But it did save Skye from having to answer the usual questions about her plans for the day.

Ethan was right; there was no way she would have been able to keep a faerie hidden here. Her mum had way too many boundary issues. What Skye thought of as her own personal space, her mum treated like a communal lounge, coming in whenever she wanted, even if it was to just have a chat and a cup of tea. It was almost as if her mum had forgotten what it was like to be a teenage girl—well, almost teenage. Her mum made it a point to continually remind her that she was only twelve years old, and that meant she was still a kid. She couldn't wait to turn thirteen. Her mum had promised to stop going through her things and to let her watch whatever she wanted on the telly when she became a teenager.

Goodbye problems; hello freedom!

Until her discovery in the woods yesterday, it had been Skye's main ambition in life to become a dance star. But finding out that faeries were real changed her priorities pretty fast. All Skye wanted to do now was go see Neevya as soon as possible. It had been hard, letting the little thing go home with Ethan.

She tried to act as normal as she possibly could around her mum—as if she had absolutely nothing exciting to talk about. Of course, on the inside she was exploding with anticipation. It took all her patience to sit through breakfast, keeping two pieces of toast handy. If her mum asked a question, she would stuff a piece into her mouth and pretend not to hear her. She knew how much her mum disliked it when she spoke with her mouth full, but was still surprised when it actually worked. She would have to remember this strategy for the future.

When she thought it was safe to escape without being interrogated, she went to the front door and shouted, "I'm off to Ethan's house to study!"

"Not yet, young lady," her mum shouted and came rushing to the door. She snatched Skye's phone from her hand, crossed her arms, and eyed Skye skeptically. "Don't you have some chores that need finishing?"

Skye groaned. "Sure, but that'll take forever, and I have so much stu—"

"But nothing." Her mum tapped her foot impatiently. "You're not going anywhere. And don't expect to get this phone back until all your chores are finished."

"Can't I at least text Ethan to let him know I'll be late?"

Her mum studied the phone as if considering Skye's request. Then her expression turned into a resolute mask of authority. She stuffed the phone into her back pocket. "The sooner you get your work done, the sooner you'll get your phone back. Now get upstairs and clean your room. After that, bring down your laundry, clean your bathroom, wash the dishes, and sweep the floors. Then we'll see if there's anything else that needs doing."

Skye felt powerless. Once her mum put her foot down there was no getting out of it.

It was well into the afternoon when Skye raced out the front door. Before hopping onto her bike, she sent a text to Ethan saying, "On my way!"

Ethan's house was a ten-minute bike ride away, and she pedaled as fast as she could to get there. He lived in a small terrace house, one of many identical houses that lined a narrow, winding street. If you didn't know exactly where you were going, it was easy to get lost.

When she arrived, she saw Noah's bike parked near the end of Ethan's driveway. She snorted, came to a skidding stop, and scoffed, "He's probably been here for hours. Stupid chores."

Skye let her bike fall to the ground as Ethan opened the door.

"What took you so long?"

"My mum made me do bloomin' chores," she grumbled. "What about you? What'd I miss?"

He stepped to the side and propped the door open with his knee. "Mum's taken Olivia out shoppin'. Dad's at the pub. Restocking day, you know."

His father had inherited a pub named, The Ugly Duckling. Ethan often had to go straight there after school to mop floors, wash dishes, and take out the garbage.

"I barely got out of havin' to go with him." Ethan's smirk said he thought he was quite clever.

"What'd you do? Pretend to break a leg?"

Ethan chuckled. "No. Noah showed up and said we had to study for some big science project. Dad bought it, and now Noah's waiting inside."

Skye eagerly marched past Ethan and into the house. She found Noah sitting on a beanbag chair in the front room. He stood when she entered.

"Where's Neevya?" Skye looked around but saw no trace of the faerie. "What have you done with her?"

Ethan motioned to an antique wooden table sitting against the far wall. A shoebox was turned upside down on the tabletop; its lid sat propped against the wall. Presumably, Neevya was under the box.

"She's fine, just a bit shy," Ethan said.

"How could you trap her like that, Ethan Castleton? I oughta…" Skye reached to lift the box.

Noah rushed up and blocked her way. "She put herself in there. I think she's scared."

"Oh really?" Skye crossed her arms indignantly. "She seemed okay last night. What happened?"

"I don't know." Noah shrugged. "She was like this when I arrived."

Skye glowered at Ethan.

He shrugged, palms up. "What? I didn't do anything."

Skye searched his expression. He seemed to be telling the truth, so she decided to ease up on him. Besides, how could she really expect him to figure out the reasons a faerie might hide? That would be a difficult task for anyone.

Trying to look at things from Neevya's point of view, Skye closed her eyes and allowed her shoulders to relax. Perhaps spending time alone while everyone slept wasn't such a good idea. Maybe it gave the faerie time to imagine all kinds of horrible things. Maybe she missed her home. Maybe being in a new and strange world was too overwhelming. Having to deal with that kind of stress might be enough to put anyone on edge, or even drive them crazy.

She opened her eyes to see Noah and Ethan staring at her.

Being as careful and as quiet as she could, Skye sat at the table and gradually lifted the edge of the box. A wing that looked like a colorful, velvety flower petal slipped out, but quickly retracted.

Skye put the box back down. She spoke over her shoulder, "Have you been talking to her?"

Noah shook his head. "Not hardly. She hasn't said a word to us all day."

"I reckon she's been reading our thoughts a bit though," Ethan scratched his ear.

"What makes you think that?"

Ethan joined Skye at the table. "I dunno. Just a feeling, I guess."

Noah offered, "She muttered to herself a few times, but I couldn't understand anything she said."

Skye slowly lifted the box again, peeking inside. There in the shadows sat Neevya, her knees curled up to her chest.

Something was different about her today. She appeared more cautious and defensive than she had the previous night.

Skye felt as if she were starting from scratch to win the faerie's trust. She softened her voice, "Good afternoon, Neevya."

A tiny hand poked out from under the rim of the box. Together, Skye and Neevya lifted the box so it no longer shielded her. Skye let go, stood, and backed away to give Neevya a bit of room. She nudged Ethan and Noah back as well.

Neevya turned around and dropped the box; it landed softly on the table.

Noah scrambled to his book bag and retrieved a notepad and pen. He sat on the beanbag chair and immediately began jotting things down.

Skye hissed, "What are you doing?"

"I'm not sure if you're aware of this, Skye, but this is the most important discovery in the history of science. Someone has to take notes."

By the look on Neevya's face, Skye thought she might crawl under the box again.

"I just want to make sure we record as much information as possible."

Skye lowered her voice in an effort to keep Neevya calm, but that didn't keep her from making her point to Noah, "What are you going to write—that you met a mythical creature in the forest? That some pixie showed up and you were there to help?" Skye ripped the notepad from Noah's grasp. "Do you want to turn her into some kind of science experiment and put her on display for all the world to see?"

She waited for Noah to answer, but he sat there on the beanbag, as if he were letting her words sink in.

Exasperated, Skye set her hand on her hip. "I think the best thing for us to do right now is listen to Neevya and see what *she* wants. Look at her. She needs our help. It's our job to protect her, not take notes."

That did the trick. As much as she knew Noah wanted to be a man of science, she also knew he didn't have an uncaring bone in his body.

Skye looked at Neevya, who was standing on the edge of the table.

As soon as their eyes met, Neevya crossed her arms. "I'm not a pixie!" She practically spat the words out. "It's best you remember that. Pixies can be dreadful things. You wouldn't want to run into one."

Had Skye mentioned pixies? She hadn't known pixies were bad. She bent forward and explained, "I'm sorry. I didn't mean to call you a pixie. It was an honest mista—"

"And I suspect you're not what you seem to be, either," Neevya interrupted.

Her change in attitude threw Skye for a loop. Why had she suddenly gone from being a scared, timid creature to such a mouthy little thing? "Neevya, what's wrong? Did we offend you?"

Neevya wrinkled her eyebrows and shook her head.

Noah added, "We didn't mean to upset you. We truly didn't know about pixies."

Neevya sighed. "It's not that. It's just, when I met you three, I thought you were dwarves. But something's happened to make me think otherwise."

Skye wondered what Ethan had done to turn the faerie against them. She gave him a quick glare, totally missing the faerie's comment about dwarves.

"I can't figure it out. Humans are mythical monsters meant to keep young faeries in line. Plus, they're bigger and scarier than you three. They're real nasty."

Neevya looked at Skye as if everything she had just said was totally normal.

Skye wondered why faeries had such strange ideas; humans weren't monsters. "Well, Neevya, I'm not sure how you're going to take this, but we *are* humans, regular people. Not monsters or anything. Just three normal kids."

Neevya darted back to the box, but before lifting it, she squinted at the three of them intently. "If humans are real, that means the stories are true!" Her face suddenly turned pale and her eyes grew wide. "This cannot be happening. I cannot be in Suntamor!"

Skye mouthed a question to the boys, "Suntamor?"

Shrugging, they seemed just as confused as she felt.

The look on Neevya's face made Skye feel as if Neevya completely distrusted, even despised her.

Skye shrugged and spread her palms wide. "We're sorry. We don't know what Suntamor is. We didn't even know faeries existed until yesterday. Your existence is a shock to all of us."

Ethan nodded.

Skye continued, "We know this must be extremely difficult for you, to be trapped in a place you believe is full of monsters. I know I would be scared. But people are not monsters."

Noah raised his hand as if asking permission to speak. Skye did not call on him, but that didn't stop him from saying, "Well, that depends on how you look at it. Take Grucker, for example. He's—"

Skye shot him her meanest look, cutting him off. What was he trying to do, scare the poor thing to death?

She turned back to Neevya. "We are not monsters, and believe it or not, we are just as confused as you. We were very surprised to find you in the woods, and we really have no clue what Suntamor is."

Neevya slowly eyed each of them. "You're not just trying to bamboozle me? You really don't know?"

Noah made a hand gesture. "Scout's honor."

Skye rolled her eyes.

How would a faerie know what that meant?

She tried to clarify, "Truly, we don't have a clue what you're talking about."

Skye let out the breath she had been holding when Neevya's expression turned from suspicion to acceptance.

"Suntamor is the name given to your realm, the human realm."

"Wow," Ethan said. "I didn't know we had our own realm."

Neevya traced her toe on the table and clenched her hands behind her back. "I suppose we all have a lot to learn."

"That we do," Noah said.

"Yeah, and on top of that, you've been through a lot." Skye tried to make her smile as tender and caring as possible. "I'm sure it's difficult to know what to think. I would be freaking out if I were you."

"Freaking out? What does that mean?" Neevya looked puzzled.

Noah spoke up. "It's a slang word that means to think and act irrationally; or to experience emotional instability."

As if fully embodying the words, Neevya suddenly started acting irrational, and she definitely seemed emotionally unstable as she patted her side and looked around frantically. "Good Mother! I'm freaking out! Good Mother! What did I do?"

Ethan rushed to her side. "What is it? What's wrong?"

Neevya zipped through the air above Ethan's head, excitedly waving her hands. "This is impossible! I've lost my pouch!"

"What pouch?" Skye eyed Ethan accusingly.

Ethan shrugged. "Don't look at me. I don't know what she's talking about. She didn't have one last night."

"That pouch is really important! I can't believe I lost it." Neevya landed on the table and buried her face in her hands. "I'll never forgive myself."

Skye wanted to help but had no clue where to even begin. "When did you last see it?"

"In the woods." Neevya paced back and forth.

Skye tentatively stepped toward Neevya, trying to recall the scene where she had discovered the faerie, but she didn't remember seeing a pouch anywhere. She slowly knelt and hesitantly reached toward Neevya, hoping not to scare her away; the poor thing was probably in shock.

Neevya stopped pacing and looked up at Skye, her expression a reflection of distress and uncertainty.

Skye gently scooped Neevya into her cupped hand and pulled the delicate faerie close to her heart. "Poor little sweetheart," she cooed. "It'll be okay. Everything will work out. You'll see."

At first, Neevya went rigid, but then she melted into Skye's comforting embrace and wept. Between sobs, Skye thought she heard the little faerie say, "I'm sorry, little acorn. I'm sorry, Mr. Oak."

Skye hugged Neevya as best she could as she rocked side to side and hummed a soothing lullaby her mother sang to her years ago. It was a tune that always made Skye feel safe and comforted.

Noah sat brooding in the beanbag chair, feeling as if the day was slipping away. He couldn't take his eyes off Skye, who was coddling the now sleeping faerie in her palm.

A sense of foreboding congealed in the pit of his stomach.

Besides Neevya's obvious misery, the chance that she could be discovered at any moment had been weighing heavily on his mind since Skye had chastised him for taking notes. For supposedly being so smart, sometimes Noah felt utterly senseless, and taking notes would have proven his foolishness. He was glad he didn't have any evidence that could endanger her, and he would have to be careful not to take anything home that might reveal her existence to his keenly observant father. How might his dad react if he learned Noah was hiding a faerie? Would he ground Noah to his bedroom and lock Neevya away in a top secret laboratory? And why was he so jumpy throughout his late dinner last night, taking every opportunity to get up and glance out the kitchen window? If it hadn't been for his strange, mumbled comment—"Just think, I used to read you fairy tales,"—when Noah was getting into bed, Noah might have been able to dismiss his father's odd behavior. But, that particular comment seemed too coincidental. Plus, this morning, his father had gotten an early phone call that was quite mysterious. Noah tried to listen in and thought he heard his dad say, "A gateway?" When his dad noticed Noah standing outside his study door, he quickly shut it and lowered his voice. A short while later, he'd darted out of his office, bumping into Noah and fleeing out the front door without even saying goodbye.

The more he thought about it, the more Noah was certain he needed to do everything he possibly could to protect Neevya from being discovered. If the government, his dad, or his dad's security firm got their hands on what they would see as an exotic specimen and not a living being, he would never forgive himself.

Noah stood, walked over to Ethan and started to speak.

Skye whispered, "Quiet voices, please."

Neevya stirred.

Noah lowered his voice, "What are we going to do?"

Ethan shrugged. "No clue, mate. But Mum and Livvy will be home any minute."

Noah nodded. "Right. We need to get out of here."

Ethan's voice rose, "I didn't mean we should leave!"

"Quiet!" Skye hissed.

Neevya lifted her head and looked around through squinted, puffy eyes.

Ethan whispered, "Oops, sorry." Then he turned his attention back to Noah. "What I was trying to say is that we need to take Neevya back to me bedroom. That's all. There's nothin' stoppin' her stayin' here with me. This can be her new home. I can protect her. And maybe, eventually, I can tell me parents and Olivia about her, too. We can be her new family."

Neevya stood and stretched.

"We can't trust anyone, Ethan." Noah raised his voice a tad louder for emphasis, "Don't you understand? Nobody. Not our parents, not our teachers, not our friends."

Ethan scoffed, not even trying to be quiet this time. "What friends? When did you become Mr. Popular?"

Noah frowned with indignation. "Listen, we all know what we have here is the discovery of a lifetime. We have proof there is more to life than we can see. Neevya is definitive evidence that what most people believe to be only legend and fiction is actually real. We're seeing the existence of the supernatural, and there are a lot of not-so-nice people who would do anything to get their hands on her. Plus, we must remember there's a natural order to things. Faeries do not belong in our world. As much as I hate saying this, she must go back, and *we* have to help her."

"Great, you two. Now see what you've done?" Skye asked.

Neevya rubbed her eyes and flitted into the air. "No, it's okay. I rested well." She looked at Skye. "And thanks. You've been so kind to me."

Skye's smile reached her eyes. "You're welcome."

Neevya turned away from Skye and flew until she hovered in front of Noah and Ethan.

Skye joined the boys so they all faced the faerie.

Neevya addressed Noah, "Thank you for your concern. You clearly know what's at stake here."

She spoke to Ethan, "Your hospitality is much appreciated."

Lastly, she looked at all three of them and smiled apologetically. "I'm sorry I called you monsters."

Noah's heart melted. He wanted to banish her remorse. "It's okay, Neevya. There's no need to apologize."

Ethan agreed, "Yeah, it was an honest mistake. I can definitely see how you would think Skye here's a monster. She scares me, too."

Noah couldn't stifle the snicker that unexpectedly escaped.

Neevya chuckled as well.

Skye slapped Ethan's shoulder. "I can't believe you just said that." A broad grin spread across her face.

They all laughed, letting the moment live and breathe.

When the laughter died down, Skye was the first to speak. "So what do we do now? Should we find you a new home? Do you think you could be comfortable staying here with Ethan?"

Neevya graciously bowed. "I would be honored to stay with any of you, but Noah's right; I need to get back. It's not safe here for me. Humans and Fae do not mix. The last time our two worlds met, things didn't end so well for either of our realms. If you could help me get back to Ayin, my home, I would be eternally grateful."

There was something about the way she said 'eternally' that made Noah think she meant it, literally. He also noticed she tended to use her hands a lot when she spoke, almost as if she were signing everything she said.

"I don't know exactly how I got here. And I know even less about how to get back, but one thing I am sure of is that we need to find my pouch. Once we find that, I believe I can locate the portal that brought me here, if it still exists."

Noah was glad to see the spark of hope in her eyes.

"You mentioned a portal before," Ethan said. "Is that how you travel from one world to another? I mean, from the faerie world to our world?"

Noah was reminded of the sci-fi novels he'd read. He used to think the notion of portals was entertaining, but not necessarily plausible. Now, anything seemed possible.

To Noah's surprise, Neevya landed on his head and slid down his body and onto the floor, where she sat cross-legged. Ethan, Skye and Noah sat around her in a circle.

"Yes and no. Yes, we use portals. No, we don't travel to Suntamor, your realm. Like I said, humans and Fae don't mix. Most portals between our realms were shut down and laws were made to prevent their creation. But obviously, they're still around if you look for them. Or in my case, I think one came looking for me."

Noah propped his head on his fists. "How *did* you end up here, anyway? I want details."

Neevya shrugged and rocked from side to side, tilting her head. "I'm not exactly sure." She scooped a ball of dust off the floor and held it lightly in her palm. She looked at it so lovingly that Noah thought she must think it was alive. When she rested her chin on her palm and whispered something to it, he was convinced.

Neevya looked directly into Noah's eyes. She gave him a soft smile and blew the dust bunny from her hand. "Seeing as none of you are likely to tell anyone, I think I can tell you the story—even if it wasn't my finest hour."

They drew nearer. This was one story they didn't want to miss.

Neevya cleared her throat and lifted her finger. "It all started when I was harvesting sunbeams."

CHAPTER TWELVE
The Trap

$\mathcal{S}$ caretaker's muscles quaked under the pressure of the chondour's telepathic assault. It felt as if an enormous pressure squeezed his brain and threatened to crush his skull; although the old man resisted with all his might, the chondour was strong, much stronger than he should have been—another sign of the misfortunes that lay ahead.

The pain from the chondour's attack sent Scaretaker to his hands and knees. The cold stones of the dungeon floor pressed into his bones, and he felt as if he carried the weight of ten men on his back. His voice was strained when he spat his words, "Ye can't get the best o' me." Drool dripped from his lips and landed in a puddle on the stone floor. "Ye've been me family's prisoner for thousands o' years, an' I aim to keep it that way."

A deep voice resonated inside his mind, *You can try, but as the world's balance weakens, my powers grow stronger. You knew this time would come. Release me now and I will spare you. Release me now and we will work together. We will rule the world.*

Scaretaker ignored the chondour, passing his promises off as lies. He used all his strength to push himself to his feet. Even though the dungeon was cold, sweat drenched his body. His steps were heavy as he moved away from the circle of magic that imprisoned the chondour.

The chondour spread its black, leathery wings wide as its deep voice boomed inside Scaretaker's mind. Scaretaker instinctively grasped his head as though he could silence its intensity, but covering his ears was just a useless reaction.

The chondour's telepathic message pierced Scaretaker's brain as if it were a well-aimed arrow. *I've been around since the beginning of time. You, like all humans, are just a babe. I have the wisdom of a thousand of your sages. I knew your ancestors—the order of Serptorian. I knew their secrets, their magic. I can teach you. I can show you their ways.*

Scaretaker didn't need his help. His pa trained him well; Scaretaker had read all the scrolls, practiced all his spells to the point of perfection, and studied with the greatest Serptorian teachers of the age. He didn't come down to the dungeon to bargain with the chondour. No, he came for answers. "Don't waste yer time, or mine."

The chondour paused as if considering. Then he said out loud, "We found the correct offspring. They are the ones we seek. Magic runs deep within them. They must be destroyed, for both our sakes."

"That's not what I asked. The Prophecy—is it true?"

The chondour approached the edge of his magical prison and eloquently spoke, "Not if you let me loose. Not if you give the children to me while there's still time to thwart it."

Scaretaker pressed his back against the large iron door and contemplated as he whispered to himself, "But they're just bairns." He eyed the chondour suspiciously. "Ye'd say anythin' to escape."

The chondour crossed his arms and folded his wings around his body. "Would I? Are you certain?"

The Trap

The rattle of the doorknob startled Noah and the others into momentary silence.

Skye darted across the room and grabbed the shoebox.

Ethan flung the lid to her. "Quick, they're home!"

Skye caught the lid and held the box steady as Neevya darted inside.

The front door flew open and Olivia bolted through the doorway. She hastily glanced around; her gaze fixed on the shoebox. A huge smile spread across her face and she waved.

"Darned lid," Skye huffed.

Noah glanced just in time to see a tiny waving hand retract into the shoebox as Skye secured the lid.

What just happened?

Ethan moved to block Olivia's view as his mum stepped into the entryway, carrying shopping bags.

"Hey Skye!" Olivia craned her neck to peer around Ethan.

"Hey," Skye replied, nonchalantly.

Olivia looked at Noah and blinked shyly. Her voice was soft when she said, "Hi, Noah."

Noah nodded his greeting.

Turning her attention to Ethan, she asked, "So, what are you guys up to?"

Ethan waved his hand behind his back, signaling Noah and Skye to make their way out of the front room and toward the stairwell.

"Who, us? Uh, we have a huge school project and it's gonna take all weekend to finish."

"What kind of project is it? Maybe I can help."

"Nope, sorry. It's uh, you wouldn't understand."

Olivia looked so pitiful, for a moment Noah was almost convinced she should join them.

Mrs. Castleton glanced at Olivia, her expression compassionate. "Just let her join you while I put these things away and start some dinner. It won't take more than twenty minutes."

"Nope. Can't do it. Need to focus. No distractions." Ethan shoved Skye and Noah up the stairs, toward his bedroom. "Sorry Livvy, really."

Her shoulders slumped in disappointment, Olivia wandered through the front room and turned on the television.

His mother called after him, "Well then, love. I'll give you half an hour. Then you and Olivia can ride your bikes to the pub and fetch your dad for dinner. It'll be good for you to get out of the house. You can also get me favorite mug back. It's been there for weeks, and he keeps forgettin' to bring it home."

Ethan rushed into his bedroom and slammed the door behind him. "That was close."

Noah asked, "Do you think she saw her? Olivia, I mean? Did she see Neevya?"

Skye set the shoebox on Ethan's desk. "I don't think so. I'm sure I got the lid on in time."

Ethan fell against his door and slid down it until he sat on the ground. "We need to be more careful."

"You can say that again," Skye agreed.

Noah raised the shoebox lid and lifted Neevya out of the box. He walked toward the bed but tripped on Henrietta Hoot, Olivia's purple stuffed owl that had somehow made it onto Ethan's floor.

"Ouch," Neevya said.

"Oh sorry, did I hurt you?" Noah kneeled and gently placed her on one of Ethan's pillows.

Neevya rubbed her leg. "No, it wasn't you. It's this injury."

Noah bent forward to have a closer look. "You're hurt? Let me see."

Neevya raised her leg for him to inspect.

Finding a small mark that was slightly discolored, he asked, "How did this happen?"

Neevya traced her finger around the wound. "There was this trap—"

"That's right!" Skye swiftly crossed the room to peer over Noah's shoulder. "There was this tiny trap out in the middle of the woods. I've never seen anything like it."

"Who would do something like that?" Noah scratched his head.

Ethan said, "I bet it was Scaretaker. No telling what kinds of things he likes to hunt in those woods. I bet he even has traps for kids, like nets that scoop you up into the trees when you step on a stick or something."

"I wouldn't put it past him." Skye eyed Ethan knowingly.

Neevya shrugged. "Well, I'm not sure if what you say is true, but I do know that trap was made of iron."

By the look on Neevya's face, Noah knew she expected him to understand the significance of her statement, but it went right over his head. Without trying to hide his confusion, he asked, "So what does that mean, exactly?"

Neevya seemed perplexed by his lack of understanding. "It could mean I have iron poisoning." She covered the injury with her hand. "But it's too early to tell."

"Iron poisoning?" Skye gasped. "That sounds bad. What is it? How can you tell if you have it? What are the symptoms? Is it serious? What does it do? Does it hurt? Can it be cured?"

Both Ethan and Noah looked at Skye.

Neevya gingerly pressed the wound. "Yes, iron poisoning is serious. Without the cure, it's dead—"

"Say no more," Noah quickly interrupted. His mother had taught him that spoken words had power. "We get the picture."

Ethan had his eye so close to her leg that a single nudge might've blinded him. "Looks like it's nothin'. I can barely even see it."

Neevya pulled her leg back. "Even so, iron poisoning can be tricky. One moment you think you're well. The next—"

Noah interrupted her again. "You mentioned a cure. Do you know where we can get it?"

She nodded. "There's only one sure-fire cure I know of, and it's in my realm."

"Are you certain that's the only one? Maybe there's something here that can work. Do you know what it's made of?" Noah questioned.

"I don't know the lesser ingredients, but I do know the main one."

Noah waited but she didn't offer any additional information. "Well, what is it?"

Neevya smiled shyly. "Magic."

Noah was amazed. He'd expected her to say it was made of something like rosemary, rose petals, or even beetle dung—but magic? That wasn't something they could pick in a field or purchase at the local supermarket.

Skye must've been thinking the same thing he was thinking because she said, "Guys, you know what this means, don't you?"

"It means we *really* need to get Neevya back to her home." Noah stood. "We have no time to lose."

Skye glanced out the window. "It'll be dark soon."

Ethan started pacing. "Yeah. And there's no way we can survive those woods at night. It's too dangerous. No chettin' way."

Ethan was right; it was too dangerous. But what choice did they have? If there was even a remote chance that Neevya might be dying, they had to do whatever it took to save her life.

His decision made, Noah turned to face them. "It doesn't matter if it's dark outside or not. Neevya needs to get home, and we have to get her there." He picked up the shoebox and sat on the bed beside Neevya, offering her the chance to crawl inside. "You ready to go?"

Neevya started to climb inside, but paused and glanced out the window. "The darkness will awaken soon," she muttered. She clambered off the box and sat back onto Ethan's pillow. "We don't have to go tonight. I mean, I'm okay for now." She inspected her leg again. "Now that I see it in this light, it looks good. I highly doubt that I could get iron poisoning from this tiny mark."

"Really?" Noah eyed Neevya suspiciously. "Are you sure?"

"Absolutely, see?" Neevya lifted her leg again and held it toward Noah. "I don't see any black tendrils crawling out of it. Do you?"

Noah turned to Ethan. "Where's your magnifying glass?"

Ethan smirked. "I'm not a scientist like you, mate. I don't keep lab equipment just lyin' 'round me room."

Noah inspected Neevya's leg once more, paying closer attention to the details this time. The place on her calf was tiny, but it wasn't very dark. It looked more like an indentation than an actual wound. He asked, "So it hurts?"

Neevya winced when he gently prodded it. "There's definitely pain, but it's not anything I can't handle."

Noah frowned as he continued to study her leg. "I don't see any black veins or tendril thingies. It doesn't even look like your skin was broken."

Neevya sighed. "That's good. It's probably just a deep bruise that hasn't come out yet." She looked around as if trying to find something. She spotted what she was searching for. "If only Henrietta Hoot were real."

Ethan looked at her, puzzled.

Noah glanced at the stuffed purple owl. "Who?" he asked, pun intended.

Neevya pointed. "That owl. If she were real, she might be able to soothe my pain. An animal with powerful restorative magic might even be able to cure iron poisoning if it's caught early enough, but that's very rare and there are no guarantees."

"That's amazing. Do *all* animals have healing abilities?" Skye asked.

Neevya nodded. "I wouldn't call them healing abilities. Their magic is more restorative in nature. There's a big difference. But to somewhat answer your question, yes; most animals are able to help others feel better to some extent. But like anything else, some are better at it than others. I've actually spoken to some pretty powerful owls, wolves, deer, rabbits—"

Noah had an idea. "You said wolves?"

"Yes, wolves often have extremely powerful abilities."

Noah repeatedly tapped his finger on his chin as he peered out the window in contemplation. *Wolves are ancestors to dogs. Hmm...I wonder.*

He fixed his gaze on Neevya. "This might be too much of a stretch, but could a dog help you feel better, possibly heal your leg?"

Neevya thought about it. "A dog? I've heard of them, but I've never met one. Which forests do they live in?"

Skye giggled. "They usually don't live in forests. They live here, with us."

Noah added, "Yeah, but they are descended from wolves."

Neevya seemed to consider their statements carefully. "There's really no way to tell what a dog's abilities might be. Like I said, each individual animal is different. Each has its own unique talents. But if they're related to wolves, chances are good they're quite gifted."

Noah thought Neevya must really love animals. The more she spoke, the more excited she got.

Ethan rubbed his palms together and gave Noah a sly grin. "Are you thinking what I'm thinking?"

Noah nodded. "I think so."

Skye bumped Ethan's shoulder. "I think I'm thinking what you're thinking, too."

They all exchanged knowing glances and said in unison, "Madison."

CHAPTER THIRTEEN
Operation Forest Storm

Noah knew leaving Ethan's house would not be as easy as just walking out the front door. Mrs. Castleton's demand for Ethan to go to the pub with Olivia to fetch his father meant they needed to sneak out without being noticed.

Ethan pressed his back against the wall near the top of the stairs and took a quick peek around the corner. He whispered into an imaginary spy watch, "Operation Forest Storm is a go."

Skye eyed him doubtfully and whispered, "Seriously? You're going to play games at a time like this?"

Ignoring Skye's comment, he flattened himself to the ground, used his hands as fake binoculars, and peered down the stairs. "All clear. Let's move out."

Noah spoke into his pretend cufflink, "Roger that. Skyefool."

Skye eyed Noah incredulously. "Not you too."

Creeping down the stairs with all the grace of a wounded badger, Ethan cocked his imaginary gun and spoke into his spy watch. "Radio silence, please."

When he got to the last step, he ducked and rolled across the floor to the opposite wall. Then he pointed his fictional weapon into the front room.

He glanced up the stairwell and waved for Noah and Skye to join him.

They started down the steps, Neevya tucked away in the backpack fastened to Skye's shoulders.

Ethan jerked his hand up.

Skye and Noah froze.

Ethan launched himself to the side, toward his dad's study, and disappeared out of view.

What was meant to be a simple get-out-quick plan had been transformed into Ethan's personal spy adventure.

Noah grinned.

Skye, on the other hand, tutted, "Poor kid."

Noah and Skye crept halfway down the stairs.

Noah ducked and peered over the wooden banister.

Ethan popped back into the hallway and slid along the wall, giving a thumbs-up to Noah. He whispered, "Madame Mum's lair is clear. Time to check on Dr. Livv."

Noah figured he could imagine what Ethan was up to when his friend stood tall and gestured. *He's adjusting his imaginary pin-striped suit. Pulling a cigar from his inner coat pocket. Smelling it.*

Ethan looked up at Noah and stretched his hand out.

Oh, how nice. He's offering me a poisoned cigar.

Noah declined his offer.

Ethan winked. "Wait for my signal." He crept toward the kitchen.

"What's that nutter up to now?" Skye stretched to look over Noah's shoulder.

"He's checking the top secret vault—I mean the kitchen."

Noah suddenly heard what he thought sounded like a bad impression of a screeching bird.

Skye whispered into Noah's ear, "Was that the signal?"

"Affirmative. Apollo has landed." He motioned to the front door, mimicking the spies he'd seen in movies. "Let's move out."

"Really, Noah. This is serious."

Noah shrugged and grinned. "I'm not Noah. I'm Noahmadeus Maximus; a secret service agent with a mission to save the earth."

"Ugh," Skye scoffed. She took the lead and tugged his arm. "Come on." They crept down the stairs.

Noah knew she was determined to act as casual as possible and not at all as if she had a mythical creature in her bag, but he thought she was overdoing it.

Noah, on the other hand, pretended to have a laser gun and some spy glasses with x-ray vision. He pressed a button on his imaginary earpiece and spoke into his cufflinks, "No alien lifeforms to report yet, Mr. President."

Skye reached back and slapped his thigh. "Stop it."

Ethan's mother appeared at the bottom of the stairs. She was absentmindedly leafing through a magazine, paying no attention to her surroundings, and bumped right into Skye.

"Houston, we've made contact. I repeat, we've made contact," Noah spoke into his cufflinks.

Skye reached back with her foot and stomped his toes.

Noah bit back a curse.

Mrs. Castleton looked at him quizzically before turning to Skye. "I'm sorry, love." She peered behind Noah and Skye, apparently looking for Ethan. "I thought you were all upstairs. Are you leaving?"

"Yes," Skye said sheepishly as she opened the front door. "Gotta go. Thanks awfully for letting us study, Mrs. C. See you soon."

Noah craned his neck to peer down the hallway, looking for Ethan. When he couldn't find him, he nudged Skye forward. "Yeah, thanks, Mrs. Castleton. We've got something important to do...it's, uh...top sec...I mean, top priority, ma'am." Noah clicked his heels together and saluted her.

Skye glared at him. She pushed past Mrs. Castleton and accidentally hit the bag against the woman's elbow. It would have been a perfectly normal event if it weren't for the distinct *ouch!* that emanated from the bag.

"What have you got in there?" Mrs. Castleton reached out to touch it.

Skye quickly moved the bag to her other shoulder and answered, "Oh nothing. It's just a thing that says 'ouch.'"

Noah eyed Skye as if to say, "Is that the best you can come up with?" He grabbed her shirt and tugged. "Yeah, you know, it's one of those new toys everyone's got. They're all the rage. What will they think of next, eh?"

Mrs. Castleton reached out and grabbed the shoulder strap of the backpack. "Isn't this Ethan's bag?"

Skye yanked the strap from Mrs. Castleton's hand. "Uh, yeah. He said I could borrow it. Mine broke uh, because I was uh, carrying so many books? All that studying we're doing—too heavy, you know?"

Olivia joined them in the cramped entryway. In a bland, bored tone she said, "Mum, Ethan's in the kitchen pretending he's a spy again."

Mrs. Castleton stepped onto the front porch. "Tell him to get out here this instant."

Olivia didn't move. She was too interested in inspecting the backpack.

Skye stepped out of the house, away from Olivia's outstretched hand.

Noah joined her on the front porch.

Mrs. Castleton folded her fingers together. "Would you two like to join us for dinner? Ethan can help me in the kitchen while you take Olivia to fetch Mr. Castleton, and by the time you get back, dinner should be ready."

Olivia suddenly looked hopeful.

Noah glanced at Skye, hoping she could come up with a good reason to skip out.

Skye simply shrugged as she inched away from Olivia, who was now on the first step leading down to their driveway.

"Good, it's settled." Mrs. Castleton leaned toward Noah. "I'm not sure if you've noticed, love, but Olivia really looks up to you."

Olivia's face turned beet-red. Blonde hair streaming behind her, she bolted back into the house shouting, "Thanks a lot, Mum. I'm not going chettin' anywhere now!"

Mrs. Castleton looked confused.

Noah cleared his throat. "Thanks for the offer, Mrs. Castleton, but we really should be on our way."

Noah and Skye had almost made it to the driveway when Mrs. Castleton called, "You two have a good evening!"

Ethan chose that moment to burst through the front door, firing his imaginary gun. He imitated the sounds of gunfire. "*Pft! Pft!*" He turned to Noah and Skye. "Go now! *Pft pft pft.* I gotcha covered!" Then he turned to his mother.

Mrs. Castleton flinched when Ethan aimed just over her shoulder. "Look out, Mum!"

Noah and Skye backed away until they reached their bikes.

Ethan pretended to shoot his target. "All clear, Mum. You're safe now." He stuffed his gun into its imaginary holster, which happened to be strapped to his ankle. "Gotta go! Don't wait up." He winked at her and joined his friends at their bikes.

Mrs. Castleton crossed her arms and shouted, "Fetch your dad and come straight home."

Ethan ignored her.

"Ethan, did you hear me? Ethan Castleton!"

She looked furious as Ethan waved her off. All three of them hopped on their bikes and quickly pedaled away. After they were out of sight, they dismounted and unzipped the backpack.

Neevya glared up at them. "Next time, I'm flying."

Chapter Fourteen

Madison

Twilight began its descent before they even made it to Stillwater Street. Noah was glad to be out of Ethan's house. He was also hungry, and he looked forward to grabbing a snack once he got home.

As they walked their bikes over the uneven cobblestones of Chester Road, Noah glanced at Neevya, who was sitting on top of a portable speaker in Ethan's backpack. The bag had been tied to Skye's handlebars, its lid peeled back.

Neevya looked a bit sickly. "You're pale," Noah said.

She smiled weakly. "Yeah, I'm just a little woozy. Not used to traveling by backpack. It's really bumpy."

Noah reached down and offered his hand. "Want to ride on my shoulder?"

Skye slapped his hand away. "What are you thinking? You can't parade her around like she just won *Britain's ExtravaDance!*"

Noah shrugged. Perhaps he hadn't really thought it through. He just hated seeing Neevya suffer. He decided to try to distract her. Maybe thinking of something pleasant like animals might make her feel better.

"Neevya, you said you spoke with animals? So you've actually had real conversations with them?"

Neevya pushed herself to her feet and peeked over the edge of the backpack. "That's a good question, Noah."

His ploy was working. She was already looking a bit better, peppier at least.

Excitement filled her voice. "Most faeries don't speak with animals. Our interests usually lie in caring for plant-dwellers." She proudly placed her hand to her chest. "But a few years back, *I* befriended a couple of elves, Isaac and Elliana. They live in my city as emissaries. Elves work closely with animals."

Her dreamy expression made Noah think she was quite fond of those elves.

"First, they taught me how to communicate with squirrels. Later, I spoke with deer and all sorts of animals." The faraway look in her eyes told Noah she was reliving happy memories. "They're all so different, the animals, and yet they're the same. Such kindness and playfulness." She tilted her head and looked at the sky. "The first owl I met had restorative magic. Isaac and Elliana summoned it when the faerie king fell ill. The owl gave him insight, which allowed him to make a critical change in his perceptions. I guess you could say it saved his life." She paused, deep in thought. "If I weren't already a faerie, I'd sure love to be an elf."

"I'd just like to meet an elf," Ethan said with enthusiasm.

Noah chuckled. "Yeah, me too. I bet they're really cool."

"I wonder how tall they are," Skye mused.

"I don't actually know. They're shrunken when they enter my realm. But that's beside the point," she looked at Noah with large, innocent eyes. "I'm really looking forward to meeting Madison."

Noah beamed, unable to contain his excitement. "It's going to be amazing!"

The prospect of communicating with his bestie was more than he could ever hope for. He regarded Neevya with awe. If she could talk with animals, what else could she do? What other wonders passed as normal for her?

"It's going to be chettin' brilliant!" Ethan looked over his shoulder at the setting sun. "But if we don't get there soon, Skye and I will have to leave before we even get started."

Neevya nodded and crawled off the speaker. As they mounted their bikes, Noah thought Neevya and Madison were probably very much alike. Even though Neevya hadn't felt well, she didn't let it stop her from trying to be upbeat. Madison too, pushed her way through various illnesses without much whining.

"Hold on tight," Skye zipped the bag, leaving a small opening to let in some evening air, "this is going to be a bumpy ride."

Noah lived among the hilly meadows on the outskirts of town, just off Stillwater Street and down a winding driveway that may have been gravel at one time, but was now hard-packed dirt with clumps of grass. Their bicycle tires made a rhythmic hum on the dirt, interspersed with the occasional sounds of stones scraping against rubber. Noah's favorite sound, however, was Madison's faint barking coming from the front window.

He gazed at her fondly. The mini schnauzer's paws were perched on the windowsill and her nose was pressed against the glass. Noah grinned at the foggy clouds on the surface of the glass that grew with each panted breath.

Gesturing to the left side of the house, Noah directed Skye and Ethan to park their bikes.

The moment they walked into the house, Madison rushed up to Noah and ran circles around his legs.

"Hey there, Madi." Noah bent down, chuckling and scratching the backs of her ears.

"Who's my girl? Who's my baby girl?" he said in a high-pitched voice. "That's right! You are. You're my baby girl."

Madison tenderly rolled her head into his palm, panting and looking up at him, but she tensed when she spotted the backpack. The fur on the back of her neck raised, her ears perked up, and she gave a trilled bark.

Noah could feel excitement mounting in her quivering muscles. He reached for her collar, but before his fingers could close around it, Madison slipped from his grasp and pounced.

Skye automatically jumped back, almost crushing Neevya against the front door frame.

A lump rose in Noah's throat. "No!"

A voice from the backpack resounded throughout the entryway. "Be still."

Madison immediately calmed down, along with Noah, Skye, and Ethan.

Noah's mother hurried into the entryway. "Everything okay in here?" She glanced around, taking inventory.

Noah knew his mother didn't miss much, but that didn't keep him from trying to play the incident off as being a boring, everyday occurrence. He casually said, "Yeah, everything's fine. No problems here." He thought about making up an excuse for the commotion, something to throw her off, but stopped. He'd never lied to his mother before, and he wasn't about to start now.

She met Noah's eyes. "Well, I'm glad you're okay."

Thankfully, she didn't pry.

She nodded at Ethan and Skye. "Welcome."

They answered with nods of their own.

"Would you like to join us for dinner? Noah's father was called away to work." Something flashed in her eyes. Was it worry?

She gestured to the kitchen. "We have plenty of food." Her penetrating gaze fell on Noah.

Noah broke eye contact, stuffing his hands into his pockets and gazing down at his shoes. He liked the idea of his friends staying for dinner, yet he was still nervous she might ask questions he wasn't prepared to answer.

Mrs. Walters turned her gaze on Ethan. "Well?"

Noah figured Ethan had trouble understanding his mother's thick accent because he just stood there with a blank expression.

Skye cleared her throat, attracting Mrs. Walter's attention. "I would love to stay for dinner, Mrs. Walters," Skye eyed Ethan before turning her attention back to Mrs. Walters, "but I'll need to call my mum first."

Noah glanced at the stairs. "Mum?"

His mother smiled curiously. "Since when did you start calling me *Mum*?"

Noah shrugged nonchalantly. "Can Ethan and Skye call their parents from my room? We have a few things we need to discuss in private."

Ethan's eyes went wide.

"Very well. Just let me know if their parents agree so I can set the table." She walked to the kitchen.

Ethan grabbed Noah's shoulders. "I can't bloomin' believe you just told your mum that!"

"I can't lie to her. If I try, she'll know."

"Sucks to be you," Ethan joked.

Skye slapped Ethan's shoulder. "Quit messing around."

Noah led the way to his bedroom. Madison trailed behind them.

The first thing Skye did when entering his room was to slip the backpack from her shoulders and open it.

Neevya coughed as she emerged from the bag. "That's the last time I agree to hide in there." Her voice was weak.

"Not to be rude, but you look terrible." Ethan helped her out of the bag.

She rasped, "I've felt better."

"Would food help?" Noah asked, ready to dart down to the kitchen and grab them both a snack.

"Ugh, food's the last thing I want right now." Neevya clutched her stomach.

Noah fluffed his pillow and laid it on the foot of his bed. "I totally get it. I can't ride in a car without feeling at least a little carsick."

Ethan gently laid her on the pillow's soft surface. "Rest here. I'm sure it'll pass."

Madison

Madison came to the edge of the bed, giving Neevya her full attention. She let out a trill. There was a hint of a whine mixed in. Even though Noah didn't know if Madison had actually said anything, he knew she was concerned—like the time he had fallen from his bike; she didn't leave his side as he laid there and waited for help.

Neevya gave Madison a tired smile and reached out to the dog. "Thank you."

Madison jumped onto the bed, laid down beside Neevya, and nuzzled her nose into the faerie's open hand.

Neevya took a deep breath and laced her fingers into the shaggy fur around Madison's muzzle.

Noah watched in amazement. Madison didn't let anyone except him touch her mouth or nose. How had Neevya won her trust so quickly?

Madison sighed and closed her eyes.

"*Pureheart*," Neevya whispered. Reverence emanated from that single word.

Noah's skin suddenly broke out in chill bumps and the air around him seemed charged with electrical currents of energy. There was no way to describe what he was feeling except to say it was magical. Everything inside him felt lighter, brighter, almost weightless—like he was flying off the top of a hill and soaring through the air.

It must be working. Madison must have restorative abilities.

He looked at Neevya. Her skin had a faint yellow glow. Madison opened her eyes and gently licked Neevya's face. Neevya took a deep breath.

"Did you feel that?" Skye whispered, wide-eyed.

"Yeah, it was...it was..." Ethan was having trouble finding the right word, so Noah helped him out.

"Magical."

Ethan nodded. "Yeah, it was magical."

They watched in amazement as Madison licked the entirety of Neevya's back, between her wings, and groomed her the way she might a puppy.

Neevya curled up against Madison's stomach, closed her eyes, and within seconds, fell asleep.

"I think maybe we should let them be," Ethan suggested.

Noah reached to pet Madison, but she lifted her head and tossed his hand away with her snout. She trilled her song for him, as if to say, "No need to worry. All is well. She needs rest."

Noah wanted to say something, but Madison cuddled up to Neevya, sighed, and closed her eyes.

Skye whispered, "I guess she told you."

Noah felt blood rush to his cheeks.

He opened his bedroom door quietly and motioned for Ethan and Skye to join him in the hallway. "Don't you have to call your parents?"

Skye gasped. "Flippin' heck! I forgot. My mum's going to throw a fit." She reached into her back pocket and pulled out her phone.

Noah grabbed her wrist. "Let's go outside first. Follow me."

Ethan and Skye followed Noah to the front yard, where a large, scraggly tree stood, its twisted branches reaching for Noah's bedroom window. The sun had faded.

Skye called her mum.

Ethan began to call his mum, but Noah stopped him. "Hold on. I have an idea."

Ethan looked at him expectantly. Noah held up his hand and darted into the house to ask his mum an important question. He returned slightly out of breath. "How would you like to spend the night?" Noah couldn't stop his grin from stretching ear-to-ear. If Ethan agreed, it would be the first time in Noah's life that he would get to have a sleepover.

Ethan opened his mouth, but whatever he was going to say got cut off by Skye's pleading whine.

"But Mummm…" Even without using the speakerphone, Noah could hear Ms. Williams' firm and loud response.

"Now see here, Skye Grace Williams, at no point did you ask permission to go to Noah's house. It's past six and you are on the other side of town."

Skye's response was hissed through clenched teeth. "I'm sorry, Mum.

We left Ethan's and came here to work on a project. I was calling because Mrs. Walters invited me to dinner."

Her mum's reply was lost as Skye rolled her eyes. "Sure, Mum, just a sec."

She held the phone against her chest. "I'll be right back. *My* mum wants to talk to yours."

She stormed up the front steps and into the house. The old wooden steps creaked under her furious stomps.

"Woah," Noah said.

Ethan chuckled. "No kidding. That was brutal. Time for me to have a go at it."

Thankfully, after Ethan turned on his charm, Mrs. Castleton stopped chastising him for not fetching his dad at the pub and agreed to let him sleepover. Ethan hung up with a wide smile. "Too bad Skye wasn't here to see how it's done."

Noah shot his fist into the air. "Yeah! This is gonna be brilliant!"

Noah's mother opened the front door and beckoned for them to come inside. "Dinner's ready."

"Come on, let's eat and make sure Skye isn't killing her phone." Ethan threw his arm around Noah's shoulders as they made their way into the house.

Two things were evident when they entered the kitchen. One, Skye hadn't smashed her phone to pieces on the floor. And two, Noah's mother was taking full advantage of another pair of hands to help set the table. As Skye placed a fork next to a dinner plate, she looked up and glared at them. The next moment, she flashed Noah's mom a perfect smile.

"Staying for dinner?' Ethan smirked, his blue eyes dancing with mischief.

Skye wrinkled her nose in a snarky manner and opened her mouth to answer, but Noah's mother beat her to it. "Yes, Ms. Williams was very nice to let Skye stay. She will pick her up in about an hour."

Skye smiled, but Noah knew it was all for show. Her voice was calm, and anyone but he and Ethan might think she was being pleasant when she said, "Yeah, Mum's worried about me riding my bike home in the dark."

Noah's mother nodded. "As she should be." She turned away to grab a pot from the stove. "Night is a time for mischief and mystery."

A shiver ran up Noah's spine.

He chanted:

"Night is a time for mischief and mystery.

When monsters come out to play.

So gather your young and tuck them in bed.

Let them not out until day."

Noah locked eyes with his mother. She nodded, holding the pot and eyeing him gravely.

He started to examine her face but she turned away.

She's hiding something.

He wanted to confront her, but then he thought of Neevya curled up against Madison's belly.

Better not tempt Fate.

Instead of prying, he asked, "What's for dinner?"

CHAPTER FIFTEEN

Pureheart

Breathing in Madison's scent, Neevya stretched the boundary of her mind to encompass her furry companion. She welcomed Madison's unexpected gift—currents of energy, sweet and pure, circulated between them like a lazy river. This was different than any animal connection she had ever experienced before. Life-essence pulsed into Neevya to the rhythm of Madison's heartbeat. How could she ever repay this charitable creature?

Images and sensations filled Neevya's attention—a bright day, running in a field, Noah racing alongside—happiness...light.

Thank you for sharing, Madison, Neevya said silently.

Madison wagged her tail and curled closer to Neevya.

It felt so good to be connected to one so radiant, one so dear to Good Mother. Ever since Neevya had entered Suntamor there was a horrible, gnawing emptiness that squeezed her insides. The utter lack of connection to anything natural around her made Neevya feel isolated and disoriented. She hadn't even realized how much Suntamor had affected her until she met Madison—grace-filled, loving Madison.

Visions of Noah cuddling Madison when she hurt her paw swam into Neevya's consciousness. Noah saying, "It'll be okay, girl. I'll take good care of you," resounded in Neevya's mind. The vision transitioned into another scene where Noah had twisted his ankle from a bicycle crash. Brown rocks, leafless green trees with thorns, and dried out bushes surrounded them, Noah lying on dry, sandy gravel. Madison stuck by his side for over an hour without wavering, which was saying something because it was blistering hot that day.

That Noah had earned such devotion from a pureheart like Madison gave Neevya a new appreciation for him.

Another scene infused Neevya's mind—a scene where Madison crawled into Noah's lap as he sniffed back a tear, his arms wrapped around Madison's body. It was a memory of love and tender care.

"I understand. Thank you," Neevya whispered back to Madison.

Neevya opened her eyes and stretched. Madison's paw cocooned her in a warm, delightful hug. She wasn't sure how long she had been lying there, but it must've been quite a while. Darkness had swallowed the room.

Clomping footsteps echoed outside the door just before Noah and Ethan entered the room.

"It's too bad Skye's mum was so upset. I hope she won't be grounded. We need her tomorrow," Noah whispered.

"I know; did you see her mum's face when they left? She was furious."

"Yeah, sucks to be Skye," Noah added.

Madison lifted her head and grunted.

"Hey, Madi-girl, did you sleep well?" Noah whispered.

Neevya ducked out from under Madison's paw.

Noah flipped on his bedroom light. "You're awake."

Neevya stood, but suddenly felt dizzy and used Madison to stay upright.

"What's wrong?" Noah hurried to her side and knelt.

Neevya placed a hand to the side of her head and waited for the room to stop spinning. "Nothing to worry about; I just stood up too fast."

Noah sat on the edge of the bed and caressed Madison's back with broad, sweeping strokes.

Instantly, Neevya received feelings of contentment and pleasure from Madison.

"She really likes that," she said with a smile.

Noah looked questioningly at Neevya. "So you really do understand her?"

Neevya nodded. "I really do."

Ethan clapped his hands. "This is brilliant! I've always wanted to know what dogs think about all day. Do they obsess over bones and chew toys? Or do they actually have intelligent thoughts?"

"You'd be surprised." Neevya suddenly felt weak and sat back down, leaning against Madison's chest.

Ethan asked, "Are you sure you're okay?"

Neevya held out her left leg and inspected the wound. She gasped. There, a little way above her ankle, was a black dot with a few spindly tendrils crawling out of it like tattooed snakes. "Oh no," she whispered.

"What do you mean, 'oh no'?" Noah asked.

Ethan knelt beside the bed next to Noah and directly in front of Neevya.

Neevya tucked her wounded leg beneath her. Her heart thudded against her ribcage as the reality of her predicament hit home.

What am I going to do? What should I say?

Neevya looked at the boys, feeling as if she needed to apologize. What she needed to apologize for, she wasn't quite sure, but she felt guilty for something. Maybe she was afraid of the remorse these kids would feel when they realized Madison couldn't heal her. Perhaps she was sorry for the pain her death would cause if they couldn't find the portal in time. Or maybe she was afraid of what they would face if they did find the portal. Why hadn't she thought about the real and possible consequences before entangling three innocent humans in her troubles?

Ethan pleaded, "Neevya, speak to us. Are you okay? You still just have motion sickness, right?" Worry colored his blue eyes and Neevya wished she could reach out and smooth the frown from his face.

Should I tell them the truth? She shook her head. *No. Finding a Precarious Portal is hard enough. Finding one before the poison takes hold is next to impossible.*

She rubbed her eyes with the palms of her hands.

Besides, if I tell them, they'll want to rush into the forest tonight. It's too dangerous to enter the forest when the darkness is awake.

Nothing, including her possible death, would make her let the children venture into that forest at night.

No, I will not tell them.

She looked at Madison.

But she knows.

Madison snuggled around her, encompassing Neevya in a cocoon of warmth and comfort. Neevya closed her eyes. Visions of Madison sleeping beside Noah came to mind as life-energy pulsed into Neevya. Then another scene unfolded where Noah rolled on the floor with Madison and rubbed her belly. Love and playfulness spilled through the waves of energy shared between them. The last image Madison shared was of her licking Noah's cut arm, and the wound healing in half the time.

Yes, Neevya responded, *I understand. You're a pureheart and Noah is your bond.*

Neevya opened her eyes and said with confidence she didn't feel, "Yes, Madison has restorative magic. No need to worry. I'm okay. I just felt a bit overwhelmed for a moment. She's very powerful."

Noah exhaled. "Thank goodness. For a second there, I thought you were going to tell us you had iron poisoning."

Noah's relief sent a surge of regret through Neevya. The look of concern on their faces had startled her. She never imagined seeing such horror on the faces of ones she loved.

Loved?

She looked at the two boys, memorizing their features, the tiny nuances in their appearances, and their innocent and soulful eyes. How could she have ever thought them to be monsters?

She smiled.

Yes, Neevya loved Ethan and Noah. She looked at Madison. She loved Madison, too. She thought of Skye, the girl who found her, the fun-loving delightful girl with pink braids. Yes, she loved Skye as well.

How extraordinary.

CHAPTER SIXTEEN

The Dern

The next morning, Noah watched Neevya prance through the tall grass on the hillside. He was glad to see her color and vitality had returned. Madison seemed happy too, as she romped through the field, snapping at passing butterflies.

Instead of taking Stillwater Street on their way to The Dark Wood, they decided to cross a large field to the south of Noah's house. They hoped to be able to speak freely, as well as to give Neevya a chance to fly without worrying about passersby. It was a fairly safe bet. Besides the occasional kid who traversed the field on their way home from school, no one ever came out here, especially on a Sunday.

Madison leapt into the air and barked at a butterfly.

Neevya mimicked her, barking and snapping as if she were a little dog.

Skye, who had met them before the sun had even risen and was caught up on all the latest happenings, giggled and pointed. "She's so playful. I love that."

Ethan added, "I wish I could blinkin' fly."

Noah agreed, but he also figured this might be his last chance to get some questions answered. He called out, "Hey, Neevya, hold up a minute."

Even though it was a sunny day, Noah thought he heard a rumble of thunder in the distance.

Neevya waved goodbye to the butterfly she had been playing with and fluttered in front of Noah. As he walked forward, Neevya flew backward, as if she were swimming through the air. There was no end to the awe Noah felt when he looked at her. Not only was she beautiful, he also felt they were becoming friends, true friends. That realization warmed his heart more than he wanted to admit. After all, he was trying to return Neevya back to her home—a home whose only entrance was in the middle of a dangerous forest—which would make frequent visits quite challenging. He cleared his throat, along with his feelings. "I'm interested in learning more about where you come from. Can you tell us about it?"

"I wanna hear this too," Ethan said.

"Me three," added Skye.

Neevya suddenly darted toward the ground.

Noah had to put on the brakes to keep from stepping on her. He held his arms to the side to halt Skye and Ethan as well.

Neevya buried her face into a flower and inhaled deeply. When she looked up, she had a blanket of pollen covering her nose and cheeks.

Madison licked her face, sending Neevya reeling back.

She giggled, hopped onto Madison's head and explained, "Well, you see, besides having much greater vitality, my realm actually looks similar to yours. We share the same planet, after all. We have the same soil, the same hills, and although my realm has many of the same plants and animals as yours, from what I've seen, we also have more varieties."

She launched herself into the air as they resumed their trek to the forest.

"And see? Father Sun looks down on both our realms. Although in mine, I don't think he's on a strict schedule like he is here."

Noah thought that sounded odd. What did she mean? Did time work differently there?

Neevya abruptly stopped and threw her arms wide. "Hoppin'

hobgoblins!" She pointed to a tree. "See that sapling over there? I planted her just a few cycles ago. She looks so healthy."

"Wow, really?" Noah gestured to the meadow all around them. "What about this? Did you plant all this as well?"

"Not me personally, but one faerie or another probably did."

"So does that mean faeries are essentially responsible for all life on Earth?" Noah said it more to himself than to Neevya, but she responded anyway.

"We give Good Mother the credit. She *is* Earth; a wonderful, loving provider—one who shares. She is the one who sustains life here, not faeries like me. We just help."

To say his mind was blown would be an understatement. And to think, he hadn't even known faeries existed until a couple of days ago.

Neevya suddenly seemed to be getting tired. She perched atop Madison's back and buried her face in her fur.

Noah thought she was beginning to look pale again.

Skye must've noticed too. "We need to speed this up if we're ever going to get you home."

Neevya lifted her head. "But without my pouch, I don't know how to find the portal."

Noah tried hard to sound optimistic. "Don't worry; we'll find it if it's the last thing we do."

Their second visit to The Dark Wood brought a sense of doom Noah could not ignore. Dark gray clouds formed swiftly overhead, and the scent of copper on the wind promised a coming storm. As they approached, dim shadows between the trees looked even more ominous than they had the last time. Goosebumps attacked Noah's arms and the hairs on the back of his neck warned of imminent danger. This was not going to be fun.

Neevya straddled Madison's back as they surveyed the edge of the forest.

Ethan stepped forward. "Let's do this."

Skye joined him. "No time like the present."

Noah wished he had something clever or courageous to say, but he remembered that deep and guttural growl from the last time they were here. His heart screamed, *Are we nuts? Let's get the heck out of here!*

Skye took the lead. Noah, refusing to be last, pushed past Ethan and placed his hand on the back of Skye's shoulder. He didn't think he could make himself enter if he weren't at least touching one of his friends, and holding hands seemed too babyish.

Ethan muttered under his breath, "Figures, I'm chettin' last again."

Noah tried to ignore his comment, but it didn't stop him from feeling a little ashamed; so he said, "Madison's got your back."

Unlike the last time, when they'd practically made themselves moving targets, this time they tried to move as stealthily as possible. They darted from tree to tree, stopping several times to listen for danger. When they did have to speak, they gathered in tight huddles and whispered.

About an hour into their journey, Neevya fluttered off Madison's back and held up her hand. She rushed Skye, making the poor girl yelp and jump back.

Neevya landed on Skye's shoulder and wrapped herself in a curtain of Skye's hair.

Ethan tugged Noah's shirt. "Did you hear that?"

"Over there. Look!" Skye warned them.

"Scaretaker," Ethan whispered.

"What? Where?" Noah asked.

Ethan pointed. "He's seen us."

Scaretaker strode toward them with the determination of a predator. Despite his unkempt appearance, there was nothing slothful or shambling about him.

Madison placed herself between them and Scaretaker. She barked wildly, her fur standing up in a ridge along her back, her teeth bared.

They started to run, but it was too late. Scaretaker was on them. With a grace that was at odds with his age and stature, he sprang over a fallen tree and reached Noah before they could take two steps. He grabbed Noah's collar and jerked him so they ended up face to face.

Noah could smell the sickly-sweet tang of pipe tobacco on his breath as he snarled through yellowed teeth, "What'r ye doin' back here? I told ye t' stay away."

Madison jumped up and grabbed Scaretaker's shirt sleeve, yanking and forcing him to drop Noah.

Noah backed away and watched in horror as Madison growled, refusing to let go.

"Let's get out of here!" Skye yelled.

Ethan and Skye took off, but Noah just backed slowly away. He couldn't leave Madison behind.

Scaretaker planted his feet firmly on the ground as Madison shook her head, jerking his arm from side to side.

Noah felt a tug on his elbow.

"Come on," Ethan whispered. "She's doing this for you. She'll catch up."

Ethan was right. The longer Noah stood there, the longer Madison felt the need to protect him, which meant he was putting her life in danger.

Noah turned and ran.

As he was catching up to Skye, Noah heard what sounded like a dog's yelp in the distance, and his heart sank. He looked over his shoulder and his foot hooked on a vine. He went flying and landed flat on the ground.

He moaned and cradled his elbow. It felt like he had hit a rock. Ethan suddenly appeared above him. He reached down, grabbed Noah under his armpits, and started to pull him up.

"Come on," he huffed, breathing hard.

Noah shoved Ethan's hands away. "I can get up on my own."

Skye was next to appear. Her eyes darted from one spot to the next. "Is he gone? Did we lose him?"

"I blinkin' hope so." Ethan bent forward, resting his hands on his knees to catch his breath.

Noah pushed himself to his feet. "Do you see Madison? Is she okay?"

"I'm sure she's fine. She can take care of herself." Ethan straightened and wiped the sweat from his brow. "So what do we do now?"

Neevya peeked out from behind a curtain of Skye's hair. "If we can find somewhere to hide for a while, I might be able to summon Madison."

Noah immediately began to search for a cave, a thick group of trees, anything that would allow Neevya to contact Madison.

Finding a safe place to hide in The Dark Wood was more challenging than Neevya anticipated, especially since she had been distracted by that old man. He looked familiar, but she didn't know why. As they travelled deeper and deeper into the forest, the wind grew stronger and whistled ominously through the trees; thunder rumbled overhead. No rain had reached them—yet.

A short while later, they were sitting in a huddle within a makeshift fort they had hastily thrown together on the side of a steep incline. Large ferns and downed limbs stacked in a brush pile covered their heads and provided enough foliage to conceal them. Neevya sat on Noah's knee and reached into the forest with her mind. She knew it could be dangerous— especially with that old man nearby. She had a feeling there was much more to him than met the eye. But Madison was worth the risk.

Ethan asked, "Anything yet?"

Neevya paused her search. "I need silence. This is very difficult. I need to concentrate."

Ethan covered his mouth. "Oh, sorry."

Neevya looked around and eyed each of them before closing her eyes and starting again.

She expanded her mind so that it brushed against every tree, every insect, every blade of grass. The forest was alive, though it was a different kind of vitality than she felt in her own realm. The Dark Wood was more guarded. The plants were harder, more contained within themselves. The insects had cocooned themselves in skeins of energy they wore like armor. When she tried to push her thoughts toward a dragonfly, it quickly bounced off the edge of her mind and flew away.

This is going to be more difficult than I thought.

She reached farther out.

Where are you, Madi? Why can't I feel you?

She caught a glimpse of something different, something dark and dangerous. She quickly withdrew, hoping to escape its notice. She shivered.

I can do this…for Madison.

She tried again.

Are you there? Please let me find you, Madison. Noah is so worried about you.

She honed in on an energy pattern that exuded all the qualities Madison possessed—compassion, loyalty, kindness.

There you are! I'm so happy to find you!

Visual images of Madison sitting patiently at the forest's edge flooded Neevya's consciousness. After revealing to Neevya that she was safe, Madison showed Neevya how she had held Scaretaker at bay for quite a while, but then he managed to kick her, forcing her to let go. The kick was more shocking than painful. When he ran away and into the woods, Madison headed back to the field to wait for Noah. Madison's pride and contentment rushed into Neevya and brought a smile to her lips. *Yes, you did a wonderful job,* Neevya communicated.

With her inner eye, Neevya saw Madison wag her tail and understood her to say, *What now? Where do I find you? Where's Noah?*

Neevya wanted to ask Noah if he'd like her to join them, but thought better of it. She couldn't afford to break her concentration, so she made her decision. *Go back to your home, Madison. Noah is well. I'm watching over him.*

Visions of Madison trotting beside Noah with Neevya riding on her back came to mind, and Neevya felt Madison whine.

Neevya whispered her thoughts, *I understand, but we are too far away, and asking you to join us might attract too much attention. Please go home. Noah will return safely, I promise.* As she said it, Neevya summoned all the peace that still existed within her and directed it at Madison.

It worked.

Madison turned and trotted away, snapping at a weed or two along the way.

Such a loyal creature.

As Neevya reeled her mind back into her body, she brushed against the darkness. But instead of pulling away, this time she focused on it and gasped.

It noticed her. It even looked back.

Neevya quickly cast a spell of glamour to shield herself and the kids. Oh, how she hoped she'd done a decent job of it!

Maybe if I can mirror the darkness's energy back onto itself, it will think it's made a mistake. I need to make it think it hasn't sensed anything unusual, or anything at all.

Her magic worked.

The darkness lost interest and withdrew its attention. Neevya took the small window of opportunity to learn more about it. She hurriedly explored its edges and qualities, realizing there was much to watch out for in this woodland; things they should avoid at all costs.

She gasped again as the darkness unexpectedly morphed into a beast.

CHAPTER SEVENTEEN

Darkness Awakens

"Did you find her? Is Madison okay?" Noah asked as soon as Neevya opened her eyes. He had felt completely helpless just sitting there watching. What if Scaretaker had hurt Madison? How could he ever live with himself?

Neevya shook her head and massaged her temples.

Did she hear me? Should I ask again?

Just when he was about to open his mouth, Neevya looked up at him. "Madison is well. She is headed back to your home."

Noah let out a long breath. He had been so worried when he heard her yelp. Now his mouth curled into a smile, but it quickly faded when Neevya's expression turned more serious than he had ever seen, which said a lot.

"We may have planted more than we can harvest." She examined her palms as if seeing them for the first time.

"What do you mean?" Ethan asked.

Neevya answered gravely, "There's something dark in these woods; something dangerous."

Noah wanted to ask her all kinds of questions but couldn't find his voice.

Skye shifted, shaking her foot nervously. "What's out there?"

Neevya glanced up. "The clouds are weeping."

Her choice of words caught Noah off guard, making him wonder if it was a coincidence, or possibly a sign. Maybe there was more going here on than any of them actually knew.

Neevya zipped through the air and stuck her head through an opening in their makeshift fort like she was expecting someone, or some*thing*. "This is not good, not good at all."

Ethan blurted out, "Why? What's wrong?"

"Hush, keep your voice down." Skye slapped his knee.

"Hey, that hurt."

"Sorry, just don't be so loud."

Noah was glad he hadn't spoken up.

Neevya ducked her head back in. "Have any of you ever heard of a chondour?"

Skye asked, "What's that?"

Neevya sat on Noah's knee. "It's a bellwether gone bad."

"A bellwether?" Noah was totally confused now.

"I don't exactly know how to explain so you will understand." Neevya looked at Noah appraisingly, pressing her finger to her lips.

Noah suddenly felt a foreign force press on his mind. Dormant memories unexpectedly surfaced. He was walking home from school in Las Vegas where he lived when his father was stationed at Nellis Air Force Base. Next, his mother was reading him a book. Then he sat alone on the school playground, wishing he had friends.

Noah massaged his temples. "Are you reading my mind?"

"Just taking a peek, looking for a point of reference."

Noah was at the circus, watching a lion tamer and feeling sorry for the lions.

He was at a museum, and his mum was showing him a painting depicting a battle between angels and demons.

"That's it," Neevya said.

The pressure on Noah's mind withdrew. He scratched his scalp, but it was pointless.

How do you scratch the center of your brain?

A clap of thunder made the forest sound hollow as rain began pelting the top of their fort. A few drops entered here and there.

"I need to make this quick." She raised her voice to be heard over the echoes of raindrops splashing through the forest canopy. "Bellwethers are like angels, and chondours are like demons. They are winged beings who are invisible to most. The bellwethers may act as guides, messengers, or protectors, and they can manipulate the light. Chondours, on the other hand, are all about darkness. Shadows can be dangerous when a chondour is around, which, by the looks of things…" She trailed off and shivered. "Let's just say, coming across one may be the last thing you'll ever do."

Noah rubbed his arms. "Is that why you're scared? Are chondours out there, right now?"

Neevya pointed up. "You hear that? That's a storm. Chondours live in storms."

Noah felt as fearful as Skye and Ethan looked.

Neevya continued, "And from what I've heard, if a chondour captures you, it's not just your life at stake, it's your soul."

That sounded worse than anything Noah had heard yet. His stomach churned, making him queasy.

Ethan's voice seemed to be trapped in his throat as he asked, "Wh… what do you mean, from what you've heard? Haven't you ever seen a bellwether or a chondour before?"

Neevya shook her head. "No, it's impossible for the Fae to see them without a Betwixter."

Noah had to stop himself from shaking, imagining Betwixters to be creatures even worse than chondours.

The kids exchanged glances, wondering who was going to ask the next, obvious question. The battle of stares ended on Noah; Ethan and Skye drilled him with invisible lasers shooting from their pupils. Noah fidgeted, straightened, and grimly asked, "What's," he cleared his throat, "what's a Betwixter?"

To Noah's surprise, Neevya smiled and regarded him thoughtfully, all traces of distress had vanished. It seemed she was remembering something pleasant, joyful even.

Neevya's reaction went a long way to ease some of Noah's tensions, and he found himself suddenly hopeful.

"Betwixters are extraordinary humans who can see beyond the realms. They can see beings such as Bellwethers and Fae." She looked down. "They can see faeries like me."

"You mean not all people can see you?" It seemed Ethan was feeling more optimistic too.

Neevya shook her head. "Nope."

Noah jumped to the next logical conclusion, but Ethan beat him to the question. "Does that mean we're Betwixters, the three of us? Are we extraordinary?"

Noah was eager to hear her answer.

"Well, I think you're extraordinary, and it's clear all three of you are remarkably gifted. But there's more to it than that; you must be tested and qualified. You must learn a new way of life, and although most humans possess dormant abilities, only a rare few are awakened to their gifts and allow the magic to blossom within them."

A sense of wonder and amazement flooded through Noah. *Gifted? Awakened?* Since he could see Neevya, did that mean that he, Noah Wayne Walters, was somehow *magical?*

Neevya held up her finger. "And know this; even if you were born with tremendous abilities, you would still have to achieve the understanding needed to harness and wield your gifts accurately to become an official Betwixter."

Noah, Skye, and Ethan sat there looking at Neevya, stunned into silence.

A sudden rustling just outside their shelter jerked them out of their trance as Neevya took to the air and flew over to where the noise had come from. She peeked out. "I hope that's not what I think it is."

Fear swiftly conquered the fleeting amazement Noah was bathing in and commanded him to be fully alert.

Neevya zipped to the center of the fort. "If there's a chondour in these woods, we need to rethink things."

Ethan stood, but the fort was too short for him to straighten up completely. "Right, if we're gonna get you home, we need a good plan."

"Yeah." Skye joined him. She also had to stoop.

Noah continued to sit, wanting to agree, but his mind kept going back to the possibility that monsters, real monsters, were right outside, waiting to eat them and steal their souls.

Neevya zoomed to the other side of the fort and peaked out from under a silver maple leaf. "There's only one safe thing to do."

"What's that?" Ethan asked.

"Go back to Noah's house and return after the storm clears."

Ethan looked up. "I don't think that's an option."

Noah pushed himself to his feet. He was short enough that he didn't have to worry about hitting his head on the fort's roof. "Why?"

Ethan looked at Noah and then at Skye. "I don't know if you've noticed, but it seems every time we come into these woods, a storm rolls in. It makes me think the storm is here *because* we're here."

Skye grimaced. "It's only our second time. That's not enough to count as anything but pure coincidence."

Ethan shook his head. "Normally, I'd agree. But—"

Neevya interrupted, "The longer we stay here, the more danger we're in. We should go back to Noah's until this clears up. If we're facing a chondour, we'll need a solid strategy before we return."

Skye opened her mouth to object, but Neevya held up her hand. "My word is final. I'm not sure if what I felt during my search for Madison was a chondour or not, but I do know one thing—darkness is out there, and it's awake. We need to leave."

Ethan usually loved storms, but that was before he knew about chondours, back when he was in the safety of his home, not when his back was pressed against an enormous oak tree in the middle of The Dark Wood.

"Do you feel that?" he yelled to Noah, who was hiding behind a tree to his right. The rain was falling so hard, the only way they could hear each other was to yell.

"What?"

"Do you *feel* that?" Ethan emphasized.

Noah shrugged and shouted, "Feel what?"

"Th-that feeling, like there's something just 'round the corner."

Skye jogged up and pressed her shoulder against Ethan's.

She pointed. "Neevya says to go that way."

Neevya, who was perched on Skye's right shoulder, nodded in the same direction.

Ethan took in the landscape that lay in the distance. A twisted bramble of vines and bushes crept along the ground between the crooked trees; shadows created mysterious shapes and forms. His stomach sank as he shook his head. "Nonononononono."

Neevya looked at him with such questioning eyes that Ethan felt the need to explain. He leaned over. "I'm just gettin' a bad feelin', like maybe one of those chondour things is over there."

Neevya continued to scrutinize him.

"What?" he asked.

Neevya nodded and spoke into Skye's ear. Her voice had become so weak from yelling over the storm that she could no longer carry a conversation.

Skye pointed in a different direction and shouted, "She says to go that way."

They headed toward a trail in the distance. Rain pelted down, soaking them. Jagged lines of lightning and booming thunder filled the air.

"Too much rain! There's no way we're getting out of this alive," Noah yelled.

The wind, ripping through the trees along with Noah's comment, made Ethan shiver.

Up ahead, Skye stood at the top of a small hill and waved for the boys.

When they reached her, Ethan surveyed the area. On the other side of the hill, thick, grayish fog covered the ground. Tendrils of ghostly vapor licked around the trees and crept among the ferns. It looked alive.

Ethan took a step back. "Tell me we're not going into that."

Skye eyed him gravely. "That's exactly where we're going."

"Can't we go another way? That fog looks so…"

"We either go down there," Skye gestured, "or that way."

He glanced to where she pointed and recoiled. Tortured branches clawed the ground, making it uneven and jagged. Ethan imagined the shadows were streams of dark blood oozing from the scratches in the soil.

"The fog's got my vote, I guess," Ethan said.

They plodded down the hill, Ethan next to Noah, who was holding onto Skye's elbow. Mud pulled at Ethan's shoes like suction cups. The farther he descended, the thicker the fog became, until it was impossible to see even his own hand. He threw his arm to the side expecting to find Noah.

No one was there.

A blast of adrenaline suddenly rushed through him, making his heart race and his palms sweat. He whipped around, frantically searching for his friends and becoming disoriented. Goosebumps crept along his skin and his breath came out in white puffs that mixed with the fog. The air pressed in on him, making him feel claustrophobic.

Where the bloomin' heck are they? They were just here a second ago.

"Skye?"

He waited.

Answer me. Please!

It had been risky to say her name the first time. He didn't want to call out into the looming mist again; it might alert prowling monsters to his location.

He worked up his courage and tried again. "Noah?"

Nothing.

A chill crept down his spine. It felt like he was being watched.

The rain stopped.

Ethan's chin quivered, making his words choppy when he whispered, "Where are you guys?"

Suddenly, darkness slithered through the fog and coiled around his body like a sneaking serpent. His heart pounded so hard he felt it in his throat.

What sounded like sharp claws scraping against a tree echoed behind him.

He spun around, balling his hands into fists.

"Who's there?"

The wind carried the stench of rotten eggs on its tides. Dread clutched his stomach and twisted it into a hard knot of anxiety.

What should I do?

Ethan scampered in several directions but couldn't pick one to follow. The fog thickened. It was getting harder to breathe.

Where are they?

A low rumble sounded to his right.

Tell me that was only thunder.

A tear slid down his cheek.

"Noah? Skye?"

A thick, wet growl, seemingly coming from the fog itself, resounded from every direction. Then a man's deep voice demanded, "Leave the boy alone!"

Ethan froze and listened intently. Was someone there to save him? He moved a few steps forward, but was distracted by another call.

"Ethan!" Noah's voice sounded muted as it trailed through the air.

Had Ethan not known better, he would have sworn there was a thick wall between them.

Ethan desperately searched through the heavy mist.

Noah's words were louder this time, "Ethan! Where are you?"

Ethan sprinted toward the voice, tears now streaming down his cheeks. Two silhouetted figures suddenly emerged from the fog. He ran to them, closing the distance.

"I'm so glad to find you guys," Ethan gasped, wiping his eyes and trying to catch his breath.

Skye threw her arms around him. "I can't believe we've finally found you! We looked everywhere. We were so worried!"

"Finally?" Ethan hugged her back, surprised by her extreme reaction.

Neevya soothingly patted the top of his head from where she stood on Skye's shoulder.

Skye released him and wiped a stream of tears from her cheeks.

Noah came in for a hug. "It's so good to see you! We were just about to go for help."

Ethan accepted Noah's hug, all the while wondering why they were acting so strange.

Skye took his hand, "Where have you been?"

Ethan gestured over his shoulder. "Just right over there. What's up with you two anyway? By your reactions, you'd think I'd been gone for hours."

Noah cocked his head to the side and appeared as though he were confused.

Skye shared a moment of understanding with Noah before she said, "Come on. We've been here long enough. We'll explain later. For now, we have to get out of here."

"Wait, did you hear that growl back there?"

Noah answered, "All we've heard is thunder."

Pulling them along with urgency, Skye led the way. On high alert, they proceeded through the heart of the forest; no one said a word. It took some time to get there, but they finally relaxed when, in the distance, they caught a glimpse of Stillwater Street through the trees.

Ethan stepped over a fallen branch. "Have you guys noticed how dark it is?"

Skye looked around. "Yeah, it's hard to see anything."

"Tell me about it," Noah said. "It seems like it's nighttime already."

"I think the chettin' sun is completely gone."

Skye threw up her hands. "But that's impossible!"

Neevya said, loud enough for everyone to hear, "Nothing's impossible."

Skye counted on her fingers as she spoke under her breath, "We left early this morning. Madison attacked Scaretaker. We built a fort. Neevya talked with Madison. We walked back here. Ethan was lost for an hour—two at the most."

Shocked, Ethan asked, "I was gone for an hour or two? Are you sure?"

Skye nodded. "I think so." She looked thoughtful when she said, "I figure we left Noah's house roughly six hours ago."

Noah pulled out his phone and looked at its black screen. "Darn, my battery's dead." He stuffed it back into his pocket. "I agree. My guess is that it should be around one or two o'clock in the afternoon by now."

"My phone's dead too," Skye muttered.

"I was missing for a full hour or two?" Ethan looked at his phone and winced. It wasn't working either.

"Yes, how many times do we have to tell you?" Skye looked at him as if he were losing his mind.

He couldn't believe what he was hearing. How could he have been missing for so long? It didn't make sense. "Something very strange is going on here. I was only gone for a few minutes, not a full hour, let alone two. And now we've lost the sun! Where's the chettin' sun?"

Noah looked up. "The storm's probably just blocking it."

As if on cue, it started to rain again.

Terrifying screams erupted from somewhere within the forest, distracting Ethan from all previous concerns. His knees went weak, and he leaned on Skye for support.

He couldn't stop his hands from trembling. Heck, his entire body was quivering.

Skye asked, "What was that?"

"I don't know, but I don't want to find out." Noah shuddered.

Ethan whimpered, his voice cracking, "Sounded like a man being torn apart to me."

A wolf's howl suddenly cut through the dense gray fog; the bellow was eerie and bloodcurdling.

They picked up their pace.

The howl came again, this time closer.

Ethan glanced over his shoulder, the hair on the back of his neck raised.

At first, he couldn't see anything unusual, but then movement caught his eye. There, in the darkness, was a shadow, low and wolf-like, stalking toward them.

"Wolf!" Ethan screamed. "Run!" His foot landed in a puddle of mud. He tripped and fell face first onto the slippery ground.

Skye anchored his arm around her free shoulder, opposite Neevya, and hoisted him up. As soon as Ethan found his balance, they ran for their lives, ducking under branches, leaping over rocks, and sidestepping mud puddles. Closing in on Stillwater Street, Ethan shoved Noah ahead of him, almost making him trip. He grabbed Noah's wrist and pulled him along. Neevya clutched Skye's hair like a horse's mane to keep from falling off her shoulder.

They ran like wildfire, fueled by terror.

They sprinted right past Stillwater Street and didn't stop until they reached the iron gate at their school.

Ethan glanced back at the forest and squinted. "Is that a ginormous wolf pacing just beyond the tree line?"

Its black fur looked more like smoke than actual hair.

Drops of rain were splashing on his face. He wiped his eyes and blinked the water away as he glanced at Noah and Skye. They were both staring into the forest, trying to catch their breaths.

He snapped his fingers and pointed to Neevya. "Oi! Is she okay?"

Neevya whispered in Skye's ear, "Back to Noah's, *now*."

They ran.

Scaretaker heard the forlorn howls and recoiled. He was now convinced that some kind of dark Fae had come through the portal—not a faerie. But what kind of creature was it? He knew there were all sorts of beasts on the other side of the veils just waiting to have the chance to travel through a portal and destroy the human realm. That's why he had to stay in this abysmal forest. In all the world, this is where the veils were weakest. A blood curdling scream bounced off the trees. His heart suddenly began to race. Had the creature gotten hold of one of those kids? He hoped not. He was supposed to protect humans from the Fae, not let them get eaten.

Away through the forest he went, searching for the source of the screams. As he ran, he summoned all his magic and prepared for battle. Whatever the creature was, he would be ready. He slowed his pace and sniffed the air.

There it was—a faint scent of blood. There was something else, too—the air felt charged, like something magical and terrible had happened nearby. He slowed to a walk and searched for anything that could lead him to the person who had screamed. Dry leaves crunched under his feet and sounded too loud in the now, unusually quiet forest. As he neared a clearing, he saw a shiny, metallic object laying amongst the leaves.

Was this some sort of trap?

On high alert and ready to fight whatever might spring from the shadows to attack him, he stalked toward the object and bent down for a closer look. It was a ring. He picked it up and inspected it. The markings on it told him the ring belonged to a member of the Order of Serptorian. He had summoned reinforcements from the order the previous day and had issued strict instructions to only enter the forest while the sun was high in the sky, when the darkness was at its weakest. Who would be foolish enough to enter the woods at night? Even *he* only went out in the evening when it was absolutely necessary. He figured there was no point tempting Fate, whom he knew personally. She wasn't the most pleasant supernatural being he'd ever met, and he got the distinct feeling she didn't particularly care for him, either.

He refocused his attention on more pressing matters and held the ring up to the light. There was an inscription on the inside of its band. He rolled it in his fingers so the moonlight shone on it just right. Now he could read what it said. It was a name; the ring belonged to Drueth, Scaretaker's dearest friend and mentor from the Order of Serptorian.

A sudden sense of approaching danger compelled him to stand and search the shadows behind him. He squeezed the ring tight in his palm as he whipped around. His instincts were right; there, in the darkness, was a wolf. He crouched and prepared to throw a spell at the creature, but then quickly realized it was not a wolf at all; it was the chondour from his dungeon. Somehow, the chondour's mind had escaped its magical prison and used the shadows to take physical form. Scaretaker knew that only the most powerful of chondours could break through that kind of magical barrier. The chondour was growing stronger indeed.

Scaretaker forced a devious smile. Even though he was nervous, there was no way he would let this chondour see his fear.

The shadow-wolf locked eyes with him and telepathically communicated, *You found my hunting grounds.*

Scaretaker stuffed the ring into his pocket. "What'd you do with him? Where's Drueth?"

The shadow-wolf grinned, which made chills creep up Scaretaker's spine. He never knew wolves could smile.

Are you speaking of the shrieking man? The shadow-wolf shrugged and eyed Scaretaker as if he wanted to eat him. *You'll find out soon enough.*

Scaretaker summoned magic into his hands. "Tell me where he is!"

The shadow-wolf blinked slowly. *Unleash me so I can leave this forest. Unleash me and I will tell you.*

Scaretaker looked around; his gaze landed on a torn piece of cloth. It had belonged to Drueth's cloak, the one Scaretaker had given him just a year ago for his birthday. Scaretaker glared at the shadow-wolf with an emotion close to hatred; he figured he knew exactly what had happened to his friend—he would never see Drueth again.

The shadow-wolf slowly strode toward him. *I almost had the children in my clutches. They are more than what they seem. They are dangerous, I've seen it. Surely, you've sensed it too? Loose me and we will work together. Loose me, and I will bestow upon you powers beyond compare.*

Scaretaker snorted in disgust. "Ye promised me powers eight years ago. I unleashed yer mind, and look what ye did." He spat on the ground. "Had t' reign ye back in, I did."

The shadow-wolf howled and thrust his thoughts into Scaretaker's head. *As I recall, I came back to you willingly, and I gave you a taste of that power. Do you forget so easily?*

Scaretaker shook his head in denial even though he did remember; he remembered feeling a burst of exquisite power—a supremacy he had never felt before. It was magnificent. "All I recall is that it didn't stick. Ye tricked me."

The shadow-wolf's breath came out in pants of white fog. It languidly glanced around and then turned its red eyes on Scaretaker. *All I promised was a taste, so that's all you got. This time the offer is for real. This time, your powers will last. Loose me. Give me the children and we will be kings of this dominion.*

Skye was more than relieved when they made it back to Noah's house in one piece and were safely tucked away in his bedroom.

She sank into Noah's computer chair and sighed. "That was too close."

Ethan was sitting on the floor with his back against the wall. He wiped stray water droplets from his forehead. "Tell me about it."

Sitting quietly on his bed, Noah was inspecting Madison's body for possible wounds as Neevya slept curled up next to her belly.

Skye watched Noah for a bit, and then fiddled with his computer keyboard. She traced her fingers around the keys as she thought about all the things that went wrong with their trip to The Dark Wood.

She swiveled the chair to face the boys. "The next time we go into that forest, we definitely need to be more prepared."

Ethan glared at her. "You think? In case you hadn't noticed, it's not a typical forest. That chettin' thing's got teeth!"

Sometimes she wished Ethan could be more supportive. Why did he always have to be so rude? "Regardless, we've got to find a way to deal with the challenges."

"Is that what you call that gargantuan shadow-wolf creature—a challenge?"

Skye crossed her arms over her chest and snorted. "You're just being mean. At least I'm trying to sort this out. What are you doing?"

Ethan didn't answer. He just sat there, banging his feet together as if keeping the beat to a song only he could hear. He truly seemed remorseful when he finally said, "I'm sorry, all right? I'm just a bit shook up."

Noah agreed, "Yeah, that was the most scared I've ever been."

Skye watched as he stroked Madison's fur. She had never really taken the time to appreciate Noah's gentle nature before. Now it stuck out like a sore thumb, especially compared to Ethan's cheek.

"How's Neevya?" she asked.

Noah nodded. "Good, I think."

She couldn't help but twiddle her thumbs, her telltale sign that she was thinking hard. "Why do you think Neevya got so weak? Do you think she's sick, or maybe exhausted?"

Noah leaned over and inspected Neevya. "She looks okay. She could be experiencing something like jet lag."

"What about that place on her leg?" Skye asked. "Is it still there? Does it look any worse?"

Noah craned his neck for a better look. "I can't tell. She has it tucked underneath her."

Ethan was coughing and shivering. "Well, if she feels anything like I do, she might be catching a cold."

Skye nodded. "That makes sense. She did lose her voice."

Noah scratched the top of Madison's head. "You're probably right. Madi-girl will make her better by morning."

Ethan crossed his ankles. "Speaking of morning. Is it just me, or did we lose like six hours today?"

Skye had hoped no one would bring that up. It was too scary to even think about.

Noah stood and looked out the window. "I don't understand. It was day, and then suddenly it was night. Just like that." He snapped his fingers. "I don't get it."

Ethan offered, "Maybe the forest is magical. Maybe it can cast spells that warp time."

Skye carefully considered this. "Well, if that's true, why didn't we lose a few hours when we entered the first time?"

Ethan shrugged. "I don't know. Maybe we didn't run into any time-warping spells the last time."

"Or maybe we crossed into a different realm. Neevya did say that time runs differently in her realm than it does in ours. Maybe we went through a portal and didn't even know it," Noah said.

"*I* must've gone through two portals if that's the case," Ethan scoffed.

"At this point, it's all guesswork. We're wasting our breath. There's no way we can figure it out on our own. We should ask Neevya when she wakes up." Skye swiveled to face Noah's computer.

She was quite surprised when, for once, Ethan didn't argue.

Grabbing a pencil from Noah's desk, she made notes on an old notepad she found tucked away behind one of his school books. "I'll make a list of all the stuff we need for tomorrow morning when we try again."

"Tomorrow morning? But we have school," Noah objected.

Skye pivoted to face him. "The longer we wait, the more chance she has of being discovered. Plus, nothing says we can't bunk off."

Noah stopped petting Madison. "I can't. I have a test."

"Which subject?" Ethan asked.

"Art. Mr. Willard assigned us to research impressionist painters over the past month. He says it will count for a quarter of our marks."

"So you won't bunk off just because of a measly test? Are you saying your marks in art are more important than helping Neevya?" Skye tapped the pencil against the side of her chair.

Noah shook his head. "No, no. That's not what I'm saying at all. It's just that if my grades start dropping my parents are going to ask questions."

Ethan picked up a tiny scrap of paper from the floor and wadded it between his fingers. "And you can't lie to your mum."

"Right."

"That's fair." Ethan flicked the paper under Noah's bed. "Don't worry. We can go without you."

Skye thought Noah suddenly looked hopeful, as if getting out of going was exactly what he was trying to do. She stopped that thought from blossoming immediately. "We need Noah. We're in this together."

Noah's shoulders fell, reminding Skye of a dying flower in a vase of water; all it could do was sit there and wait for its death, dismal and forlorn.

Skye placed the notepad back on the desk. "Which period is your art lesson?"

Noah mumbled, "Fourth."

Skye thought for a moment. "So lunch is next. It'll be easy to bunk off then."

Ethan stood and patted Noah on his back. "It's settled. We leave at lunch."

CHAPTER EIGHTEEN
The Assembly

Monday mornings were the worst, especially after repeatedly dreaming about being chased by a monstrous wolf all night. Ethan felt as if he had run for an eternity. His muscles ached and his legs were stiff. He yawned and strained to take an extra-long stretch before crawling out of bed. Saying he was tired was a colossal understatement. He felt as if he'd had a negative amount of sleep, as if someone had snuck in and stolen it from him.

He forced his legs over the side of his bed and pushed himself to his feet. After a bit of wobbling, he managed to get washed and dressed. Too bad it was a school day. If he hadn't already promised to help Noah and Skye sneak out at lunch, he might have tried to convince his mum he was ill. He didn't think she would buy it a second time that month though.

Trying to walk down the stairs with aching legs was proving to be more challenging than he'd anticipated. He paused at the bottom of the steps, stumbled through the hallway, and then practically fell into the kitchen. A bowl of his favorite cereal, Coco-Pips, was waiting for him on the kitchen table.

Ethan didn't know exactly when he had made it home last night. He just remembered it was late and his mum wasn't too happy about it. He recalled constantly looking over his shoulder as he rode his bike back to his house. He also thought about how they had escaped The Dark Wood, and how Neevya had practically fainted.

"But no one will ever know about it," he said wistfully.

"Know about what, love?" his mother asked as she sorted through a large pile of mail. She paced around the room in a way that made him dizzy. There was clearly something on her mind, and Ethan did not want to interfere.

"Oh nothin', just thinking out loud."

"That's nice, love."

The milk had turned just the right shade of chocolate-brown for Ethan to dig in; he was very particular about that. What was the point of having chocolate cereal if he didn't wait for the milk to change color? He slurped down the contents of the bowl and checked his phone—five minutes before he had to leave, ten if he took the shortcut through the neighbors' gardens. He wondered whether he had the strength to navigate that particular obstacle course this morning. He doubted it. Plus, something else was bothering him, besides his concern for Neevya and the huge wolf waiting in the woods.

"Mum?" Ethan looked around.

"Yes, love?"

Ethan scratched his head. "Where's Olivia?"

Usually, his younger sister joined him for breakfast. Her absence made him feel even more out of sorts, if that were possible. One of his favorite moments of any day was to see her smiling face in the morning when he entered the kitchen. Unlike what he'd heard from the other lads at school about their younger siblings, Ethan was proud to have Olivia as his sister. Of course, that wasn't something he'd ever let her know.

Mrs. Castleton looked up from her papers and glanced at Ethan with a vacant stare. Her voice held an edge of worry when she said, "Oh, she's gone to work with your dad today."

That's odd. Why would they take her out of school?

Ethan tried to search his mum's expression, but she had already turned back to her papers.

"Mum? Why did Dad take Olivia to work?"

His mother looked up. She made eye contact for only a second and quickly looked away, tucking a lock of hair behind her ear. Ethan had seen that nervous gesture before.

She's hiding something.

His mother cleared her throat. "Well, Dad wanted…" She paused. "Dad wanted to show her a new painting he recently acquired." She shrugged. "You know how she wants to be an artist."

What kind of answer was that?

Ethan started to ask more, but a text from Noah came through on his phone, saying, *U OK? Where R U?*

"Blimey, I'm late. Got money for school dinner?"

"Sandwiches on the side." His mother pointed without looking up. The foil-wrapped block on the counter looked unappetizing.

"Let me guess, ham chettin' sandwiches again? Can't I just get somethin' at the canteen?"

Ethan's mother apparently found the letter she was looking for and quickly opened it. She winced when she saw what was inside.

"Well, if the number on this bill is correct," she waved the letter like it was a dead rat she'd found behind the couch, "I won't have any money for you before you leave for university. You're having homemade sandwiches from here on out. And yes, they are ham. You said you liked ham."

Ethan snatched the package from the counter and tossed it into his bag.

"The first time I liked it. The fifth, sixth time? Not so much. I can't live on bloomin' ham alone, Mum."

She didn't reply.

Ethan offered a quick goodbye and made his way out, taking the shortcut.

"He's late," Noah complained.

Skye searched the road. "I hope he made it home okay last night."

"Yeah, me too." Noah shifted his backpack and pulled the zipper open. "Sorry, Neevya. I know you don't like it in there."

"It's okay. I'm getting used to it," a tiny voice drifted from the small, unzipped portion of the bag.

Noah and Skye were waiting for Ethan by the iron gate. A trickle of students walked by, oblivious to them.

"We should text him again." Skye was now pacing.

"I'm sure he's fine." Despite his eager confidence, Noah pulled his phone out of his pocket and sent Ethan yet another text. "Nine and counting."

"Ugh, I wish he'd just get here already."

Noah touched her arm. "We still have a few minutes. Let's go sit."

He led Skye to the football pitch.

They sat on the ground and waited.

"We'll see him from here, if he shows up, that is," Skye said.

"He'll show up." Noah peeked inside the backpack. "How are you feeling?"

Neevya tentatively popped her head out of the bag.

"Your backpack smells nice." She looked down. "And I really like these clothes you gave me, too."

Noah grinned. Upon waking, Neevya had mentioned being cold, so he raided his action figure collection and found a pair of knee high cloth boots plus a long coat from a wizard that fit the faerie perfectly. All he had to do was cut a couple of slits in the back of the coat for her wings and tie her sash. "Thanks, I'm glad you like them. But, you looked really sick last night. Are you feeling better?"

Neevya waved him off. "Oh, that? I don't do so well in the rain."

Skye leaned in. "You're avoiding the question."

Neevya bashfully batted her eyelids. "Madison helped me greatly. She is what we call a pureheart." She lowered herself back into the bag so that her head barely stuck out the top. "You're very lucky, Noah."

He looked at her questioningly.

She explained, "Aside from possessing the most powerful kind of restorative magic that exists, purehearts have a special ability to bond with the one they love most. It's the kind of bond that is never broken, even beyond death."

"Beyond death? What do you mean?" Noah asked.

"It means that she will never leave your side, even after her time in your world has passed. It also means that if you ever find yourself facing the Grim Reaper, she can save your life by giving her essence to you when you need it most, or vice-versa."

Although Noah was initially taken aback by the mention of the Grim Reaper, waves of appreciation and love engulfed him. He wished Madison was with him now; he longed to hold her in his arms, stroke her fur, and scratch her belly.

A weight tugged on his mind. *I need her to know how much I love her.*

"She already knows," Neevya said.

Noah looked at her, confused. "What?"

"Madison," Neevya confirmed. "She knows how much you love her."

"Really?" His voice cracked, his throat suddenly raw.

Neevya nodded. "Really. And she loves you very much, too."

With a smile, Skye reached out and put a hand on his knee. "Madison's amazing."

He smiled and tried to think of something else, something that wouldn't make him all teary-eyed. Fiddling with the zipper on his backpack, Noah focused on Neevya. "I'm so glad you're feeling better. You had me scared."

Neevya's little hands grabbed the lip of the backpack, and her violet eyes looked straight at him. "I'm glad too. But..." She looked at Skye.

Noah waited for her to say something, but he had to prod her to finish her thought. "Yeah?"

Neevya pulled herself up, bringing her face closer to his. "You need to promise me you won't be scared for me, ever again."

Noah thought her request was strange, and he didn't answer for a moment. How could she expect him to make a promise like that and keep it?

"Promise me, Noah," Neevya said. She looked at Skye. "You promise me too."

Noah looked down, wanting to please her, but he couldn't bring himself to lie. So instead, he said, "I'll do my best."

Skye nodded. "Yeah, me too."

The odd request dredged up another thought, forcing his mind to revisit The Dark Wood.

"Neevya?" he asked. "Can you tell us why it got dark so fast yesterday?"

Skye visibly stiffened as she withdrew her hand from his knee.

Neevya frowned. "Hmm, that's a good question. I don't really know." She looked off to the side, considering. "The only explanation I can think of is that we may have passed into Thunderstone, the realm of the chondours, when we entered that cloud."

"You mean the fog?" Skye asked.

Neevya took a moment to ponder before she said, "Yes."

"So you think we passed through a portal?" Noah asked, excited.

Neevya shrugged. "Well, I don't really know if portals exist between Suntamor and Thunderstone, or if your two realms just sort of overlap, like they do with Haventhrone."

"Haventhrone?" Skye asked.

"That's where the bellwethers live."

"So we don't need portals to get to the bellwether realm?" Noah asked. This was getting more confusing by the minute.

Neevya shrugged. "You're asking the wrong faerie. I haven't studied it much, to be quite honest. I just heard a few tidbits here and there, and I didn't really pay attention. I mean, after all, I thought humans were just lore until I met you lot." She chuckled.

Noah joined her, not really knowing what he was laughing about.

A broad grin unexpectedly lit up Skye's face.

Noah looked up to see Ethan running through the iron gate shouting, "Guys! Guys! I'm here. Did you miss me?"

Skye tugged on Noah's sleeve. "And Mr. Castleton arrives," she said with a sigh.

Noah couldn't tell if she was relieved or angry—maybe a bit of both.

Ethan jogged up. "What're you sittin' around here for? School's about to start."

Neevya ducked into Noah's backpack and they made their way to registration.

Noah aced Mr. Willard's art history test during fourth period, but his good mood evaporated as soon as he walked out of class and heard the rumors circulating around the hallways. On his way to meet Ethan and Skye for lunch, he overheard some older kids.

A dark-haired boy named Jacob said, "I heard he were torn to pieces, a lot like that lad they found eight years ago."

Lexi Morgan, a girl from Year Ten, gasped. "Blimey! Do you think it'll all start happenin' again?"

Ethan walked up and placed his arm around Noah's shoulders. "Have you heard the news?"

Skye joined them. "If you're talking about the lad that went missing, then yeah. It would be pretty hard to miss."

Ethan pulled Noah and Skye into a secluded corner. "D'you think it was that person we heard screaming in The Dark Wood?"

Skye slapped his shoulder and glanced around nervously. "Keep it down! Do you want the whole school to know where we were last night? Besides, we don't know what we heard. For all we know, it could have been an old barn owl with a bad cold."

Ethan sneered. "That was no owl."

"Well, regardless, we can't start jumping to conclusions."

Ethan considered her statement for a few moments, then clapped his hands together, startling Noah.

The Assembly

"So, we ready to do this or what?"

Noah just looked at him. He wanted to stay in the safety of the school for a little while longer. Besides, there was no need to rush into the forest on an empty stomach.

Ethan cocked his head and addressed both Skye and Noah, "We are still bunking off now, right?"

Noah shrugged.

Skye waved them to come in closer. "There's a few things I want to check into first. If somebody's been torn to pieces, we need to get as much information as we can. I heard Tomas O'Heaphy say his dad found part of the body. We need to know where."

Noah was horrified by that bit of news, but also relieved they weren't going to rush off just yet.

They grabbed their food and made their way outside to the lowest portion of the stone wall surrounding the school. Ethan sat on the wall. Noah gently placed his backpack beside Ethan and unzipped it a sliver, handing Neevya a goji berry.

Her jaw worked hard as she munched the chewy fruit.

Noah tried to soak in the moment as lunch dwindled away and the inevitable bunking loomed closer. It wasn't that he didn't want to help Neevya. He did. He just didn't want to get torn to pieces or lose his soul in the process.

Skye spent the hour keeping an eye out for O'Heaphy, but he was nowhere to be seen. She muttered under her breath and took a vicious bite out of her sandwich, "Hate going in blind."

Ethan, as usual, ate his lunch as if he didn't have a care in the world. A few minutes before the bell rang, he stood and gestured to a group of students who were walking into the school. "Well, time to leg it. Looks like lunch is almost over."

"All right." Skye dusted off her skirt. "Let's get out of here."

Noah's heart leapt into his throat. Why couldn't he be as brave as his two friends? The thought of going back in those woods brought a sense of fear so dense, he wondered if he could reach out and touch it.

Before he knew what he was saying, Noah blurted out, "O'Heaphy's in my next lesson. If we wait another hour, I can ask him where they found the body parts." Inwardly chastising himself for being a coward—a coward who put his own safety before Neevya's—he looked down and shook his head in shame.

Skye grimaced. "Ugh, you can't just mention dead bodies like that, we just finished eating."

"Sorry," Noah murmured as he gathered the uneaten portion of his lunch and stuffed it into his backpack, careful not to crush Neevya.

A soft wind whispered through the trees. Skye looked over the school wall. "Okay, Noah, we bunk after next period. Talk to him and then we go. We'll meet by the iron gate."

Noah nodded and they headed back into the school.

Just as they reached the entrance, Noah happened to look over his shoulder and see Scaretaker walking in from the parking lot; he was closely followed by a man in a dark suit, but Noah only had eyes for the intimidating, scraggly man. He froze, blocking the doorway and causing Ethan and Skye to bump into him.

"Watch it," Ethan said.

Noah pointed, his heart pounding.

A small crowd of students started to gather, trying to get past them.

Ethan looked over his shoulder and whispered, "Scaretaker."

A boy shouted, "What's the hold up?"

Skye whipped her head around, her braids slapping Noah's face. "What's he doing here?"

Noah cradled his backpack and tried to back out of the doorway, but there were too many kids pushing to get through.

Once inside, Ethan pulled Noah and Skye aside. "I don't know why that creep is here, but I say we bunk off now while we have the chance."

Noah vigorously nodded. "Let's get out of here." Before he could take a single step, a great oaf strutted through the doorway.

Noah tried to hide behind Skye, but it was no use.

The Assembly

Grucker waddled up to them. "Well, well, well. If it ain't the Kamikaze Kid and his loser friends."

Skye puffed herself up. "Pick on someone your own size, you overgrown baboon."

Grucker stepped forward so he loomed over her. "I dare yeh to say that to me face."

Skye shuffled back. "Just leave us alone," her voice held less bravado.

Grucker grabbed her shoulders and shoved. She tripped and landed hard on her bum.

Ethan rushed to her side as Grucker descended upon Noah.

"So, little baby. What'll you give me to not smash yer face in?"

Noah looked down at his backpack, anxiety seizing his stomach.

"Gimme that." Grucker reached for the bag.

Noah quickly pushed it behind his back and shouted, "No!"

Grucker looked at him with disbelief. "No? You dare say no to me?"

Noah glanced at Ethan, who had pulled Skye to her feet and now had his hands in position to catch the backpack. Noah quickly tossed it to him.

Ethan caught the backpack, careful not to squeeze.

"Go," Noah hissed.

Ethan took off down the hallway.

Grucker watched and then shoved Noah against the wall. "That's not gonna save you. You still have to pay yer dues."

Noah chanced a glance at Skye and was surprised to see she was talking with a teacher named Mrs. Tremball. She pointed in his direction.

Skye and the teacher walked over.

Backing away from Noah, Grucker mouthed, *Watch yer back.* He turned and sprinted in the same direction as Ethan.

Mrs. Tremball crossed her arms. "Hmmm," she said, staring after Grucker. "Seems Cordell has his work cut out for him."

An announcement blared over the school speakers. "All students, please report to the main hall for a mandatory assembly."

Mrs. Tremball regarded Skye and Noah. Like a hen gathering her chicks, she ushered them down the corridor. "Report to the main hall, you two."

CHAPTER NINETEEN
Double Trouble

Skye elbowed Noah. "Look over there."

Scaretaker stood beside a small stage, dressed in the same tattered and dirty clothes they had seen him in before. His lanky body reminded Skye of a brittle branch, old and ready to crack. But his face, with its severe lines and long nose, reminded her of a vulture. His head even moved like a bird of prey as he scanned the crowd.

"This is not good." Noah grimaced. "Not good at all. What kind of assembly is this, anyway?"

Skye's stomach churned as she pushed through the crowd of students toward the far exit. "We have to get out of here and warn Ethan."

"I can do it." Noah whipped out his phone and texted, *Hide. Don't come 2 assembly. Scaretaker here.*

With Noah in tow, Skye snuck closer to the exit, but a teacher stepped through.

There's got to be another way out.

Mrs. Grimes, the head teacher, walked up a short flight of steps to stand on stage.

Skye strategically pulled Noah into the crowd of students so they could try to blend in near the back of the room.

Double Trouble

Mrs. Grimes motioned for the students to sit. They obeyed in unison, dropping to the floor with a synchronized thud.

Her horn-rimmed glasses balanced on the tip of her nose, Mrs. Grimes looked over the student body. She commanded silence and attention with her posture. Nobody wanted to mess with that old woman. Resembling her personality, her appearance was harsh and angular, making her seem less like a human and more like an insectoid-type alien; a praying mantis maybe?

Skye had been listening to too many of Noah's sci-fi stories.

"I regret to inform you of some troubling news," Grimes began in her abrasive, metallic voice. "As I am sure many of you have heard, there has been a casualty of the most violent nature in our town of Herogate."

A hush fell over the student body. Not a whisper could be heard.

"Therefore, by recommendation of the city of Herogate, it is my duty to inform you that a curfew is now in effect. Any pupil under the age of seventeen caught outside after dark will face suspension."

A low murmur erupted throughout the room.

Mrs. Grimes tapped her microphone, demanding complete silence. "Additionally, it has come to my attention that we have delinquents in our ranks who may be involved in the unfortunate incident."

Gasps flooded over the crowd like waves crashing onto the shore.

"She means us," Skye hissed at Noah. This was getting worse by the second.

"We will be conducting a thorough investigation, questioning each pupil as to their whereabouts last evening. I have been made aware by Mr. Solomon here," Mrs. Grimes gestured to Scaretaker, "that at least three of you have been caught repeatedly entering the Forest of Shadowen. All pupils should know the forest is private property and entry is prohibited."

His name was Solomon? Scaretaker seemed way more appropriate. Even though he wasn't looking at her, Skye was certain Scaretaker had already picked her out in the crowd. Of the three of them, she stood out the most, with her dark skin and pink braids.

Grimes continued making her announcements but Skye stopped

paying attention. If Mrs. Grimes knew what was really going on she'd kick Scaretaker out of her school and never let him return.

Noah let out a curse under his breath.

Skye flinched. "What's wrong?"

Noah stuffed his phone back into his pocket. "Accidently called Ethan. I only wanted to check the time."

Skye scowled. There she sat, trying her best to hide her pink braids, imagining them to be flashing beacons that screamed, *I'm over here! Look at me!* And all the while Noah was playing with his phone.

She glanced up just in time to see Scaretaker look her way, and she hunched behind the tall boy who sat in front of her.

Noah whispered, "He's not looking over here anymore. It's okay."

Skye focused on the stage. "We have to get out of here. He's searching for us."

"Just how do you suggest we do that?"

"Don't worry, I've got a plan."

Noah looked at her, amazed. "You do?"

Skye didn't actually have a plan. But she didn't want Noah to know that. She said, "Just follow me."

Ethan checked his text message from Noah and then stuffed his phone into his pocket.

"Thanks for the tip off," he mumbled to himself.

With a sly grin, and Neevya secured safely in the bag, Ethan skulked away from the main hall, pretending he was sneaking through The Dark Wood and evading Scaretaker.

Pay attention! Gonna get yourself caught at this rate, Castleton.

But Ethan couldn't stop the images of pelting rain, thick fog, and shadowy figures from flashing through his mind.

The sounds of squeaking shoes alerted Ethan to the imminent arrival of Mr. Cordell. That trademark squeak had saved many a stray pupil from detention. Ethan slipped into a nearby classroom; strong smells of burnt chemicals, sulfur, and disinfectants assaulted his senses. He was in the science lab. Too bad it wasn't Mr. Bell's history classroom. Ethan would have had a field day in that room with all the cool and unusual things Mr. Bell kept on display.

Mr. Cordell passed by the door's window. By the sound of it, he was going to be late for the big talk. Ethan smirked, hearing the squeaking fade away. "Ooh, you're in big trouble now, Cordell, mate." Mrs. Grimes made no exception for pupils or teachers.

Ethan considered staying in the science lab for the remainder of the assembly, but the air reminded him of the scent he'd smelled in The Dark Wood. When he couldn't take the stench any longer, he stepped into the hallway which had taken on an eerie emptiness. As he walked, he imagined he was aboard a ghost ship, quietly sailing into harbor with almost no crew on board, except for Neevya, of course. Neevya was his stowaway.

Ethan imagined a peg-legged man with an eyepatch and a see-sawing gait approach him and say, "Ahoy matey, shall we visit the seas of the sirens?" He pointed to the girls' toilets.

Ethan chewed on it. "Argh, scallywag. It would be the last place anyone would look fer us. But perhaps it's not such a good idea." If he was going to get caught, he'd rather keep at least a shred of dignity.

The imaginary pirate said, "Arrr, right ye be, Master Castleton. Set sail fer Latrine Lagoon."

As he entered the boys' toilets, Ethan squatted and checked for feet. "Oi," he said loudly, cringing when the sound echoed off the walls.

No one answered.

"The coast be clear," Ethan said.

A small voice from within the backpack asked, "Who are you speaking with?"

"No one. I was just messin' around." Ethan took up residence in the stall farthest from the door. He sat on the back of the toilet to keep his feet off the floor as his ghost ship fantasy evaporated.

He placed the backpack on his lap and unzipped its top. "How're you holdin' up in there?"

Neevya poked her head out. "Not so bad. Noah's bag is much cleaner than yours."

He chuckled. "Everybody's chettin' bag is cleaner than mine." He may have prided himself on being able to make almost anything stylish, but organization was not his forte.

Neevya started to fly, but on the other side of the door came Grucker's chilling voice. "All right, lads, keep it down. First sign o' trouble, we leg it."

Ethan waved Neevya back inside the bag.

The door leading into the restroom creaked open.

"There's no way I'm goin' to that bloody assembly, and I'm not gettin' caught out here, neither," Grucker complained.

Same here, Ethan thought to himself. Just as long as Grucker didn't check the cubicles, he would be okay. All Ethan had to do was stay absolutely quiet.

"Hey, you! What're you lads doin' out here?" Mr. Cordell's voice trailed through the open doorway.

Ethan heard a few curses accompanied by shuffling feet and someone opening a stall door and slamming it. The thuds of other footsteps scurried away, chased by Mr. Cordell's squeaky strides.

Mr. Cordell shouted, "You get back here! Detentions for the lot o' yeh!"

Someone in the stall next to Ethan mumbled, "Bloody Nora."

Ethan sat as still as possible, hoping it was one of Grucker's bullies and not the man himself.

"Can't wait till I get outta school and be on me own."

Ethan recognized that voice and listened as Grucker paced outside the stalls, all the while mumbling to himself.

One of Ethan's favorite songs started blaring from inside his pocket. "Blimey!" he hissed.

How the flippin' heck did me ringer get turned on?

He yanked the phone from his pocket and slid the ringer to silent. Then he hastily peeked in at Neevya. "Whatever happens, stay in there. Do not, I repeat, do not come out for any reason." As carefully as he could, he set the backpack on a small window ledge that was high on the wall beside the toilet.

"Who's that talking to himself?" Grucker sneered. In an instant, the bully was banging on the stall door.

Ethan looked at his phone to check the caller ID. It was Noah, probably calling to find out where he was.

I'm knee deep in it, that's where I am—about to get pulverized by Grucker. Feel free to stop by and rescue me.

"All right in there?" Grucker kicked in the door and rubbed his hands together. "It must be me lucky day."

CHAPTER TWENTY

Bamboozled

Compared to Grucker's massive size, Ethan might as well have been an ant. He certainly felt crushable as he stood in front of the great lump who towered over him.

"Well, well, well, what have we got here?" Grucker jabbed a stubby finger into Ethan's shoulder.

Pain shot through his arm and fear clenched his stomach. It was enough to make him nauseous, but Ethan didn't make a peep.

Grucker glanced at the backpack. "I see you've got me bag." He started to reach for it, but Ethan blocked his way.

"So tell me. What're you doin' in here anyway? Shouldn't you be in the girls' loo?" Grucker spat his words, spraying Ethan not only with his drool but with the venom of his insults.

Ethan wiped his face. How could he get Grucker away from Neevya?

Stepping forward until they were chest to chest, Ethan played every escape scenario he could think of. He could try to sidestep Grucker and make a run for it, but that would leave Neevya vulnerable. What about shoving Grucker back and picking a fight? That wouldn't work either. Grucker's size alone would prevent Ethan from shoving him an inch. He even considered calling for help, but that might lead to Neevya's discovery. Ethan couldn't think of a single thing that might save him. Then he realized there was only one thing left to do.

I must sacrifice meself.

Grucker jeered, "What's that look in yer eyes fer? Daydreamin' about what dress you'll wear when you get home?"

How can I play this idiot's insults to me advantage? Ethan considered his options. It suddenly came to him. He had no choice but to roll with it. Summoning all his courage, Ethan stepped into character.

His hands were shaky when he slowly and deliberately ran his fingers through his hair and smoothed his collar. He let out an uneasy sigh. His voice cracked when he said, "I'm so sorry. I must have lost me mind. Can you repeat the question please?" He made a bold attempt to look Grucker up and down appreciatively, but wasn't sure if he was pulling it off, so he said, "I mean, I forgot to listen. I was too busy admiring you."

Grucker straightened. A trace of a smile formed on his lips for the barest of seconds. Ethan realized the big buffoon was actually flattered.

But the moment didn't last. Grucker's face turned steam-engine-red and contorted into outright rage.

"You'll be sorry fer that."

Ethan licked his lips nervously. "Sorry for what, appreciating the view?" Certain he was about to get clobbered, Ethan prepared for a blow, but Grucker just stood there, nostrils flaring and hands balled into fists.

For several complicated moments, they simply eyed each other. Grucker's shallow breaths warmed Ethan's face with each exhale, making him feel confused and even more queasy.

He had to do something to get out of this mess. But what?

Ethan decided to push his luck. Placing his hand on Grucker's shoulder, he gave it a gentle nudge. To his surprise, Grucker stepped back as if in shock. Ethan held Grucker's gaze as he tiptoed past him, and out of the stall, shutting the door behind him. Backing toward the exit, his confidence grew with each step. His plan was to lure Grucker away from Neevya. To do that, he would have to make Grucker chase him. Ethan figured he could lose the great lump fairly easily in the hallways and make it back before Neevya even realized he was gone. It was the only way she would be safe.

Ethan grabbed the door handle and said with disgust, "I'll tell you what I'm sorry for. I'm sorry no one likes you because you're so mean. I'm sorry I'm wasting me breath on you. I'm sorry you're so pathetic."

Ethan pulled. The handle slipped out of his sweaty palm as two vise-like hands gripped his shoulders. Before he knew what was happening, Ethan went flying back and landed sprawled on the tiled floor.

Grucker loomed over him. "You think yer smart, don't yeh?"

Ethan scooted away as quickly as he could, but it wasn't nearly fast enough.

Grucker pulled Ethan to his feet and slammed his back against the far wall. The look in Grucker's eyes sent shivers down Ethan's spine. He felt as if he stood in the eye of a hurricane; the worst was yet to come.

He gulped.

Grucker's eyes were full of menace, his voice low and composed. "I don't have to be smart. I don't have to know all the answers. Kids like you think they can talk back to me, but it doesn't change nuttin'. I'm still in charge 'round here."

Like two slabs of meat slapping against a butcher's table, Grucker punched the wall on either side of Ethan's head.

"No matter how much yeh cry, or how much yeh beg, I always get me way." He jabbed his thumb into his own chest. "*I* always win."

There's a point where sarcasm fails, and Ethan had just found it. There was nothing he could do to save himself.

"Yer goin' to the girls' loo where yeh belong." Grucker forced Ethan to the floor.

Even though Ethan knew it was impossible to talk his way out, he tried his best. "You know we're in this together, you and me?"

This seemed to make Grucker even madder. He grabbed Ethan's ankles and began to drag him across the floor.

Ethan pleaded, "We're both bunking off, aren't we? We both escaped

Bamboozled

Mr. Cordell's notice. That's because great minds think alike, which is why you and me ended up here."

Grucker reached for the door.

Panic flared inside Ethan as he grabbed for something, anything that would keep him from being pulled away from Neevya. Without considering the consequences, he called out, "Neevya, stay here. I'll come back for you." He didn't know what made him say it. But once it slipped out, he couldn't take it back.

Grucker dropped Ethan's feet, slowly turned, and glanced around the toilets. "Who're yeh talkin' to? There's no one here but you and me."

Those were words Ethan never wanted to hear. Being alone with Grucker was as bad as being trapped in a giant spider web without scissors.

A flash of pale yellow streaked behind Grucker. Ethan gulped. Why was Neevya hovering above the sinks?

Grucker reached for one of Ethan's flailing feet and kicked him in the stomach, knocking the wind out of him. Ethan rolled on his side and cradled his belly.

Neevya hovered above Grucker's head and chanted.

"Go back inside!" Ethan huffed, his eyes fixed on the flying faerie.

"What th'?" Grucker looked up.

There was a time Ethan would have paid good money to see terror on the great lump's face. But now that he was actually watching it, he didn't feel the tiniest bit of pleasure; if anything, it made him feel worse.

Neevya darted behind Grucker.

"Flippin' heck! What were that?" Grucker shouted, whipping around.

Ethan, still clutching his stomach, tried to will Neevya to hide in the stall as she flew right in front of Grucker's face and screamed, "You hurt one more hair on his head and you will face my fury!"

Grucker stumbled back.

As if in slow motion, Ethan tried to tuck in his feet, but it was too late. Grucker's oversized shoes lodged between Ethan's knees, sending the bully reeling. He fell like a great oak tree, his weight driving him hard onto the tiled floor. His head was the last thing to hit. To Ethan's dismay, it bounced.

Grucker's eyes closed.

Ethan sat up and scrambled away on all fours. Then he locked eyes with Neevya.

She held her hands over her mouth, horrified. "I didn't mean to kill him!"

Ethan crawled to Grucker's side. He lowered his head and placed his ear near Grucker's mouth and nose, hoping to hear, or at least feel the oaf's hot breath.

Grucker groaned.

"Thank goodness he's alive," Ethan sighed with relief. "I think he's trying to say something."

Grucker whispered, "I'm going to kill you, Castleton."

Ethan hastily pushed himself to his feet and looked at Neevya. "What should we do?"

Grucker moaned and rubbed his eyes.

"I'm delighted he's not dead," Neevya's voice was full of elation.

Grucker tried to sit up but fell back to the floor.

Ethan hastily hopped out of his reach. "That's not any help. As soon as he gets up, *I'll* be dead! Is there anything you can to do make him sleep; at least long enough to give us time to make a plan and get out of here?"

Neevya shrugged. "I might be able to glamour him."

"What's glamour? It won't hurt him, will it?"

"It's a kind of magic. It's totally safe. I use it all the time."

Ethan nodded. "Do it."

Just as Neevya hovered above Grucker's face, his eyes flew open, and he screamed.

Neevya muttered a few words as Grucker closed his eyes, and his head lolled to the side.

Ethan looked at Neevya appraisingly. "Nicely done. Glad you're on my side."

Her cheeks turned a bright shade of pink as if she were embarrassed.

Nudging Grucker with his feet, Ethan sneered, "How's that for getting a taste of your own medicine?"

Grucker squirmed.

Ethan hopped back and shot a questioning glance at Neevya.

"He must be having a bad dream." She hovered just above Grucker's nose and inspected his eyelids. "Nobody deserves nightmares. Stand back." With a wave of her hand and a few unrecognizable words, Neevya cast her spell.

Grucker continued to twitch and started to breathe heavily.

"Something's not right." Neevya repeated the spell.

Nothing happened at first, but then Grucker suddenly pushed himself to his feet and began spinning in circles while singing an old folk song. To Ethan's surprise, the brute had a nice voice. With each new word, Grucker's singing grew louder and louder; his melody echoed off the walls.

"Keep it down, will you?" Ethan opened the restroom door and quickly peeked out.

As if noticing Ethan for the first time, Grucker raised an eyebrow and staggered over to him. "Hello sir. Would you care to dance?" Bowing and almost falling over, Grucker held out his hand.

Ethan pressed his back against the door. "Neevya, what did you do?"

"Oh dear Mother, I have no clue. That spell never affected the flowers this way."

Grucker took off his necktie and draped it over Ethan's head. His voice rose and fell to a cheerful melody as he sang, "Why is it so hot in here?" He proceeded to unbutton his trousers.

Ethan tossed the necktie in a nearby corner and eyed Neevya. "You have to do something. He's gone mad!"

Grucker sustained his tune; his trousers now completely unfastened.

"Certifiable; he's chettin' mental! Neevya, fix him! He'll be naked before we know it."

"What went wrong?" Neevya anxiously flitted around the room, muttering, "I was careful to wield the weaves. Did I confuse the commentary? Maybe I crossed the currents."

Ethan figured it was best to stay out of her way; she needed time to think. For that matter, he also did his best to stay out of Grucker's way as the bully sang and pranced around.

A short while later, Grucker's trousers were tossed on the floor, his shirt was hanging from one of the stalls, his vest decorated the sinks, and his shoes were in the toilets. The only piece of clothing Ethan was able to convince Grucker not to remove was his briefs.

"Seriously Grucker, put your clothes back on. You're going to regret this."

Grucker's pupils were dilated, his face was flushed, and he was drenched in sweat. He answered with a deep, operatic bellow. "Regret? Regret. Reeegrehttt!" He even used vibrato on that last, drawn out word.

His next verse was upbeat and to the tune of a popular kid's song. "Dance, dance, move your feet firmly with the beat; merrily, merrily, verily, verily, Ethan come with me." Grucker grabbed Ethan's wrist and pulled him out into the hallway, all the while singing his heart out.

Too shocked to resist, Ethan soon found himself dancing in the hallway, being whipped from side-to-side and twirling around in spins he didn't know he could perform. Grucker even dipped him before passing out and collapsing on top of him.

"Flippin' heck, he's chettin' drenched!" Ethan wriggled out from under Grucker, stood, and wiped away the bully's salty sweat. "Ugh, it got in my mouth. Disgusting!"

Ethan spat on the floor several times and dabbed his face on his shirt. When he felt somewhat dry again, he looked at Neevya curiously. "Neevya, what just happened?"

She was hovering over Grucker, pulling at his eyelashes. It seemed she was trying to wake him up; or she had an odd way of examining him. She turned to Ethan and threw her hands wide. "Well, that was unexpected."

A shimmer of light escaped her palm and hit Ethan squarely between his eyes. "Oops," Neevya giggled and halfheartedly shrugged before turning back to Grucker.

Ethan suddenly felt an odd sense of insecurity. He stood there, reliving the moment over and over. He had just been humiliated, tossed, twirled, and soaked in someone else's sweat. Now, he was watching a faerie inspect a sweaty, half-naked bully, who just happened to be unconscious in the middle of his school's hallway; a hallway that would probably soon be filled with students. What would happen next?

Neevya unexpectedly zipped over to him and snapped her fingers in front of his face. "What are you just standing around for? We need to get him dressed."

Ethan didn't respond. He just looked at her with a blank stare.

Neevya batted her eyelashes. "Well, I suppose it can wait. I mean, I understand if you're tired from all that dancing. You're quite good, you know?"

Ethan blinked.

Neevya gestured to the toilets. "I may be able to summon his clothes and magic them on him."

That did it; Ethan snapped out of his trance. "I think you've done enough magic for one day."

"You're probably right."

They locked eyes and stared at each other for several moments. Neevya began to giggle, sending them both into fits of laughter. Ethan laughed so hard tears streaked his cheeks and he had a difficult time catching his breath. His ribs even hurt.

"You should've seen the look on your face," Ethan was saying when a noise distracted them.

Neevya impulsively hid behind his back.

Daring a quick glance in the direction of the sound, he saw a classroom door slowly crack open; behind it was a couple of students who were also bunking out of the assembly. His first thought was of hiding Neevya, but he quickly realized she was already safely tucked away behind him. Then he followed their gazes, which were fixed on Grucker, making Ethan's cheeks flush with embarrassment. Feeling as awkward as a thief caught with stolen loot, Ethan grabbed Grucker's fat ankles and whispered, "Quick, to the toilets."

Just then, they were distracted again.

"Castleton! Just what do yeh think yer doin'?" Mr. Cordell stomped toward them.

Grucker groaned.

The teacher closed in on them. Seeing Grucker, his expression changed from anger to shock and then to outrage.

Ethan held up his hand to calm the livid teacher. "It's not what it looks like, mate." He stepped to the side, out from between Grucker and Mr. Cordell. "I was trying to help."

A muffled snigger caught Ethan's attention. He glanced in the direction of the students hiding out in the adjacent classroom.

When they realized Mr. Cordell was following his gaze, they quietly pushed the door shut.

Mr. Cordell turned back to Ethan, crossed his arms, and clenched his jaw shut. He looked as if he were angrier than a bull in a bullfight.

Ethan tried to look as innocent and hopeful as possible. "I won't mention this to anyone if you don't."

The teacher's glare blazed with fury, his grinding teeth causing tiny muscles to pop out on his jaw.

Ethan slowly backed away.

"You stay right where you are, Castleton."

Neevya flew to Ethan's shoulder. He waited for Cordell to react, but when he didn't say anything, Ethan whispered out of the corner of his mouth, "Can't he see you?"

"What did yeh say?" Mr. Cordell questioned.

Neevya fluttered straight in front of Cordell's face. "I don't think so."

"I didn't say anything, sir."

Grucker's eyes fluttered open as he sat up and looked around.

Mr. Cordell patted him on the back. "Get up and get yer clothes on."

Grucker scrambled to his feet, took one last look at Neevya, and rushed into the toilets, wide-eyed and struggling to keep his balance. Ethan was surprised to see wet trailing footprints; even the soles of his feet were sweaty.

Mr. Cordell turned all his attention on Ethan. "This is unacceptable, Castleton. I'm taking you to Grimes."

"But I didn't do anything wrong, sir."

Neevya stuck her tongue out at the teacher.

Mr. Cordell put his hand on the back of Ethan's neck. "Yer comin' with me."

Ethan glanced up at Neevya, who looked from him to the toilets.

"Go back and wait with the bag. Stay out of Grucker's sight. I'll come back for you."

The last thing Ethan saw was Neevya fluttering down the hallway.

No! Not that way!

Skye gestured with a jerk of her head. "That door's our only shot."

Noah slowly turned and looked over his right shoulder.

Skye felt him stiffen at her side. "What? What's wrong?"

Mrs. Grimes paced the stage as her voice echoed throughout the main hall.

Noah looked at Skye nervously as sweat began to glisten on his forehead. "This doesn't make any sense." His breath became quick and shallow.

"What are you talking about?" Skye looked over her shoulder and saw what she had previously missed. There, standing inconspicuously in the far corner was a slender, athletic man with dark, wavy hair. He was dressed in a black suit. "Is that?"

"My dad." Noah looked back over his shoulder.

Skye asked, "What's *he* doing here? Did he come with Scaretaker?"

"How should I know?"

"If anyone should know, it's you. You do live with the man, after all. Has he said anything?"

"My dad's job is top secret, remember? He doesn't tell me squat."

Skye looked back at the stage just in time to see Scaretaker throw a nervous glance at Mr. Walters. "Maybe Scaretaker's under investigation and he's in your dad's custody. You can't have a murder without suspects, and that lad was ripped to shreds in Scaretaker's backyard."

"But wouldn't the local police handle that? Why would my dad be involved?"

"Who knows? Maybe Scaretaker is an international spy."

"Maybe, or he could be some kind of monster from the portal. If Neevya got out, there's no telling what else came through." Noah eyed the stage nervously.

Grimes stopped speaking and motioned for Scaretaker to join her. She placed the microphone in a stand that sat on a wooden podium.

Noah whispered, "He's going to see us for sure."

Scaretaker climbed the steps and walked to center stage. He peered over the crowd, leaning forward and squinting. Then he lifted his notes with a shaky hand and cleared his throat. "Me name is Mr. Solomon. I am here to…" He cleared his throat again and dropped his paper. "Ah, t' heck with it. Be friendly, they say. But it's not a friendly matter, is it? It's a scandal, I tell ye." He grabbed the sides of the wooden podium. "So let's get down to it, then. Some of yer lot have been creepin' around me land and it has t' stop." He slapped his hand down hard on the podium, causing a boom to blare through the sound system. "Them woods are dangerous. I can't be gettin' blamed for what happens t' bairns creepin' 'round a forest that has a mind of its own. I know ye be out there, ye three. Ye'd better show yerselves now, or next time I catch ye I'm gonna skin ye alive. I'm gonna let the devils eat ye."

Mrs. Grimes rushed the stage and placed her hand over the microphone.

Scaretaker yanked the microphone from its holster and held it out of Grime's reach.

Noah's father crept closer to the stage, preparing to intervene.

Mrs. Grimes said, "Now, Mr. Solomon. That's no way to speak to children. How dare you come into my school and make threats?"

Noah whispered, "We have to get out of here before he sees us."

Skye pointed at a door to her left. "Let's leg it. If we run fast enough, we can make it."

"That's the dumbest idea ever! We'll get caught for sure!" Noah broke the cardinal rule of assembly. He spoke out loud.

The commotion on stage suddenly stopped as all eyes turned to Noah.

"Who's talking back there?" Mrs. Grimes yanked the microphone from Scaretaker's skeletal grip. "Stand so I can see you."

Scaretaker leaned forward to get a better look.

Mr. Walters, now standing next to the stage, looked as well. He met his son's eyes.

Noah froze. "He's seen me."

"Stand up, I said," Mrs. Grimes blared over the sound system.

Everyone around him was staring at him, waiting.

Skye shook her head. She couldn't let him give himself up. Not now. There was too much at stake. This wasn't simply about getting detention or getting an earful from old Grimes; this would jeopardize them from being able to go back to the forest ever again.

To Skye's horror, Noah started to stand, his gaze locked on his father.

She had to think quickly. What could she do?

"What's your name?" Grimes called out, her voice sharp and pointed, like a dart tossed across the room.

Noah stood the rest of the way.

Scaretaker pointed and shouted, "It be one of 'em! It be one of th' lot on me land!" He jumped off the front of the stage, causing a group of students to scatter out of his way.

Clearly shocked, Mr. Walters seemed glued to the spot as he questioned Noah with his eyes.

Mrs. Grimes raised her voice, "Mr. Solomon! Get back on stage this instant!"

At the same time, a commotion on the other side of the hall suddenly erupted. A boy yelled, "I promise I'll pay attention in lessons. Anythin' but Grimes!"

Several hundred heads swiveled in unison, including the heads of Mrs. Grimes, Mr. Walters, and Scaretaker.

"Ethan!" Skye hissed.

There Ethan was, being led into the main hall by Mr. Cordell, and saying, "How would you like some Sweetkats? I have a whole bag of 'em at home. I'll bring you some tomorrow."

Scaretaker stalked toward Ethan. "There be another'n!"

As Ethan's gaze landed on Scaretaker, a mask of horror settled on his face; his chest heaved as he pushed against Mr. Cordell and struggled to back away from Scaretaker.

Mr. Cordell forced Ethan forward.

Skye bolted to her feet. "We're flippin' doomed!"

Ethan jabbed his finger at Scaretaker. "Monster!" He frantically twisted and shoved Mr. Cordell. Three more teachers joined in to subdue him.

"He's going to kill me! He's going to kill us all!" Ethan shouted at the top of his lungs, flailing his arms, contorting his body into seemingly impossible positions, and appearing mad. The more he struggled, the more his veins popped out along his temples and down his neck. His face turned crimson. "Don't let him rip me apart!"

Scaretaker's nostrils flared as his hands balled into tight fists. He leapt over a group of sitting students. When he landed, he sneered at Ethan, his yellow teeth bared.

A young girl pointed at Scaretaker and shrieked, "Monster!" Other students joined in, until screams erupted from every direction. Students stood and scattered.

Mrs. Grimes clapped her hands in front of the microphone and shouted, "Order! Order!"

No one listened.

Ethan slipped out of Cordell's grip and fled into the hallway.

Scaretaker gave chase.

Mrs. Grimes snapped her arm and pointed at Scaretaker. "Cordell! Stop that man!"

Before Mr. Cordell could react, Noah's father seemed to come out of nowhere and attack him, wrestling him to the floor. Three other teachers gathered around to help, but Mr. Walters waved them off. When he had Scaretaker under control with his hands cuffed behind his back, Mr. Walters pulled him to his feet and shoved him toward the rear exit.

"Please escort Mr. Solomon out of the building," Mrs. Grimes commanded.

Mr. Walters nodded, looked over his shoulder to eye Noah, and then shoved Scaretaker out the door.

Cordell directed his mob of teachers into the hallway, presumably to chase Ethan.

The only thing Skye could do was watch the pandemonium all around her.

Noah grabbed her hand and tugged. "Let's get out of here."

CHAPTER TWENTY-ONE
Finding a Faerie

Noah kept a firm grip on Skye's hand as he pulled her through the crowded hallway.

"We're in real trouble, now. There's no way my dad's not going to give me the third degree. He'll find out about Neevya for sure."

"Relax, we'll come up with something convincing to tell him."

This made Noah even more nervous. "I can't lie! He'll see right through me. My dad's a trained expert, remember?"

All around them, kids darted into classrooms where teachers were waving them in. Trying not to get caught up in the shuffle, Noah stood on his toes for a better look down the hallway.

"Don't worry about your dad right now. We have more important things to think about, like finding Ethan and Neevya. Where do you think they are?"

Skye was right; Noah forced himself to abandon all thoughts of the trouble he would be in when he got home and tightened his grip on her hand. "Follow me." Leading her through a series of hallways to the back of the school, they crept out of the gymnasium and toward the football pitch.

A gust of wind carried putrid odors from a nearby garbage bin on its tide.

Noah's phone vibrated. He began to reach for it, but was distracted by a throng of teachers crossing the football pitch.

"He went this way!" Mr. Bell broke into a trot.

Ethan darted out from behind the iron gate as Noah and Skye ducked behind the large, stinky rubbish bin. They both covered their noses.

Like a lion pouncing on an antelope, Mr. Cordell dashed past Mr. Bell, tackled Ethan, and sent them both rolling across the ground.

"Mr. Cordell!" Mrs. Grimes shouted, one arm raised, "We do not tackle our students!" Her long strides ate the distance as she made her way to the tackling.

Cordell stood and dusted himself off. "I caught him, didn't I?"

Ethan rolled onto his side, gripping his elbow.

Noah smothered a laugh as he heard Ethan say, "Mr. Cordell, I thought we were mates."

Cordell offered his hand to Ethan.

Ethan just lay there, eyeing it.

"Stand up." Mrs. Grimes and her mob of teachers closed in on Ethan like hunters circling their prey. Noah watched as they escorted him back into the school.

Indignant, Noah couldn't help but to grind his teeth. "Chettin' vultures." That *chet* was for Ethan.

When the coast was clear, Noah and Skye came out from behind the rubbish bin.

Taking a deep breath, Skye said, "Remind me never to hide behind that foul thing again."

"Reminder remembered." Noah nonchalantly pulled his phone out of his pocket and froze at the sight of the text message on his screen. The phone slipped from his grasp.

Skye picked it up and read out loud, "Neevya gone."

A cold chill ran down Noah's spine. He turned to Skye, who looked just as stunned.

She thrust the phone at him. "We have to find her."

"Like, yesterday." Noah quickly put the phone away and followed Skye back inside the school. They snuck through the gymnasium and toward the hallway. Just as they were about to exit, Mrs. Grimes announced over the loudspeaker, "In light of recent events, the school will close early today. When the bell rings, you may gather your belongings and meet your parents out front."

The bell rang.

Students poured into the hallway, and a group of sniggering girls gathered near the water fountains. As Noah and Skye were about to pass them, an older girl named Tracy Hollingsworth stepped forward and told the others, "O'Heaphy said Grucker was in the hallway practically naked! He said it was that Castleton lad who done it; stripped him down and left him hog tied to teach him a lesson. Probably payback for what he did to that Noah lad."

The girls broke into peals of laughter.

Noah stared at Tracy, shocked.

Skye tapped her shoulder. "Did you say Castleton? As in Ethan Castleton?"

Tracy spun around, her long blonde hair swishing through the air. She looked down her nose at Skye. "Who wants to know?"

Noah stepped forward. "We're his friends. Can you tell us where it happened?"

Tracy looked Noah up and down and smiled devilishly. "All right, cutie."

Noah felt his cheeks flush.

Skye spoke up. "Please, it's important."

Tracy sighed, "Yeah, fine. He was just outside the loo over by the Science lab."

Noah met Tracy's eyes. "Thanks."

She winked.

Noah's knees grew weak as Skye grabbed his elbow and yanked. "Come on. We don't have much time."

Noah felt his mouth curl into a half-smile as he backed away and shyly waved. Tracy blew him a kiss and turned back to her friends with a giggle.

Noah and Skye searched under all the desks and in the dusty cupboards.

They even dared to look in the teacher's desk drawers, but there was no sign of Neevya in the Science lab.

"Where on Earth could she be?" Skye asked.

"I don't think she's in the school anymore," Noah reasoned as they snuck out of the classroom. "We've searched the toilets, the hallways, every inch of this place. Besides finding my backpack, there's not a single trace of her." The word *trace* made him think of Tracy.

Skye looked at him with a scowl. "What are you smiling about?"

Not realizing he'd been grinning, Noah tried to wipe it from his face. "Nothing." To change the topic, he said, "Maybe Neevya's gone back to my house. We should check there."

Skye agreed.

Noah bolted into his house and shouted, "Mum! Mum! Are you here?" There was no answer.

Madison meandered down the stairs and rubbed against his legs.

Noah thought she didn't seem as peppy as usual, and made a mental note to thoroughly check her out after they found Neevya. She had probably just woken up from a nap or something. He bent down and stroked under her chin. "Hey, Babygirl."

She stretched her neck forward, as if asking for more.

Noah obliged. "You're such a good girl, sweet Madi."

Skye stepped up behind him. "Do you see Neevya anywhere?"

Noah gave Madison one last scratch behind her ear. "Let's check my bedroom."

They ran upstairs, threw open the door, and rushed into his room. The space felt oddly empty.

Noah knew the answer before Skye called, "Neevya? Are you here?"

Madison entered the room, tilted her head, and as soon as she caught Noah's eye, she yipped and bolted downstairs.

Noah hurried to her side; Skye followed.

"What is it, girl?" he asked.

Madison scratched at the front door, which was unusual for her.

Noah knelt. "Is it Neevya?"

Madison trilled and circled around him. She then pressed her paws on the door.

Noah looked up at Skye. "What do you think?"

She shrugged. "Let's see what happens."

Madison fled down Noah's driveway, onto Stillwater Street, and toward Herogate High School. They raced after her. When they neared the school, Madison sniffed around the edge of the stone wall, her tail wagging furiously.

"She's picked up a scent." Skye pointed. "I think she's found something."

Noah rushed to the spot, but Skye beat him to it, blocking his view.

She bent down, parted the weeds, gasped and jumped back, as if she'd found a hornet's nest.

"What wrong?"

Skye stood there, shaking her head. "This can't be happening."

"What? What can't be happening?" Noah pleaded, not wanting to look.

Skye didn't respond.

"Fine; don't answer," Noah mumbled as he tentatively stepped forward and parted the clump of weeds. He felt as if he'd been punched in his stomach, his breath slammed out of his lungs. There, curled up into a ball with her eyes closed, was Neevya. But that wasn't what made Noah's knees go weak.

Neevya's skin was a dark, purplish-gray.

He did a double take, and then bent down for a closer look. The coat he had given her was folded and propped under her head as a pillow; the boots were nowhere to be seen.

Noah looked at Skye.

Tears stained her cheeks.

As gently as possible, Noah gathered the limp faerie in his hands.

CHAPTER TWENTY-TWO

Dish Duty

A small crack in the hard, plastic seat pinched Ethan's leg as it shifted under his weight. Just like the entire situation, the seat was terribly uncomfortable. Ethan looked around the room. Mrs. Grimes's office reflected its owner—sterile, bland, and stiff. Nothing in the small, cramped space indicated she was a real person with any kind of personality instead of some automated robot that got its jollies by telling kids what to do. Diplomas and certificates lined the walls; instructional books filled the bookcases.

At least her chettin' henchman have left me alone. What a mess this is. Mum and Dad are goin' to kill me!

Presumably, Mrs. Grimes had stepped out to call his parents.

When he was being escorted to her office, he imagined he'd probably receive at least a week's suspension; Mrs. Grimes was renowned for making examples of her victims. Ethan felt she'd be especially keen to punish a lad who literally ran away from her in front of the entire student body. Besides, he knew she'd had it in for him ever since he'd started a food fight earlier that year.

Ethan laced his fingers behind his head and sighed. There were worse things than getting suspended. He wondered if Noah had received his text. For Neevya's sake, he hoped so.

The door opened, and his mum's favorite perfume wafted into the office. Ethan didn't need to turn around to know his parents had arrived. Planning to make a joke he thought his dad would appreciate, he started to say something cheeky, but the look on his father's face made him snap his mouth shut. He wasn't prepared to see the disappointment in his father's expression or the distress in his mother's eyes. And why was Olivia here?

"Please, pull up a chair." Mrs. Grimes motioned to the empty seats in front of her desk.

His parents and sister sat down. Mrs. Grimes settled into her own chair, lacing her knobby fingers into a twisted tangle as she regarded the Castletons; then her cold glare settled on Ethan.

He shrank into his seat.

This is not going to end well.

"What we have here is a problem with discipline," Mrs. Grimes said, not taking her eyes off Ethan.

Ethan's dad calmly nudged his chair closer to Mrs. Grimes. He leaned forward, placed his elbows on her desk and mirrored her, lacing his fingers together. His voice was stern and deep. "What we have here is incompetence within the management of this school."

Ethan blinked. *Come again? Is Dad blaming Grimes?*

His dad typically lived his life with a joke on the tip of his tongue and a song in his heart. Unlike other dads, he had a keen sense of humor. He also liked a good party and took things in stride. "Life's too short not to have fun," Colby Castleton liked to say.

But when Ethan noticed his father's set mouth and bitter glare, a shudder ran through him, and he sat back to watch the show.

You're in for it now, Grimey, love.

Mrs. Grimes regarded his dad over the top of her horn-rimmed glasses. Picking up a piece of official looking paper, she read, "Ethan Castleton compromised a fellow student, skipped a mandatory assembly, disrupted said assembly, and resisted authority." She laid the paper on her desk. "There's more. Shall I go on?"

More? There isn't any more! Ethan leaned forward and started to call her bluff, but his dad scowled at him, one eyebrow raised.

Ethan settled back into his seat.

His dad forcefully pushed his chair back, his finger to his mouth. "Hmm…" He stood, pulled a book from her bookshelf, and inspected it. He began to pace around the room. "I see. That does seem to be quite the list." He stopped pacing and hovered over Mrs. Grimes. "I wonder…" he drew out the word, "what would make me son, who I know to be a sensible young man, want to compromise a fellow student?" He tilted his head and straightened up. "Maybe you have the wrong lad?"

Mrs. Grimes cleared her throat. "There is no evidence to suggest anyone else was involved. Your son was caught red-handed." She stood and retrieved a glass of water without offering one to anyone else. She took a sip and sat back down. "What your son did is one of the worst misfortunes I've had to deal with in my entire career as head teacher."

His father turned to Ethan and raised a questioning eyebrow.

Ethan wasn't about to speak up without direct permission.

Olivia flashed him a grin that was meant to be encouraging.

His dad coolly strolled over and placed his hand on Ethan's shoulder. "Tell me, Son, what happened?"

All Ethan wanted to do was convince his father of his innocence, but he simply sat there, at a loss for words. He couldn't say that Grucker was hoodwinked by a misfired magical spell cast by a faerie; that Grucker stripped off his clothes while prancing around singing old folk songs. Somehow, he didn't think his father would believe him.

"He was discovered by a member of staff undressing a boy and leaving him on display in the hallway." Mrs. Grimes coughed delicately.

His dad blinked, placing the book on her desk with exaggerated coolness. "Me son would never do anything like that. He doesn't have a cruel bone in his body. I suggest you look for the real culprit; the one who started all this mess."

Mrs. Grimes seemed confused. "The real culprit?"

His dad jabbed his finger on Grimes's desk. "Now listen here, I've kept me mouth shut long enough. You've got a problem with bullies in your school, and it's well time you did something about it. I don't know who they are, but I do know they've been pickin' on me son for quite some time now—coming home repeatedly covered in bruises. I can mention a few others who are at their mercy too; his best friend was recently forced out of the gymnasium stark naked. Bullies run rampant in your hallways and you've done nothing to stop them—sitting behind your desk pickin' on decent kids, intimidatin' them while you let the tyrants roam free. Might as well give them cricket bats along with English lessons for all the good you've done; and you call this a school."

Ethan stared at his dad. *He knew about all that? About Noah?*

Mrs. Grimes gasped and brought her hand to her chest. "Why, never have I—your accusations are appalling! Bullying is not tolerated in my school; which is why I regret to inform you, sir, that your son is expelled!"

His father's cheeks flushed. Pure anger poisoned his words as he growled, "I regret to inform *you*, madam, that you're off your rocker if you think me son had anything to do with this! Instead of calling me all the way down here to pick up me son—who'll need bloomin' counselling the rest of his born days after this, the check for which I will be posting to you—you should be punishing the ones who truly deserve it!" By the last sentence, splatters of spit were spewing from his mouth.

Chettin' daisies, Dad's face has gone purple!

Mrs. Grimes stood and matched his bulldog stance. "This is unacceptable! How dare you come into my office and tell me how to run *my* school!"

Ethan's mum reached up and held her husband's wrist, as if to calm him. She took Olivia's hand and rose. "Mrs. Grimes, I don't know what kind of establishment you think you're running, but you can be sure the proper authorities will be receiving a letter from us." With that, she spun on her heels, pulled Olivia to the door, and opened it. She looked at Ethan. "Coming?"

Ethan jumped to his feet and darted to her side.

Before exiting the office, she turned back to Mrs. Grimes, who was now looking quite stunned. "I'll expect your apology in the post, love."

Ethan's mum gently shut the door with a calm smile, and the three of them walked away.

That meeting had most certainly not gone as Ethan had expected.

They waited in the car for at least twenty minutes before his dad, red as a beet and covered in hives, stormed out of the school. Opening the car door, he said, "You're not expelled anymore." He plopped himself in the car. "That old bat doesn't know up from down."

He slammed the door and peeled out of the parking lot.

Scaretaker opened the front door to his Lodge and rubbed his wrists. They were sore from the handcuffs. Even though the sun was still up, he didn't need to go down to the dungeon to feel the weight of the chondour's mind pressing against his.

Back so soon?

Scaretaker was tired and his defenses were down. As if speaking casually with the chondour were something ordinary, he automatically replied without much thought. "Not sure why they let me go. Must've needed evidence to keep me." He realized what he was doing and tried to push the chondour from his mind.

But before he could gain even the slightest bit of ground, the chondour communicated, *My offer still stands. I will make you the greatest magician the world has ever known. Greater even than Merlyn.*

Scaretaker rubbed his temples and went to the kitchen for some food.

The chondour continued, *We have found the children of prophecy, You and I. This is glorious, indeed. Yet it shall be tragic if they are allowed to stay their course. Let me loose. I will care for them. I shall invade their minds, their hearts. They will be our willing servants. Their powers shall be ours.*

Scaretaker sat down at his kitchen table, but he didn't take a bite of the food he placed before him. He rested his head in his hands, and for the first time in eight long years, he allowed himself to fully remember what it had felt like to wield the power the chondour had let him taste. His head slipped from his hands, just as surely as his resolve was now slithering away. The offer was awfully tempting.

Ethan's dad lectured him during the entire drive to the pub. "It's one thing to defend yourself, but something entirely different to humiliate someone for the sake of revenge. Even your worst enemy deserves respect."

Ethan had tried to explain that he was actually trying to help, but his dad wouldn't hear it.

When they got to the pub, Ethan's dad pointed to the kitchen. "Take over dish duty."

Ethan nodded and escaped into the kitchen, grateful to have some time to himself.

Steam billowed around the sinks, smelling of chip fat, bacon grease and mayonnaise. Dirty plates piled up as familiar pub sounds washed away Ethan's cares for the day. He took a moment to look around and wipe a lock of sweaty hair from his forehead; then he went back to scrubbing dishes as he listened to silverware clinking, the chef barking orders, and the serving bell dinging for food pickup. Cleaning dishes was mindless work, which was exactly what he needed. Not even thoughts of Neevya being lost or images of that shadow-wolf competed for his attention. He'd never thought that washing dishes could be a lifesaver.

"Ethan," his father called from the front of the kitchen.

Snapping back to reality, Ethan blinked. "Yeah?"

"Greg called in sick, and we need some help up front. Can you take orders?"

Ethan nodded, still a bit dazed. He took off his rubber gloves. "Sure."

Dish Duty

His dad gave him a reassuring smile and headed back to the front of the restaurant, letting the double doors swing in his wake.

Ethan was relieved to see that smile. It meant all was right between him and his dad again.

Grabbing a pad of paper and an apron, Ethan headed onto the pub floor.

The Ugly Duckling was loud, with several groups of locals joking over a pint. There was a long queue of people behind the "Wait here to be seated" sign, all hoping to take advantage of the early bird menu. An arcade fruit machine gargled in the corner, its orange lights flashing.

Ethan picked up a knife from the floor. It looked clean enough. Should he set it back on the table? He glanced at his mum, who was teaching Olivia to make utensil packets. He began to whistle and slipped the knife next to a plate.

"Oi! How hard is it fer a bloke t' get a pint?" A man's voice boomed through the pub like thunder. Ethan swore he saw the windows shake.

He looked at the offender and saw that it was none other than his bully's dad, Mr. Grucker, or as Ethan liked to call him, Yucker.

The resemblance between father and son was striking. Both were tall, wide, and dark-haired, but where Grucker's bulk showed he was heavy and muscular, Yucker's girth held much more belly.

Great! Not only do I have to deal with Grucker at chettin' school, his dad has to come in here and ruin me day.

Yucker stumbled into a table and nearly knocked it over.

Ethan quickly rushed to steady it.

Yucker sneered, shuffled to the bar, and wobbled for a bit, as if considering his options. He pushed his way between two men, knocking them off their barstools, and slammed his meaty fists on the countertop. Through slurred words, he hollered, "Castleton! A pint!"

Ethan's dad quickly rounded the bar. "Lawrence! That's enough!"

He pulled Yucker away from the bar and forced him into a chair.

Had the great oaf not been so legless, Ethan doubted his dad could have made him move an inch. He watched in silence as his dad helped the fallen men to their feet.

Ethan's father dusted off Mr. Holiday's jacket. "I'm very sorry about all this, Will."

He turned to Mr. Hollingsworth. "You too, Seamus. How about a pint on the house?"

Lawrence Grucker's face turned an ugly shade of purplish-red. "Oi!" He stood up and stumbled. "What about *me* pint?"

"James!" his father yelled to his bartender. "Give Will and Seamus a pint of bitter on the house."

James nodded. "Comin' up."

Ethan's father gripped Yucker's arm and ushered him to the far corner of the restaurant.

"Sit down, Lawrence. I'll get you a glass of water and call your boy."

At the mention of his son, Yucker's face contorted. "Useless, that lad is; good fer nowt and no one, if yeh ask me."

"That'll be enough of that," Ethan's dad said. "Now you stay put. I'll be back in a moment."

Ethan's dad walked to the bar and retrieved a glass of water. "James, call Mr. Grucker's son while you're at it."

Ethan's dad set the glass down in front of Yucker. He crossed his arms. "Now I want you to sit here and behave. I don't want to get the village bobbies involved."

Yucker muttered something that Ethan was not close enough to hear, but by the look on his face, he was sure it was vulgar.

"Like I said, behave." Ethan's father went to the utensil station just beyond the bar and spoke to his wife. Ethan's mum nodded and led Olivia through the kitchen's double doors.

Ethan watched Yucker out of the corner of his eye as he took orders. A group of locals sat near Yucker's table. *Why did they have to sit there? Now I have to go near the old goat.* The closer Ethan came to the man, the more he noticed something unpleasant; a foul stench of rotten eggs. What was it with rotten eggs lately? The odor made Ethan want to vomit. He decided to breathe through his mouth, at least until he could get away from Yucker, then something grabbed his attention.

Dish Duty

Is that a shadow?

Ethan turned to look straight at the man, but could no longer see a shadow or any other kind of darkness anywhere near him.

Suddenly, Yucker's shoulders curled forward, as if they were collapsing into his ribcage. His head dropped at a sharp angle, and with a loud *thunk*, hit the wooden table.

Is he dying? Ethan thought, alarmed. *I've never chettin' done first aid, I don't know what to do! I could call an ambulance, but—*

Ethan bent down so their faces nearly touched. Yucker's eyes were closed, and he sighed, emitting stale beer and rotten egg breath. Ethan doubled over and gagged, almost losing his lunch all over the floor.

Yucker wasn't dead. He was passed out cold.

That's the last chettin' time I'll be a concerned citizen!

Ethan's dad hurried over. "What's got yeh?"

Ethan swallowed hard. "It's just nerves."

His dad threw his arm around Ethan's shoulder and guided him to the bar. "Maybe you should rest for a few. You look a bit peaked."

Ethan nodded, following his dad's lead. Before he had a chance to find a good resting spot, Grucker threw the front door open and strolled in like he owned the place.

"Oh great," Ethan muttered under his breath.

"Where's me dad?" Grucker shouted. "Someone get me dad."

Mr. Castleton hurried over to Grucker and started speaking with him in hushed tones. Grucker stiffened and looked over to where his father was passed out on the table. An expression crossed the bully's face that Ethan had never seen before.

Is he about to cry?

Grucker blinked rapidly as he gritted his teeth. He opened and closed his fists several times.

In that moment, Ethan felt sorry for Chris Grucker.

When Ethan's dad put a reassuring hand on Chris's shoulders, Ethan found himself smiling. The two exchanged a few words, but Ethan couldn't hear what they were saying until his dad called over his shoulder, "Ethan, call a taxi."

Once the taxi was waiting outside and its rear door was open, Ethan walked back into the restaurant. "It's here."

Grucker, James, and his dad tried to pull Yucker to his feet.

"Give us a hand?" Ethan's dad asked.

Ethan sighed, walked over to the men, and readied himself.

"On three, lads." Mr. Castleton bent down and grabbed Yucker's arm. "One...two...three!"

With much grunting, they managed to carry Yucker to the taxi and push him inside.

Grucker stood on the sidewalk and spouted his address as Mr. Castleton handed the driver some money. Grucker pushed the door of the taxi shut.

Ethan's dad asked, "Aren't you going with him?"

The taxi drove away.

Grucker looked straight into Mr. Castleton's eyes. "Why should I? He doesn't care about me. Why should I give a flippin' heck about him?" He stormed away, bumping Mr. Castleton's shoulder.

Ethan figured his dad must be in shock, or else he'd never let himself be pushed out of the way so easily. To Ethan's surprise, his father said, "Hold up there. How about a bite to eat?"

Grucker looked at him with a blank stare.

Mr. Castleton pointed. "Go in the back and see me wife, she'll take care of you. I'll be in shortly."

Grucker entered the pub and Ethan started to follow, but his dad grabbed his arm. "I don't understand how people can get so mixed up."

Ethan shrugged. "Me either."

His father looked him squarely in the eyes. "I promise I'll never treat you like that. That bloke hasn't got one ounce of love for his son—his chettin' son, for Pete's sake." He pulled Ethan into a hug. "I love you, Son."

Ethan whispered, "I love you too, Dad."

His father straightened up and smoothed his hair out of his face. "How 'bout we go back inside and make some magic happen?"

Dish Duty

Walking back into the pub was not as difficult as Ethan had assumed it might be, given that Grucker was in there. Maybe the hug his father had just given him made his concern dissipate a little. Or perhaps it was because he knew Grucker couldn't hurt him in front of all these people. Whatever the reason, Ethan walked in with a smile and went about finishing his duties.

Grucker sat at a back table and finished off a burger and chips.

Ethan glanced at him periodically, just to check if he was still there. But as time passed, he forgot about Grucker altogether.

It wasn't until Ethan headed to the back of the lobby that he found himself face to face with the great lump.

Grucker cornered Ethan against a wall. "Not a word, Castleton. Not one word about what happened in the toilets or you'll be sorry."

The front door flew open, bringing with it a familiar voice. "We need to hurry!"

Ethan looked over Grucker's shoulder, and to his surprise saw Noah and Skye; their eyes darted frantically all over the place and then settled on him.

Grucker grabbed Ethan's apron. "Did yeh hear me? Are me threats not good enough fer yeh?" Grucker leaned in, his hot breath foul.

Ethan wrinkled his nose. "I got it. I got it. Me lips are sealed."

Something simmered in Grucker's eyes, something Ethan couldn't quite pinpoint, but mercifully, Grucker let go of his apron. He walked out of the pub without another word.

Ethan inhaled sharply, adjusted his apron, and joined Skye and Noah. "And to think, I thought I was safe in me own blinkin' pub. Can you believe it? He actually came in here, me pub of all places, and threatened me!"

Skye and Noah looked gloomily back at him. Their expressions didn't match his complaint; they were too grave to be anything but disastrous.

Ethan's heart sank and his words were barely audible when he asked, "What is it?"

Skye sniffled. "It's Neevya. She's dying."

CHAPTER TWENTY-THREE

Olivia

"What do you mean, she's *dying*?" Denial shielded Ethan's heart like armor. "I thought Madison healed her."

Skye reached over and grabbed his arm. Her nails bit into his skin. He welcomed the pain. It helped him concentrate.

She let go. "It's more serious than we thought."

He looked around, not necessarily searching for anything, but needing to give his eyes something to do as his mind came to grips with the news. *Mum and Olivia are back to working at the utensil station. Dad's behind the bar. A normal day at the pub.* He looked down at the floor. *And I'm standing here with Noah and Skye and they're telling me Neevya is dying?*

Looking at Skye with all the seriousness of a doctor delivering bad news, Ethan said, "Follow me." He nudged past her and crashed through the double doors, making them swing wildly as he cut through the kitchen.

He waited for Noah and Skye to catch up and said, "We can talk out here."

The Ugly Duckling's back door opened into a narrow alley next to a small storage building that was for sale. Ethan's father hoped to buy that building someday, but only when his pub was successful enough to demand a bigger stockroom.

Ethan knelt and picked up a small stone. "This should work," he said under his breath as he strategically placed the stone to prevent the door from shutting completely. He stood. "How do you know Neevya's dying? Did she say so?"

Noah shook his head. "Not exactly. Her skin is really dark, and I think she's having trouble breathing. We laid her next to Madison, but even that doesn't seem to be working."

By the look on Noah's face, Ethan knew there was more.

Noah's eyes became glassy. "Madison keeps whining, and sometimes she even trembles. It's not right." His chin started to quiver. "If anything happens to them, I don't—"

"It'll be okay, mate. We'll work this out. Everything'll be okay."

Noah's smile seemed half-forced and half-genuine.

Skye stepped up behind Noah and placed her hand on his shoulder. "Ethan's right. We just need to get Neevya back to her home, like yesterday."

"If you're saying we should go at this very moment, you're gonna have to leg it without me." Ethan gestured to the pub. "There's no way me dad will let me leave his sight tonight. Me parents are watching me like hawks. With that murder last night and all, I'll be lucky if they let me go to the loo by meself."

Skye shuffled some small pebbles under her shoe. "What do you suggest then?"

"I don't suggest anything. I just know me parents won't let me go. Maybe we can try first thing in the morning?"

Noah spread his palms wide. "Neevya is awfully sick. I don't think she can last that long."

Ethan laced his fingers behind his head and paced. "You two can pull it off."

Skye considered for a moment. "What do you think, Noah? Can we do this?"

Noah chewed his lip as he deliberated. "No, we need all the help we can get. Maybe if we compromise?" He looked at Ethan. "Do you think you could sneak out tonight, after everyone's asleep?"

Ethan clapped his hands together. "That'll work. Be at me house at midnight."

"It'll be dark at midnight." Skye fidgeted with one of her pink braids.

As much as Ethan wanted to help, it was the best he could do. "That's me offer; take it or leave it."

"Fine," Skye let go of her braid and kicked the side of an old rubber tire that was laying in the alleyway, "Midnight it is."

Noah leaned against the wall. "Great, it's a plan."

Satisfied, Ethan scheduled his escape attempt in his smartphone calendar, but something in the back of his mind was troubling him. It was something important. He suddenly remembered. "Chettin' daisies! Grucker!" The words exited his mouth before he realized what he was saying.

Noah whirled around. "Where?"

Ethan stuffed his phone into his pocket. "Oh, sorry. I didn't mean to scare you. It's just that, something happened with Grucker I almost forgot to tell you about."

Skye took a moment to study him. "Ethan Castleton, what did you do this time?"

There was no way to break the news softly; so Ethan braced himself for Skye's attack. "Grucker saw Neevya."

It took a moment for the information to sink in, but when it did, Ethan was glad he had prepared.

Skye shoved his shoulder and hissed, "*What*? How could you let that happen? Can't you do anything right?"

Ethan stumbled back. She was stronger than he'd imagined she would be.

She continued to advance on him, steam practically billowing from her ears.

"All right, all right! It's been a blinkin' mental day. It's not a big deal. Give a bloke a break. We're supposed to be friends, remember?"

Skye backed him against a wall. "That's not a small thing, Ethan!"

Ethan reached out and grabbed her wrists. "I said I'm sorry. Come on, Skye."

Noah pulled Skye away from Ethan.

She lowered her hands and looked at the ground, playing with a strand of hair. After several moments, her expression softened, and she met Ethan's eyes. "Sorry, I didn't mean to shove you that hard."

Ethan rubbed his shoulder. "Bloomin' Nora, next time why don't you try and put some punch into it?" He grinned at her wryly.

She smiled back.

Noah stepped between her and Ethan. "Do you think Grucker knows what she is?"

Ethan shook his head. "Hard to say. He was a bit preoccupied."

"Well, that's good at least," Noah said.

"Did anyone else see her?" Skye asked.

Ethan headed back to the pub. He paused at the door and rested his hand against it. "Well, there were some other students, but Neevya hid, so I don't think they saw her. And she flew right in front of Cordell, but she was invisible to him."

Noah asked, "Are you sure?"

"Yes, I'm chettin' sure."

Skye considered for a moment. "You know what that means, don't you?"

Ethan shrugged. "What?"

A small voice from behind the door answered, "I know what it means. I can see her too."

They all flinched as a young girl pushed her way through the door.

"Olivia!" Ethan scowled. "What are you doing out here?" He replaced the rock to keep the door from closing.

She looked at him indignantly. "What are *you* doing out here?"

"Obviously, I'm talking with me friends, which doesn't include you."

Olivia ignored him and stepped farther into the alley.

She stared straight at Noah and Skye. "She's really sick."

Ethan shook his head. "Who is? Mum?"

Olivia looked at him as if she were speaking to a baby. "Of course not Mum. Don't be daft. I'm talking about Neevya."

Surprise hit Ethan like a sack of potatoes. His sister had said some pretty uncanny things before, but he wasn't prepared to hear anything like that slip from her mouth. He had to prop himself against the wall to keep from sinking to his knees.

How does she know about Neevya?

He straightened up and tried to act casual, as if he knew nothing of a faerie named Neevya who happened to be sleeping at Noah's house this very moment. He cleared his throat, stuffed his hands in his pockets, and tried to think of something to say. "What are you bloomin' on about? Who's Neevya?"

Olivia bent down, picked up a pebble and started polishing it with her shirt sleeve. "Neevya's the faerie you've been hiding for the last few days."

They stared at Olivia as if she'd suddenly sprouted wings.

She examined the pebble, held it up as if to show Ethan how pretty it was, and calmly said, "If you want to help her, look for the glowing mushrooms."

CHAPTER TWENTY-FOUR

Mysterious Dreams

Noah studied Olivia carefully. Until this very moment, he had never spotted the wisdom in her eyes, and he wasn't exactly sure what it was he was seeing now, but there was definitely something special about Ethan's nine-year-old sister.

Ethan gestured to the back door of the pub. "This really isn't the time for games. Go back inside."

Olivia frowned. "But I can help."

Ethan stomped his foot. "Olivia, this isn't your business. Go back inside, *now*."

Olivia's shoulders slumped and her head hung low as she started to walk to the door.

"Wait." Noah blocked her way.

She bumped into him, and when she looked up, her cheeks reddened.

Noah grinned and turned his attention to Ethan. "She clearly knows something. Why are you sending her away?"

"She's me sister and I say she has no chettin' business getting tied up in this mess. It's too dangerous." Ethan put his hand on Olivia's shoulder and guided her back toward the kitchen door.

Noah grabbed Ethan's free arm. "She's already in this, whether you like it or not. We might as well hear what she has to say."

Ethan brushed his hand away, and reached for the door.

Noah blocked him. "Think of Neevya."

Sighing, Ethan slid his hand down the door and slowly turned to face them.

Skye said to Olivia, "I think it's time we had a little chat." Her voice was soft and kind.

Olivia looked up at Ethan, asking for permission.

Ethan met her eyes, dropped his hand from her shoulder, and nodded. "Just a few questions, that's it."

Olivia threw her arms around her brother's waist. "Oh, thank you, Ethan! I'll never call you daft again."

Ethan rubbed the top of her head and halfheartedly said, "I'll hold you to that."

Skye smirked as she led Olivia to an old rubber tire that had been in the alley for as long as Noah had lived in Herogate.

"Have a seat," Skye said.

Olivia and Skye sat on the tire as Noah and Ethan plopped down on the cobblestone path.

"So," Skye took Olivia's hand, "how do you know about Neevya?"

Olivia pulled her hand away and opened her mouth to speak, but closed it. She looked straight at her brother. "Promise you won't get mad?"

"Why would I get mad?" Ethan asked.

Olivia shrugged and wrapped her arms around her bent knees, which were pressed against her chest. "I don't know. Just promise."

"Come on, Ethan. We're wasting time," Skye said.

Ethan regarded his sister. "Okay, fine. I promise."

A trace of a smile graced Olivia's lips. "We met the night she stayed in your room."

"What? You were in me room?" Ethan started to stand up, but Noah grabbed his wrist and pulled him down.

"You promised, remember?" Noah said.

"But she—"

"Just listen," Noah insisted.

"No, you chettin' listen! I was with Neevya all night. The only time Olivia could have snuck in was when I was…" Ethan turned and eyed his sister incredulously. "When I was asleep!"

Olivia stared back at Ethan, her expression calm and serene, unfazed by her brother's outburst. In that instant, Olivia felt different—older.

A feeling of euphoria hit Noah; looking at Olivia was like looking at an angel. When she turned her sparkling green eyes on him, Noah felt special—lucky to be the recipient of her attention. He broke eye contact as soon as he realized he was gawking at Ethan's kid sister.

The shifting energy around Olivia must've affected Ethan too, because he was calm and much more pleasant when he asked, "Why were you in me room?"

"I had a dream about Neevya, and when I woke, I knew," Olivia answered.

"Knew what?" Skye asked.

Noah dared to look at Olivia again, wanting to grasp her answer. He was relieved that she looked like a normal kid again.

Olivia twisted a lock of her blonde hair around her finger. "I knew she was in your room, and I knew I had to meet her. So I snuck in and introduced meself."

Skye snapped her fingers. "So that's what happened that night. That's why Neevya was so scared the next morning, and that's how she figured out we were humans."

Skye was right. Now it made sense. But there was something more Noah needed to know. "Olivia? Why did you tell us to look for the glowing mushrooms?"

She answered matter-of-factly, "I had another dream."

All previous frustration gone and clearly proud of his little sister, Ethan turned enthusiastically to Noah. "Her dreams are accurate; it's how we learned me uncle was in the hospital a few years back."

Olivia nodded. "Yes, those dreams are different than regular dreams. They're more real, and I can remember them longer."

Noah didn't want to be rude, but she hadn't properly answered his question. "You still haven't told us why we need to find the glowing mushrooms."

Olivia placed her fingertips together and looked off to the side. "I was in a forest. It was The Dark Wood, but it had a different name. I think it was something like the Darn, or the Dern."

Noah and Ethan exchanged knowing glances, eyes wide.

"And there was this strange space, almost like a door. It was a door, but it wasn't. Uh, what's the right word for it?" She looked at them for help.

"A portal?" Noah offered. Their eyes met.

Olivia blushed and averted her gaze. "Yes, that's it. I knew the portal opened to Neevya's home; a land so colorful it makes this," she pointed to the alleyway, "look dull."

Skye encouraged her, "Go on."

"I saw Neevya. She was sick. Her skin was covered in black lines."

Olivia shuddered. Ethan went to her and wrapped his arms around her shoulders.

She snuggled into his side.

"Then what happened?' Noah asked, leaning in.

"I carried her to the portal, and the closer I got, the more I noticed there were loads of bright glowing mushrooms next to it. That's how you can tell when you're near it—the mushrooms are everywhere. They get bigger and thicker."

"That sounds easy enough. Look for the glowing mushrooms," Ethan said with a quick squeeze.

"In me dream, black, squiggly lines ate her body. Then there was this creature, and it looked like Neevya was covered in blood."

Noah's mouth fell open. That was not what he had expected to hear. More descriptions of the portal and instructions on how to locate it would've seemed normal—as normal as could be, anyway. But Neevya covered in blood? That took things to a whole new level.

He looked at Ethan. "Do her dreams always come true? Do we have a chance at changing things?"

Ethan regarded his sister thoughtfully. "I don't know. She's only told me about dreams where something had already happened. Like I said, me uncle was already in the hospital when she dreamt it."

Skye stood. "It doesn't matter. I'm not about to let Neevya die. Not if I can do something about it. Who's with me?" Skye held out her hand for a team huddle.

Noah and Ethan joined her, stacking their hands on hers.

Olivia stood and reached but Ethan blocked her way. "Oh no you chettin' don't. You're staying home. There's no way I'm letting you go into those woods."

Olivia looked to Noah for help. Noah shook his head. "Sorry, I'm with Ethan on this one."

Olivia tried her trick on Skye, displaying the same puppy dog eyes.

Skye ignored her.

Olivia sighed. "I don't get to have any fun."

Ethan focused all his attention on his sister; he was deadly serious when he said, "What we're going to do won't be fun at all." He put his hand over his heart. "I promise."

Olivia mumbled her understanding, went back into the pub, and held the door for Ethan.

"I need to get back inside or Mum and Dad are going to get suspicious," Ethan said. "See you two at midnight." He joined Olivia and let the heavy door slam shut behind them.

Skye turned to Noah. "I'll catch you later then?"

Noah shrugged. "Yeah. Midnight. Ethan's house."

Noah turned to exit the alley, but a small movement caught his eye. He looked at a rubbish bin that sat near the corner of an adjacent building. Someone was hiding behind it; someone with black hair. "Grucker?"

Skye hissed, "What? Where?"

Noah pointed. He tugged on Skye's arm, pulling her to the dumpster.

He peered around the metal rubbish bin, prepared for a confrontation. The alleyway was empty.

On the side of the adjacent building, a door stood open.

CHAPTER TWENTY-FIVE
The Necklace

Noah ran home as fast as his feet would carry him. It felt good to run, to feel the wind in his hair; to concentrate on his breathing and let go of his worries. He imagined that restorative breezes washed over him as he sprinted down the streets he had come to know so well.

I can't believe that just a few days ago, my biggest concern was avoiding Grucker. Look at me now.

He was running for his life; well, sort of. He may not be running for *his* life, but he was running home to check on the lives of two creatures he deeply loved. That should count, right?

He threw open his front door. The house was quiet. The grandfather clock in his father's study ticked the seconds away and trailed down the hallway.

Noah walked into the TV room and called, "Mum, I'm home!"

No answer.

Even though it was close to dinner time, it wasn't unusual for his mother to have a late night here and there. It was the busy season, after all. She must have been tied up at the shop, preparing floral arrangements for some convention, or perhaps a spring wedding.

Noah called out one more time just to make sure, "Anyone home?"

He waited for only a second before he bolted up the stairs. He slowly turned the doorknob and inched the door open. The room was silent.

There was Madison, lying on his bed with Neevya curled up beside her. Noah tiptoed across the room for a closer look.

A tangle of dark spindly tendrils oozed out of the black wound on Neevya's calf. It had created an inky web that covered her torso and was beginning to creep up her neck.

Noah gasped. It had gotten worse. Much worse.

He started pacing, trying to calm his racing heart.

What should I do? She might not make it till midnight.

It would be dark soon. There was no way Skye's mum or Ethan's dad would let them out of the house now. Maybe he should go alone. Maybe he and Madison could get the job done.

He glanced at Madison and realized she wasn't breathing.

His heart slammed against his ribcage. If he thought his heart was racing before, it was nothing compared to the sprint it ran now.

Noah fell to his knees and placed his hand on Madison's side, searching for any signs of life. He held his breath and counted.

One.

Two.

Three.

Madison's chest heaved and fell.

Noah sighed. She was still alive. If only he could see her eyes, then he would really believe it.

Madison raised her head and blinked groggily when Noah began to scratch behind her ears.

She started panting.

That was a good sign.

Madison took a deep breath, rested her head back on the bed, shivered, and closed her eyes again.

He traced his hands down her back, willing her to feel better. In his mind, he repeated something his mum would say to him when he was sick. *You are well. You are happy. We are together.*

The Necklace

From out of nowhere, Noah suddenly felt a familiar presence pressing on his brain, making it itch. He whispered, "Neevya?"

The pressing got stronger, and suddenly a tickle in Noah's mind produced a sound. The sound was vague at first, but the more he paid attention, the more he thought he understood.

The voice whispered through his thoughts, *Noahh.*

Did he just hear his name?

Noahh. It came again.

Neevya's body twitched.

Move meee. The voice was getting clearer and louder now. *Move me away.*

"Neevya? Is that you?"

Neevya twitched again.

Yesss.

In that moment, Noah had a choice, a choice he'd never imagined he'd have to face in his entire life.

Finding Neevya, a creature from fairy tales, stretched the limits of his belief system, but at least she was tangible. She was real. She could be touched. Not to mention Skye and Ethan could confirm her existence.

Allowing himself to believe that a faerie was speaking with him through telepathy was a totally new ball of wax. What proof was there that he wasn't imagining the whole thing? What if all the stress was driving him insane? Then again, what if it *was* real?

Right then and there, Noah felt something shift inside him as he made a decision that would change the rest of his life.

I choose to believe.

Noah said, "I hear you, Neevya. I hear you."

Neevya whispered in his mind, *Thank you, Noah. Thank you for trusting me, for trusting in yourself.*

Noah smiled. Every time Neevya spoke, it felt as if Noah needed to scratch an inner part of his brain he couldn't reach.

Neevya communicated, *I need you to move me. Move me away from Madison.*

Noah frowned. "Why? I thought Madison was healing you."

Noah felt Neevya's faint smile in his head. *Madison is getting weak. She can only give so much.*

Neevya didn't have to tell him twice. Noah gently scooped the wilting faerie into his hands and held her next to his chest.

The moment she had separated from Madison, the mini-schnauzer whimpered and Neevya grimaced.

"I'm sorry. I didn't mean to hurt you."

You didn't hurt me. It was a natural reaction.

Noah looked at Madison. "Will she be okay?"

Yes, in time. She will recover.

Noah sighed with relief. "You'll be okay too. We're taking you back home tonight." He sat on his bed and propped up his pillow. He leaned against it as he looked out the window, trying to make Neevya as comfortable as possible.

Thank you, Noah.

Noah was ready to say more, but he felt the soft withdrawal from his head. Neevya took a deep breath, and cuddled into Noah's palm. It felt good to have earned Neevya's trust. "We'll protect you, Neevya. You're going to be okay."

If anyone had asked, Noah would have sworn days had passed instead of just a few hours.

He was sitting at his computer desk, letting the light of the monitor illuminate his dark room. Madison continued to sleep at the foot of his bed, while Neevya lay on top of his pillow.

Dinner had been a quick and quiet event. His mum had come home exhausted from a long day's work. She stayed at the dinner table just long enough to nibble on a sandwich, yawn, and excuse herself for bed.

Before heading upstairs, she explained that Noah's father wouldn't be coming home for a few more hours. There was something urgent he was working on, some big project.

Noah fiddled with his mouse to make his screen light up so he could check the time.

11:30.

"About time," he mumbled as he jumped out of his chair and grabbed his backpack. On his nightstand sat a makeshift sling he had created out of two old pairs of socks. It was designed to carry Neevya safely within its folds. Noah reasoned it would be more comfortable for her than his backpack. Plus, it would keep her close, right next to his heart.

He reached down, grabbed the sling, and fastened it around his neck and ribcage.

"You ready to go back home?" He gently lifted Neevya from his pillow and carefully slipped her into the sling, making sure her face wasn't covered by the fabric.

Momentarily forgetting Madison was ill, he called for her, but Neevya reminded him by communicating, *she stays here.*

The pressing on his mind retreated.

Noah looked at his loyal companion; his most trusted and treasured friend. Then he knelt, kissed the top of Madison's head, and snuck out.

When Noah arrived at Ethan's house, he found Skye already there. She spat a torn fingernail onto the grass and cast a nervous glance at Noah.

He quietly rolled his bicycle to Ethan's back gate.

"Hey," Skye whispered. "Where's Neevya?"

Noah pointed to the sling across his chest. "Safe and sound."

She peeked inside and inhaled sharply. "She looks dreadful."

Noah sighed. "Yeah, I know, and Madison isn't doing too well, either. Neevya says she'll be okay, but—" His throat closed around the words and he shook his head. "Never mind. She'll be fine."

Skye touched his shoulder and gave him a sympathetic smile.

"Oh, I almost forgot." Noah carefully took the backpack off and handed it to Skye. "Here, you carry this. It's too big for me. It keeps sliding forward and I'm afraid it'll bump Neevya."

Skye took the backpack, hooked it over her shoulders, and tightened its straps. "That's what these are for."

Noah said, "I know, they keep coming loose."

A clanking noise suddenly startled them.

They both jumped.

Someone let out a string of unintelligible curses. Noah and Skye ducked behind a short, stone wall.

"Guys," a familiar voice said. "Guys, are you out here?"

"Finally," Skye hissed and stepped into view.

Noah followed.

Ethan emerged from the side of his house, dressed in black. "Had to sneak out of me dad's bloomin' study," he explained. "Shall we do this, or what?"

He grabbed his bike and mounted it.

A thin, muffled voice said, "Stay. You're too young. Don't come."

"What?" Ethan asked.

Noah threw up his hands. "It wasn't me." He looked down to where he felt Neevya put her hand on his chest. "Neevya said that."

Ethan almost fell off his bike. He caught himself just in time. "She doesn't want me to come? I'm older than you."

"Not you," Neevya said, her words just a ghost of a whisper. "Olivia."

Ethan scoffed. "Olivia? She's in bed, I just—"

Another sound came from the same direction as Ethan had traveled. Even in the dark, Olivia's blonde hair practically glowed.

"Livvy! What're you blinkin' playin' at? We told you, it's too dangerous. Get your chettin' bum upstairs right now, before Mum and Dad wake up and all of us are chettin' grounded till we turn eighteen!" He spat the words out in a low, furious whisper without stopping to take a breath.

The Necklace

Olivia didn't look at him. She stared at the bundle across Noah's chest. Walking past Ethan, she reached out to touch it.

Neevya's voice cut through the night, a little stronger, "Olivia. You must stay. If you get caught, all will be lost."

Noah, Ethan, and Skye looked at Olivia with puzzled expressions.

Neevya must've felt their confusion because she telepathically explained, *According to an ancient prophecy, there is only one direct descendant of Merlyn who is powerful enough to defeat the approaching darkness. Olivia, you bear his mark. You are his great granddaughter many times removed, and you have inherited his powers.* Neevya paused and coughed. *I grow weak. Heed my words. Do not follow us. Stay here. Stay safe.*

To say Noah's mind was blown would be an understatement. He had felt something was different about Ethan's younger sister, but learning she was a direct descendent of Merlyn was incredible. Like the others, he stood in silence, pondering her words.

Ethan spoke up, "If Olivia is Merlyn's direct descendent, then that means I am too." A smile spread across his face.

Neevya's faint voice sounded like a whisper in Noah's mind as she communicated with the group. *Yes Ethan, you and Olivia are unique in this regard.* She paused. *But Skye and Noah are extraordinary too. Each of you is special in your own way. I can't believe I didn't understand the full implications of this situation sooner. You have come together just as surely as the stars align. If Fate is to have her way, I must get back and tell the king. I must survive long enough to let him know. I am so very sorry for asking you three to risk your lives to help me get home, but the destiny of our world lies in your hands. Please, we should hurry, I am quickly fading.*

Olivia started to climb onto her bicycle.

A whisper trailed through the air as if it were a wisp of perfume carried on the wind. "Olivia, stay."

The warmth from Neevya's hand on Noah's chest grew cold as she let her arm fall limply to her side.

Noah sensed that Olivia wanted to argue, but she crawled off her bike and said, "As you wish." She walked over to Noah and gently placed her hand over the bundle. "Goodbye, Neevya. I hope we meet again."

"Farewell, Olivia."

Another noise sounded in the neighbor's backyard.

Noah jumped. "What was that?"

A cat jumped onto the stone wall that separated Ethan's yard from his neighbor's. It pranced forward and brushed a gnome figurine that sat happily on the ledge.

The gnome toppled to the ground. *Not so happy anymore,* Noah thought. He glanced at the figurine and was surprised to see the gnome wasn't broken. *Hmm...tough little fellow.*

Ethan turned his bike around. "I didn't realize I lived in such a noisy place." He put his hand on Olivia's shoulder. "Time to go inside."

She shrugged him off. "Grandma told me to give you this." She took off her necklace and handed it to Ethan.

He stared at it. "But you haven't been without it since she gave it to you." Olivia insisted.

He hesitantly took the necklace, clearly surprised. "Wait, you talked to *Grandma?*"

Looking first at Noah and then at Skye, Olivia said, "Remember, look for the glowing mushrooms."

With one last farewell to Neevya, Olivia turned and headed back to her house.

CHAPTER TWENTY-SIX

The Great Potato Head

The rhythmic hum of rubber wheels cycling along the pavement lulled Ethan into a hypnotic trance. Besides the occasional barking dog, he was surprised at how empty the city was. No cars roamed the streets, the pubs were empty, and all was quiet. It was as if the entire city had shut down.

It's like a dream. Would his alarm clock blare to wake him up at any minute?

"There it is," Noah's voice trailed through the air.

Ethan shook his head in hopes of shaking away his eerie mood; looking up at the full moon didn't help. A sense of nervousness attacked his spine.

They reached the school gate.

Noah stopped, got off his bike and leaned it against the stone wall. "We should walk from here."

Skye followed suit.

Glancing first at the school and then across Stillwater Street to The Dark Wood, Ethan mumbled, "Great, two of me favorite places."

Noah cuddled Neevya and looked down at her. "Still sleeping."

Ethan hopped off his bike and propped it against the iron gate. "Are you sure she's still alive?"

Noah observed Neevya intently for several moments. The longer he watched her, the more his expression changed from curiosity to concern.

Ethan started to walk over so he could have a look for himself, but stopped when Noah let out an enormous sigh. "Whew, thank goodness. She just took a breath."

Ethan let his shoulders relax. "That's a relief."

"I second that." Skye dropped the backpack to the ground and searched inside. "But we need to get a move on if we're going to have any chance of saving her. Here, take these." She passed around torches.

"What else do we have in there?" Ethan grabbed the bag and rummaged through it. "I don't see anything but a couple of bungie cords and this thing." He lifted a small device. "What is this, anyway?"

"A weather radio," Noah said.

Skye asked, "How's a weather radio going to help us find a portal?"

Noah snatched it from Ethan. "It's not. Chondours live in storms, remember? If one starts heading our way, this should be able to give us plenty of warning."

"Good thinking, mate." Ethan hoped beyond hope that no storm would come tonight.

Noah tried to turn on the radio. "Ugh! I forgot the batteries!" He slammed the radio to the ground and kicked it in frustration.

"Well, isn't that just our luck? It's flippin' useless." For good measure, Ethan kicked it too.

"You two stop messing around. Are we ready to do this or what?"

Ethan met Noah's eyes, and they couldn't help but snigger nervously. It was their way of dealing with the stress of the situation. Then Ethan clicked on his torch and pointed it at the woods. "Ladies first," he said with a sly grin as Noah fought back a chuckle.

"Do you ever take anything seriously? I swear, if either of you…" Skye unexpectedly froze midsentence.

Something in her expression made Ethan think things had just gone terribly wrong.

Skye slowly stepped back. "Oh no. Please no." She started waving her hands frantically, gesturing to the boys. "Turn them off. Turn off the lights, *now!*"

Ethan clicked off his torch and tossed it in the bag. Noah was having trouble, so Ethan quickly yanked it from his hands and shut it off.

Skye whispered, "We have to hide." She sidestepped to the wall and crouched, motioning for Ethan and Noah to join her.

They followed without a sound.

Ethan pitched Noah's torch into the bag and, as quietly as possible, he placed the bag on the ground, next to the stone wall. He whispered to Skye, "Put your torch down. You don't want to accidentally turn it on and attract attention."

Skye held a finger to her lips to shush Ethan, but she quickly obeyed, setting her torch in a crevice at the base of the wall.

The stench of rotten eggs permeated the air as Grucker came into view.

He sauntered around the corner as if he owned the place. When his gaze fell on the three of them, he sneered, "I heard yeh in the alley. So yeh went through with it—thought yeh were too spinelessness to show up here."

Ethan glanced at Skye and Noah, hoping they could silently communicate some kind of exit strategy, but Noah simply cradled Neevya protectively to his chest. Skye threw him a look he could not interpret.

"What's wrong? Cat got yer tongue?" Grucker eyed each in turn, as if they were slabs of meat, and he was deciding who would be served up as his main course at a dinner only he was attending.

Grucker's attention settled on Noah, "Looks like me favorite Kamikaze Kid needs a bit o' tenderizin.'"

He started toward Noah, but Ethan quickly stepped in his way. Of the three of them, Noah was the one with Neevya, which meant he needed to be protected at all costs.

Grucker seemed surprised by Ethan's boldness at first, but his arrogance quickly returned. "What do yeh think yer doin', Castleton? Playin' hero?" Grucker shoved him.

Ethan stumbled back, but he was an athletic sort, so it wasn't difficult to regain his balance. He placed himself in Grucker's path once again, this time fixing his stance so he could not be pushed aside so easily.

Skye joined in, marching up behind Ethan and saying, "Why can't you just leave us alone? What's your great potato head doing here, anyway?"

Ethan felt his jaw tense as he whispered through the side of his mouth, "Great way to diffuse the situation, Skye."

Grucker crossed his arms and regarded her as if she were an ant he wanted to squash. "I always knew you three were a bunch of freaks, but coming to The Dark Wood at midnight? Yer all kinds of mental, ain't yeh?"

Skye huffed and tightened her fists as she stepped past Ethan and faced Grucker directly. "You're just upset that Ethan got the best of you. How does it feel to be humiliated in front of the whole school with your pants down?"

As she spoke, Ethan couldn't help but cringe; he'd forgotten to tell her what happened. He could only imagine the rumors she'd heard. Each word she uttered seemed to make Grucker angrier. Couldn't she see what she was doing? What game was she playing?

Grucker's nostrils flared as he glanced between the two of them; he ground his teeth, making his jaw muscles flex repeatedly. "Ethan got the best o' me, huh? Well then, I reckon it's time fer a bit o' payback, isn't it?" His eyes settled on Noah. "There's nuttin' like gettin' some payback on a lad's best friend. Hurts twice as much, I reckon." He pressed his fist into his palm as he stepped around Skye and Ethan.

Ethan watched in horror.

Skye sprinted across the way and shouted, "Noah, over here! Come to me!"

Noah frantically darted away from Grucker and hid behind her.

Grucker changed course and teased, "Aww, Kamikaze, I thought Ethan was yer girlfriend." He glared at Ethan. "You've been dumped, lad."

Ethan darted between Grucker and Skye. "It's me you want. Like Skye said, I'm the one who pulled one over on you. Leave them out of it!"

Grucker's grin was pure evil. "I'm coming for yeh all."

"Run for it!" Skye yelled.

Ethan didn't have to be told twice. He bolted onto Stillwater Street, pushing Noah and Skye ahead of him.

When he heard Grucker's shoes slapping the pavement behind him, he whirled around near the far side of the street and spread his arms wide. "Don't do this, Grucker. You don't know what you're doing."

"Yeah, we don't want any trouble," Skye added as she and Noah stopped just at the edge of the woods.

Grucker glanced at the woods, to Skye, and back to Ethan. "Well, yeh've got trouble, ain't yeh? And by the looks of things, yer stuck between a rock," he jabbed his thumb in his chest, "and a hard place," he nodded toward the forest.

Grucker was right. They were in quite the pickle, but if the past was any indication of what they could expect, Grucker wouldn't follow them into the forest.

Ethan supposed there was nothing good that could come out of delaying the inevitable, so he waved his hands behind his back, signaling Skye and Noah to enter the woods. They followed his directions. At least in the forest they would have only monsters to deal with, and not an oversized bully to boot. Ethan backed away from Grucker, then turned on his heels and ran. But he didn't stop there, he couldn't resist the temptation to look back over his shoulder and yell, "Goodbye Grucker, smell ya later," as he plowed beyond the threshold of The Dark Wood.

"Oh, but yer wrong, Castleton. Yer gonna smell me now. I'm followin' yeh; followin' yeh till yeh can't run no more!"

Ethan's stomach sank. This could not be happening. They couldn't expect to survive against a shadow-wolf *and* Grucker.

Up ahead, Noah and Skye ducked behind a fallen log as Ethan rushed toward them, hoping to hide behind it before Grucker could see where they'd gone. But footsteps followed closely behind him, and let him know Grucker was hot on his heels.

When Ethan reached his friends, he swiftly turned to face the bully, readying himself to be tackled. "Mate, you don't understand. There's chettin' monsters in this wood!"

"Yer right, Castleton. There are monsters in this wood, and one's standing right in front of yeh. Look close, lad, cause I'm the scariest thing you'll ever see," Grucker growled, shoving Ethan so forcefully he fell onto his back.

"You seriously don't get it, do you? These woods are dangerous!" Skye stepped over the fallen log and tried to help Ethan to his feet.

"Like I said," Grucker pushed past Skye, knocking her to the ground to land beside Ethan, "*I'm* the one you should be scared of."

He stalked Noah.

Skye rolled over and inspected her scratched elbow.

Noah cupped Neevya and scrambled away as best he could, but his feet fumbled on the uneven ground and a tree blocked his way.

Grucker closed the distance.

Ethan stood, pulled Skye to her feet, and shouted, "What the bloomin' heck's your problem, Grucker? Can't stand your drunk dad's chettin' snorin'?"

Grucker whirled around and leapt at Ethan, who sprinted to his right in hopes of luring the bully away from Skye and Noah, but he didn't get far.

Grucker grabbed a handful of Ethan's sweatshirt and jerked him up by his collar. "Want to say that to me face?"

Thunder rumbled in the distance. The trees rustled as the wind picked up speed.

Ethan imagined the brewing storm fanning the flames of his building rage. Contempt dripped from each word as he said, "Think you can handle it, Grucker? Do you? Think you can handle that your dad's a wasted old *git*? Think you can handle the fact that no one in this world likes you, not even your old man? Oh, and you know what? I've figured out your little secret."

A look of alarm flashed across Grucker's face, but was quickly replaced by fury so intense, Ethan wondered if the bully had gone completely mad. His eyes grew unnervingly dark and vacant, as if he had stepped out of his body and was replaced by the Grim Reaper himself.

"Ye best be keepin' yer mouth shut, Castleton!" Grucker picked Ethan up and slammed him against a tree so hard, it felt as if a few ribs cracked. The bully whispered into Ethan's left ear, "I ain't no different than you." They locked eyes; a silent understanding passed between them.

Grucker loosened his grip.

Thunder boomed all around them, closer than before, making Ethan's insides vibrate.

He darted a nervous glance to Skye, willing her to take Noah and leave.

She got the message and pulled the back of Noah's shirt, forgetting to whisper when she said, "Let's leg it while we still can."

Grucker hastily spun around and pounced. "Yer not goin' anywhere!" He pinned Noah to the ground and reached for the front of his shirt.

But he got Neevya instead.

She screamed. Her voice rang into the air as loud as a steam engine's whistle.

Grucker leapt away, his face turning a pale shade of white. "What the…what is that?"

Skye rushed to Noah's side and eyed Ethan. "I'll take care of Neevya. You take care of Grucker."

Ethan placed himself in front of Grucker as Skye took the sling from Noah's chest and fixed it to her own.

Grucker backed away, his hands outstretched. "What the flippin' heck is going on here?"

Ethan stalked toward him, confidence building with each step. "I told you, mate. There are monsters in these woods."

As if on cue, Ethan saw something that almost stopped his heart. There, behind Grucker, was a large shadow creeping along the forest edge. He whispered, "The shadow-wolf."

The wolf-like creature seemed to suck the shadows from the ground and trees, bringing them to life in waves of smoky fur. Its body flowed as if it were half in and half out of this world. The air chilled, causing puffs of white fog to exit its mouth with each pant.

Terror soaked into every inch of Ethan's body, as if he were a dry sponge that had just been tossed into a bucket of water.

Grucker turned to follow his gaze.

He screamed and ran.

Ethan hoped the shadow-wolf would give chase, but it coolly watched Grucker stumble onto Stillwater Street and head back toward town, screaming the entire way.

Ethan backed slowly away.

The beast growled.

And lunged.

CHAPTER TWENTY-SEVEN
The Light in the Darkness

Noah didn't dare look back as he ran for his life, trees whipping past him in a blur and the chilly wind whistling in his ears. Ethan ran much faster than Noah and had easily darted past him. Skye followed suit. Pulling up the rear, Noah struggled to keep up as they barreled headfirst into the unknown with only faint beams of moonlight that shone through the canopy to light the way.

Although he couldn't see the shadow-wolf, Noah could feel it sneaking through the darkness, easily keeping pace with them as it stalked its prey. It was almost as if the beast was hunting them the way a cat hunts a mouse, taunting and teasing its food; giving the mouse hope that it might escape, when the reality was the poor thing didn't stand a chance. They wouldn't last long in this deadly game, and Noah knew it.

Storm clouds drifted across the moon as lightning flashed. The bright flash of light penetrated the forest, giving Noah the chance to spot the shadow-wolf, which was now circling ahead of them.

Thunder erupted in an ear-splitting crash all around them, causing the ground to tremble.

"Stop!" Noah screamed at the top of his lungs as he put all his effort into a quick burst of speed. Grabbing the back of Skye and Ethan's shirts, he jerked them behind him with strength he didn't know he had. "It's up ahead!"

They came to a skidding stop just in time to face the massive black wolf, its fangs exposed.

"It's the size of a bear," Noah heard himself say, but what he was really thinking was, *I don't want to die. I'm not ready to die.*

Visions of his parents and Madison flashed before his eyes.

Why hadn't he hugged his mom one last time? Why didn't he tell his dad he loved him before he left for work? And why hadn't he paid more attention to Madison instead of playing stupid video games?

Before this moment, Noah thought he had fully understood the dangers of returning Neevya to the portal, but now he realized he hadn't actually considered that he might never get to go home again.

Death is final. There's no coming back.

Noah felt a warm hand gently grip his shoulder. "Follow my lead," Skye whispered, her mouth close to his ear. She ever so slightly pulled Noah's shoulder as they slowly backed away, hoping the beast would miraculously change its mind and let them live.

The shadow-wolf inched closer, its smoky fur waving and dancing to the songs of the winds. Wet growls warned of its dwindling patience.

Noah froze, afraid to move a single muscle. Skye and Ethan froze as well.

The shadow-wolf slowly crept closer, observing each of them keenly with intelligent eyes, stopping only to focus on the small bundle attached to Skye's chest. It tilted back its head and howled, closing its deep-red eyes.

Goosebumps covered Noah's entire body. The bellow filled the forest and echoed through the trees. It seemed as though the beast called to the storm, and the storm answered.

A bolt of lightning struck a nearby sapling; its deafening boom shook the ground, and a wave of heat pulsed through the air, the blast so forceful it pushed Noah back and made him tumble into Ethan and Skye. They ended up on the ground in a tangled heap, Noah's elbow smashing into a dead branch on the forest floor.

The air around them was charged with electricity, and a sulfurous scent of burnt wood and rotten eggs floated on the mist.

Ethan was pinned face down on the ground under Skye. "Get off me."

The shadow-wolf stopped howling and glared at him, as if Ethan had interrupted an important conversation. It focused on the bundle attached to Skye's chest once more.

A deep, guttural growl gurgled in the back of its throat as it bared sharp fangs.

Skye didn't move, she just lay there, helpless and exposed, her back pressed against Ethan's.

Without taking his eyes off the shadow-wolf, Noah felt around for a dead tree limb. He found one and gripped it tightly, then slowly pushed himself to his knees, hoping not to catch the wolf's attention.

Time slowed down and several things happened at once. The wolf attacked, and Noah swung the branch like a baseball bat, wedging it in the creature's open mouth.

Skye screamed and scampered off Ethan's back, which just so happened to put Ethan between her and the beast.

The wolf clamped its jaw shut, snapping the branch in half as easily as it would a small twig. It coiled for another attack.

And that's when it happened. Ethan pushed himself to his hands and knees, and the crystal necklace Olivia had given him spilled from his shirt.

The crystal began to glow.

The shadow-wolf hunched there, coiled in wait, eyeing the crystal. Its gurgling, low-pitched snarls became even more threatening. It tried to inch closer to Ethan and Skye, but the crystal glowed brighter and made a high-pitched noise that sounded like someone tracing a finger along the rim of a crystal glass.

Noah whispered, "Olivia's necklace!" On all fours, he crept closer to Ethan, each movement deliberate and careful so as not to attract attention.

Ethan looked down at the dangling crystal. Skye knelt behind him and hurriedly adjusted Neevya's sling.

The shadow-wolf's gaze fixed on the crystal, then on Skye, and then back to the stone, as if it didn't know where to look or what to do.

Noah couldn't believe their luck. He held out his hand to Ethan and, as if the wolf couldn't hear him, he whispered, "Quick, hand it to me."

With trembling hands, Ethan quickly pulled the necklace over his head and handed it over.

Noah felt the weight of the crystal in his palm, and was surprised to discover that the small stone was hot. But it wasn't the kind of heat that burns. It was a soothing warmth that spread throughout his hand, into his arm, and it dissolved the pain in his injured elbow. He held it up in front of his face, mesmerized, almost forgetting the shadow-wolf was just inches away. But his momentary lack of awareness didn't last long.

The beast lunged at Noah, but quickly retreated with a yelp as thunder crashed all around them.

His full attention on Noah, the wolf stalked around him hungrily, drool dripping from its mouth. Its chest heaved as puffs of fog billowed from its nostrils. The thunder seemed to be in time with its growls. The wolf readied for another attack.

If Noah was going to have a chance of surviving, he'd have to act. Gathering all his courage, he pushed himself to his feet and thrust the crystal at the shadow-wolf.

The wolf cautiously backed away.

Noah took another step.

The wolf retreated again, this time whimpering.

It started to rain.

Noah advanced three more steps. The wolf looked smaller, like it was shrinking. A few more steps and it was no longer the size of a bear, but a large dog.

The realization sent a spurt of confidence rushing through Noah. Thrusting the crystal in front of him, he shouted, "Get him!" and gave chase.

The Light in the Darkness

The rain poured down as storm clouds drifted past the moon, causing the forest's shadows to appear as if they were moving.

With one last yelp, the shadow-wolf turned and hightailed it out of there. The farther away it ran, the less the crystal glowed and hummed, until it was dark and silent once more. Noah examined the stone in his slippery, wet hands. He thought the small shard looked like an ordinary, clear piece of glass. He turned it over and held it to a faded beam of moonlight that somehow broke through the canopy overhead.

"What a strange little crystal. What other powers might it have?" Noah wondered aloud.

Ethan caught up to him and forcefully clapped him on his back. "That was bloomin' brilliant! That wolf was chettin' scared of you. You, mate, of all people, it was chettin' scared of *you*!"

Ethan slapped him again, hard enough to sting. "Get him," he chuckled, "Get him. That was beau'iful!"

Skye jogged up, out of breath. "I thought we were done for."

"Yeah, me too." Noah tried to calm his adrenaline rush with a few deep, slow breaths.

Ethan flung his arm around Noah's shoulders and squeezed. "Good thing I remembered to use Livvy's necklace. I knew it would work."

Skye threw him a sarcastic look. "Sometimes I worry about you."

Noah sniggered as he handed the crystal to Ethan. "I'm siding with Skye on this one."

Ethan feigned indignation as he slipped the necklace over his head, but ended up laughing right alongside Skye and Noah as they let off steam.

Deciding their best bet was to find the stream bed where Skye had discovered Neevya, they walked deeper into the forest. By the time they reached a familiar spot, the heavy rains had lifted and the winds had died down, which was a good thing. How else would Noah have heard the crunching of leaves that told him they had company?

He reached out and grabbed Ethan's elbow. "Hold up a minute." He listened intently. It sounded like something was rustling through the forest, just beyond a small hill. "You hear that?"

"Not the shadow-wolf again." Ethan grabbed his necklace and held it up in front of him.

"That wolf didn't make those kinds of noises," Noah remarked. "Whatever's out there has real mass."

They searched the shadows and strained their eyes as they sought the cause of the commotion. Noah tugged on Ethan's sleeve and pointed. In the distance was a scraggly man wearing worn-out overalls standing just beyond a dim beam of moonlight.

Skye, who clearly wasn't paying attention because she was checking on Neevya, bumped into Ethan's back. "Hey, what'd you stop for?"

Noah whispered, "Scaretaker."

The man's head jerked up.

"Oh no, he's seen us." Noah backed away, pushing his friends behind him. "Quick, find a place to hide!"

"I think it's too late for that, mate."

Scaretaker was quickly approaching, his spindly form leaping toward them like a dear sprinting through a field.

On the run again, they darted down a hill and up another. They plowed through a familiar blackberry patch and toward a group of tall trees with crooked trunks and branches that looked like claws. Ethan pulled ahead and glanced over his shoulder, but he slipped in a puddle of mud and went crashing into a thicket. Bouncing along the ground in an explosion of moss, mud, and leaves, a thick stump ended his progress as he slammed into it.

From the corner of his eye, Noah watched the whole thing happen; it looked painful. He quickly changed course, hoping he could get there in time to help. He vaulted over a fallen tree trunk and landed on a muddy incline, hastily grabbing a branch to catch his balance. The rotten wood gave way under his hand, and he came to a skidding halt, landing in the mud next to Ethan.

Skye stopped too, but Noah waved her on. Her cargo was too precious. She darted away into the heart of the forest.

"Are you okay?" Noah huffed, clasping a trembling hand around

Ethan's and helping him to his feet. Mud soaked their clothes and painted their faces.

"I'm fine. Let's get out of here."

They struggled to run on the slippery ground, fighting for balance with every step. Scaretaker sprang over the fallen tree and reached Noah before the boys could gain any ground. He grabbed Noah's collar and jerked him up, spinning him around so they met face-to-face.

This scenario seemed vaguely familiar to Noah.

"I thought I warned ye lads. Stay away! I'll have yer hides fer this, mark me words. Ye don't have any respect, ye bairns. Should never have let ye go. Now yer comin' back wit' me. I'll sort ye out."

Noah swallowed hard; he was paralyzed with fear. Madison wasn't there to save him this time. There was something about Scaretaker's bulging eyes that reminded him of the shadow-wolf, and a chill crept up his spine. He glanced to see if the crystal necklace was glowing, but was surprised instead to see Ethan picking up an oversized branch.

What does he think he's doing? He can't defeat Scaretaker with a rotten old stick. Noah willed Ethan not to do anything stupid.

"Let him go!" Ethan yelled, lifting the branch like a weapon.

Like some nightmarish vulture, Scaretaker swiveled his head to face Ethan, his neck straining against his tattered clothes.

"What ye goin' t' do with that, lad? Are ye goin' t' hit me? I'd like t' see ye try."

"Of course he's not going to hit you, are you, Ethan?" Noah struggled weakly against the fierce grip that held him pinned to the spot.

Ethan slowly lowered the branch. "Nice one, you plank—why don't you give him me address too, while you're at it?"

"Stop yer yappin', th' both of yeh's!" Scaretaker said with an exasperated wheeze. "Don't ye know when ye've been beaten? Look here, I've seen after this land since yer pa's were lads, and I haven't had a single trespasser make the same mistake twice. I'm not about to let that change. I was fair wit' ye before, but ye chose not t' listen t' good sense, and now here we are. Don't think yer gettin' off lightly this time, lads. That's not how it works."

Ethan raised the branch once more. "I bloomin' swear if you don't let him go, I'll..."

The man snapped back with a ferocity that made Ethan recoil. "I'll tell ye what ye'll do. Ye'll suffer the penalties, that's what. D' ye think I'm some frail old man who can't take care of a couple of pipsqueaks like yerselves? Well, do ye?"

Ethan squirmed under his gaze.

"Believe it, lads, I'm anythin' but weak. Ye can't be weak and expect t' survive a place like this." Scaretaker spat on the ground. "I've seen things in these woods that'd curl yer toes. Ye don't know the half of it. If I drag ye back t' the street, it's fer yer own good. Somebody's got t' teach ye not t' go messin' wit' things that're nowt t' do with ye. And the Dern be one of them, lads. I ain't threatenin' ye, I'm *savin'* ye."

There was something genuine about the old man's words, and for no good reason other than a gut feeling, Noah suspected Scaretaker knew something about the other side, about faeries, and perhaps portals too.

Noah cringed when Ethan said, "Good thing Skye has Neevya."

Was Ethan going mad? Why was he being so careless? Had he munched a few berries when they passed through the blackberry patch?

Scaretaker's expression swiftly transformed from righteous anger to confusion, and then to incredulity. "The lass has Neevya?" His eyebrows formed a V at the center of his forehead, like the sweeping wings of a bird of prey. Somehow, he looked even more like his nickname, a twisted caricature of a man.

Noah's suspicions that Scaretaker knew more than he was letting on were confirmed when he said, "What're ye ramblin' on about no good faeries for?" He tapped the side of Noah's head. "Yer not all there, are ye, lads?"

Noah's breath caught; Ethan hadn't mentioned *faeries.*

Scaretaker's grip on Noah's shoulder relaxed, giving him the opportunity to pull away.

"I told ye this place is dangerous an' ye got no business here. Ye should want no part of it." Scaretaker was clearly distracted, sniffing the air and scanning the forest. "That's curious," he mumbled under his breath, barely audible. "Where's that lass?" He sniffed the air again and seemed to catch a scent. Abruptly, he shooed them with waving hands. "It's best time ye lads get on outta here, and don't come back, ye hear?" Scaretaker unexpectedly spun around and darted off, his long legs easily carrying him through the bracken.

Ethan looked at Noah, wide-eyed. "Blimey, I can't believe he just let us go!"

"He didn't *just* let us go," Noah said through clenched teeth, trying not to lose his temper. "He went after Skye."

Ethan seemed truly confused, which quelled Noah's rising anger.

"Didn't you hear him? He knew Neevya was a faerie. He recognized her name."

Comprehension dawned as Ethan stared after Scaretaker, shocked. "How was I supposed to know he knew Neevya's name? Flippin' heck, how was I supposed t' know he even knew faeries existed?"

"It doesn't matter." Noah looked around. "We have to find Skye before he does."

CHAPTER TWENTY-EIGHT
Glowing Mushrooms

Crunching leaves and creaking timbers let Skye know danger was near. There was no time to lose; she had to think of something, and quick.

Noticing a small hollow by the stream's bank, Skye darted toward it, jumped over its ledge, and tucked herself in.

"That was close," she whispered, and then remembered no one was there to agree. A sinking feeling formed in her stomach as she realized just how alone she really was. The boys might as well have been in Timbuktu for all the help they could give her. Neevya was passed out, something was creeping around just a short distance away, and the crystal, her only shot at defeating the shadow-wolf, was with Ethan. How much worse could it get? Answering her own question, Skye quickly glanced inside the sling. Neevya's chest rose and fell with shallow breaths.

At least Neevya's still alive.

As Skye watched from behind the stream bank's edge, Scaretaker crept from tree to tree, his nose twitching as if he were trying to sniff her out like a hunting dog.

It's a good thing I'm covered in mud, Skye thought. *It might mask my scent just enough for him to miss me.* She settled into the hollow, pressing her back to the muddy wall. An exposed tree root poked into her ribcage, but she barely noticed for fear of being discovered. Even though she knew the sleeping faerie couldn't hear her, Skye whispered, "Don't worry, I'll get us out of here."

Step by step, she slowly inched along the edge of the stream bed, away from Scaretaker.

Skye's trek down the stream bed was full of frights. In the dim light, she imagined the trees had eyes; their twisted branches reaching for her, trying to snag her in their cruel claws. Thunder crashed all around, making her heart pound as fast as a hummingbird flaps its wings. She now knew all too well what could be lurking inside a storm, and she *never* wanted to encounter that creature again.

Each bolt of lightning and clap of thunder made Skye flinch, bringing visions of claws, fangs, and piercing, red eyes. Her knees trembled and her teeth chattered, not from the cold, but from an overwhelming sense of dread. By the time she had reached a somewhat familiar spot, she was on the verge of a full-blown panic attack.

That's when she noticed something wonderful; a sight that made her heart leap. Olivia's words resounded in her mind. *Look for the glowing mushrooms.*

There, in the middle of the muddy stream bed, was a glowing mushroom with a rainbow of colors that swirled on its cap. Excitement flooded through Skye as she hurriedly dropped to her knees and crawled toward that small colorful miracle; her hands and knees sunk deep into the mud as Neevya dangled close to the ground. Glancing down, Skye realized just how careless she was being, and before she moved a single inch farther, she sat upright and pulled the sling tight, eliminating any chance of Neevya falling out. She made for the mushroom again.

Crawling was more difficult than Skye anticipated. The mud was as thick as icing, yet slippery, too. Crawling slowed her down, but she wouldn't dare walk through the muck for fear of slipping and smashing Neevya. Skye moved forward to see the mushroom more clearly, but the closer she got, the more she realized something wasn't quite right.

Surely it was a trick of the light; nothing else made sense. The more she tried to focus on the colorful cap and white stem, the more elusive the little mushroom became. It had a translucent quality, flickering in and out like a candle flame.

When she got within reaching distance, she chanced a glance over her shoulder to make sure no one was sneaking up on her, and tentatively stretched to touch it.

To Skye's amazement, her hand passed right through the tiny thing. *How strange.*

She crawled closer and bent down for a better look.

Its glow became brighter.

Skye reached for it again; this time she was able to caress its soft, velvety cap. Thrilled, she peered down at Neevya and enthusiastically whispered, "You're almost home!"

She imagined doing a victory dance while singing, "I found it! I found a glowing mushroom!" Oh, how she wished Noah and Ethan were here. She could practically see the excitement on their faces as she envisioned waving them over and saying, "Look how it shines! Isn't it beautiful?"

What would Ethan say? Probably something like, *It's chettin' brilliant!*

And Noah? How would he react? Skye concluded that Noah would probably try to look at the situation logically and say something like, "That's only one mushroom. We need to find a whole mess of them."

Skye considered this. "Noah's right." She glanced around. "Where are the others?"

It took a bit of time, and some clever maneuvering through the treacherous mud, but Skye managed to crawl to a spot that had a good vantage point. It wasn't too far from the mushroom she'd found, but it wasn't too terribly close either. If she squinted hard enough, she could barely make out its colorful cap.

Glowing Mushrooms

Still on all fours, Skye was overjoyed to see something flicker just a few yards away.

"Another one!" she exclaimed as she eagerly crawled to it. This one was bigger and brighter than the last.

Skye searched the area, and before she knew it, she soon found another, and two more in quick succession. Barely able to contain her enthusiasm, she made her way from mushroom to mushroom. Not only were they becoming larger and more solid, the mud was replaced by a soft carpet of thick, green grass.

Skye lost herself in joyful abandon as she traveled farther down the stream bed into a whole field of multi-colored mushrooms. Each one seemed to have its own inner light and a unique design of twists and twirls that decorated its cap. Some caps were round and bulbous, while others were pointy and uneven, like soft-serve ice cream. Skye was just about to bend down to admire a particularly beautiful specimen when she heard something that ripped her out of her musing and reminded her where she was, smack dab in the middle of The Dark Wood.

Snapping twigs announced the heavy footsteps of something approaching from behind. Judging from the sound, it was too late to do anything but ready herself for a fight. She might not last long, but she curled her fists, vowing to protect Neevya at all costs.

Hands suddenly grabbed her from behind.

She spun on the spot and smacked her attacker right across the cheek with the back of her hand, sending him reeling onto his back.

When she saw who it was, she hissed, "Ethan!"

"What'd you have to go and do a thing like that for?" he exclaimed, rubbing his jaw.

Judging by the pain in her hand, she figured Ethan's cheek must be on fire. "Serves you right! That'll teach you to sneak up on a girl, won't it? I thought you were Scaretaker." She massaged her stinging skin and then helped him to his feet.

Noah was right behind him, trying to suppress a laugh. "We lost

Scaretaker ages ago." He bent down to examine a glowing mushroom. "This is amazing! Have you found the portal yet?"

Skye beamed. "It's got to be around here somewhere. These little guys are everywhere." She reached for one and lost her balance, barely catching herself from falling flat on her belly and crushing Neevya.

Noah rushed to her side and steadied her. He eyed her appraisingly. "You look tired. Let me take her."

Skye thought that was his polite way of saying, *You almost smashed Neevya, you ham-fisted idiot! Now hand her over.*

She slipped the sling off and handed Neevya to Noah. He fixed it onto his chest, and they continued to search the area.

After only a moment, Skye saw a space that didn't look quite right. At first she thought she was getting a headache. She struggled to focus on the area between two trees. The more she tried, the more it seemed she was looking through a large bubble. Space seemed to protrude, and the forest on either side didn't quite match up in the middle. She stumbled toward it wordlessly, leaving the boys behind.

"Is that it?" Ethan asked as he joined her. He had a bright red handprint on his cheek.

"It has to be." Skye stared in wonder. Whichever way she looked at it, it didn't make sense. It was a mirage—an iridescent bubble that had no business being in the middle of the woods.

A tall and unnaturally thin figure suddenly approached from the other side, its body strangely distorted. "Someone's coming," she whispered.

The figure grew bigger and bigger as it approached, and Skye could tell it was human-like...well, almost. She squinted to get a better look. Its eyes were too close together and its body didn't seem to fit together comfortably.

Noah tugged on her elbow, encouraging her to move away, but she had no intention of moving. She wanted to see the other side. She wanted to see this being coming from Neevya's realm. It was Ethan who convinced her otherwise with two simple words.

"Skye. *Run!*"

Glowing Mushrooms

For a moment, Skye's legs wouldn't obey, but then she saw what the approaching figure actually was. It wasn't walking *through* the portal. It approached from behind what Skye *assumed* to be the portal, and its shape had become contorted, like an image seen through a clear glass ball. This wasn't some ethereal creature from another world.

It was Scaretaker.

Now alone, her friends already hiding, Skye ran for it.

"Bloomin' lass. I'll have ye! C'mere!" Scaretaker darted past the side of the bubble.

Ethan and Noah had made it to the stream bank and were concealed behind a thicket.

Scaretaker, consumed with capturing Skye, didn't notice them and was hot on her heels.

Skye thought about what would happen to Neevya should the faerie fall into his filthy, grubby hands, and made her decision. As much as it pained her to miss saying goodbye, making sure Neevya was safe trumped anything else. Skye knew what she had to do.

"Come and get me, old man," she shouted. "You couldn't catch me if my feet were tied together and you were in a car!"

She bolted away from her friends, away from Neevya, away from the would-be portal. Her lungs were on fire as she ran through the forest.

It was obvious that Scaretaker would catch her eventually. He was bigger, faster, and he knew the woods better than she did. But that didn't matter. All she had to do was lead him far away.

He grabbed one of her braids and yanked, bringing her to an abrupt stop. An involuntary yelp escaped her mouth and he quickly let go, pausing as if he didn't know what to do. Taking advantage of what she figured was his lack of wanting to hurt a girl, she bolted away and into a thick fog, figuring she could lose Scaretaker within its heavy mists.

Once inside the haze, Skye wondered if she'd made the wrong decision. She couldn't see much of anything, but that didn't keep her from running as fast as she possibly could. By the time she could see anything but a cloud of smoky vapors, she realized that by some miracle, she had made it all the way through the forest and had arrived near the northern meadows, just at the edge of The Dark Wood. She stepped past the threshold of the forest. How had she gotten this far? Had she taken a shortcut through a portal? Had she entered a different realm?

Shaking her head as if she could shake off her confusion, she fell to the ground and kissed the grass, exhausted and panting. She was safe, thankfully; she had lost that crazy old man and was out the forest, out of his reach, or so she thought.

To her surprise, Scaretaker approached.

Skye quickly stood and tried to think of how she might get out of this mess. What had worked in the past? Thinking about her first encounter with Scaretaker, Skye decided to take a brash approach, something to throw the old man off. Pressing her hand to her chest, Skye said, "Oh, I'm sorry. Were you looking for me? I didn't realize." She flicked her wrist in a dismissive gesture. "I guess I was too busy enjoying the country air."

Scaretaker snarled, and Skye ran away.

CHAPTER TWENTY-NINE

Ole Grum

Scaretaker couldn't believe he'd worked so hard to save such ungrateful children. Why couldn't he be coldhearted and just give the kids to the chondour? He chastised himself as he made his way back into the forest after chasing that pesky lass. Something about the woods felt different than it had earlier that night. What had those kids done? He started to search for the lads, but the shadow-wolf snuck out of the darkness and approached him. The wolf looked worn and tired.

Before he could stop himself, Scaretaker asked, "What happened t' ye? Cat got yer tongue?"

The shadow-wolf growled and communicated, *It's worse than we could have imagined.*

Scaretaker crossed his arms and eyed the wolf. "How so?"

The wolf walked closer. *The children, they possess the amulet of Merlyn.*

Scaretaker's heart leapt. "They what? Are ye certain?"

The shadow-wolf nodded and closed its eyes. Then it focused all its attention on Scaretaker and snarled. *Why else would I be here with you, instead of feasting on their tender flesh?*

Scaretaker eyed the wolf suspiciously. "So, ye nivver had any mind of lettin' the bairns live, eh?"

The shadow-wolf just stood there, watching the old man.

Scaretaker let his shoulders sag. "But, that amulet of Merlyn... why'd the younglings have to go and get into so much trouble? No clue what they're messin' with."

He locked eyes with the shadow-wolf once more. "Appears we gotta work together after all." He looked around and sighed. "But with the amulet defending 'em, there's nowt to do tonight. Back t' the lodge. We need a plan."

For the first time in known history, a member from the Order of Serptorian and a chondour walked together, side-by-side.

Noah couldn't believe how fast Skye had run. She dashed through the woods like a deer running for its life. Yet, as fast as she was, her speed would not be enough to escape Scaretaker, Noah was sure of that. Scaretaker was already gaining on her when Skye gave Noah the nod. It was a nod that said, "Take care of Neevya, I got this."

Maybe she was right. She just might buy them enough time to get to the portal and see Neevya through.

Noah didn't want to think of what might happen when Skye was caught, but she'd made her decision, and her fate was in her own hands now.

Noah followed Ethan back down the slope, one arm clutching Neevya to his chest. Ethan intercepted Noah at the bottom of the short slope and kept him from tripping over a mound that was almost completely covered in brilliant glowing mushrooms. Maybe it was a trick of the light—what light there was, anyway—but Noah swore he could see the swirling mushrooms growing before his very eyes.

The concentration of these flamboyant caps became more intense as they walked along the stream bed.

The light they produced made it easy to see the surrounding forest.

Ethan exclaimed, "Chettin' daisies!"

Ole Grum

Noah whirled around. "What?" But he didn't need to ask.

There, standing in front of Ethan, was a small creature that reminded him of the garden figurine that had fallen from Ethan's wall earlier that evening.

Was Noah seeing what he thought he was seeing? Was that a living and breathing gnome?

The squat fellow with a black hat, off-white shirt, brown trousers, and tan suspenders waddled up to Noah. "Well, are you just going to stand there like a petrified gnome, or are you going to hand over that faerie?"

Noah backed away.

The fellow stomped his foot on the carpet of lush grass. "Hoppin' hobgoblins, boy, I'm not gonna hurt you. Or her."

Noah caught a glance of Neevya's face. Black tendrils curled around her eyes and crept up her forehead.

"We don't have all night," the fellow said.

Ethan placed his hand on Noah's shoulder. "I'm not sure why I'm saying this, but I think we should trust him."

Noah threw Ethan a doubtful glance and then he gazed down at the chubby little fellow, who had a white beard, oversized feet, and big hands. "Are...are you a gnome?"

The fellow laced his thumbs into his suspenders and rocked back on his heels. "Well, if you must know, Grum's the name, Ole Grum to you; and yes, I *am* a gnome." He gestured to Noah's chest. "I just happen to be friends with that faerie you're carrying. My cousin got wind to me that she needed some help."

"Your cousin?" Ethan searched for another gnome.

Ole Grum nodded. "My cousin. He was lounging about your house this evening, serving as a garden statue. He said you had Neevya there, you did. Said she has the iron poisoning." He jabbed his thumb into his chest. "I'm here to tell you, as much as I hate to admit it, Neevya is my friend, and I'm here to help."

That was all Ole Grum had to say.

Noah knelt and gently lifted Neevya from the sling. He presented her to the gnome in his cupped palms.

Ole Grum winced at the sight of Neevya. "It's worse than I reckoned. This is gonna take a good amount of fixin' up." He closed his eyes and mumbled, "Thank Good Mother for the picking and the plant-dwellers for their participation." Then he looked around and plucked an armful of glowing mushrooms from the ground. He looked up at Ethan. "Well, don't just stand there, help me, boy. Grab ten more gnomestools."

"Gnomestools?" Ethan asked.

"The swirly caps. Like these." He dumped the gnomestools in a pile near Noah's outstretched hands, where Neevya rested, still as death.

Ethan plucked ten gnomestools from the ground as Ole Grum proceeded to pop off the glowing caps. He handed one to Ethan. "Here, peel off the outer skin."

Ethan tried to peel it off using his fingernails, but it didn't work. All he managed to do was make a mess of the cap, bruising it. He threw it to the ground, and picked another one. "How do you expect me to do that?"

Ole Grum popped off another cap from the pile and demonstrated. "You grab right under here, and then you yank, like this, you see?"

Ethan mimicked Grum's movements and the skin peeled right off.

Noah kept an eye on Neevya, and watched the gnome's progress.

When all the caps were peeled, the gnome looked around. "Now where did I put that silly thing?" He took off his hat and rummaged through it. "Ah, there it is." He withdrew a small bag and held it up to Ethan, saying, "Here, this is Neevya's pouch. Hold this."

Ethan took it and inspected it. "So this is what got her so upset."

Ole Grum searched inside his hat again. This time, he pulled out a large wooden bowl and set it on the ground. He looked up at Ethan. "Well, don't just sit there, grant me that pouch, boy."

Ethan handed it back to the gnome.

Ole Grum opened it and quickly plunged his hand inside. It seemed he struggled to grab whatever it was he was after, because he thrust his hand into the sides of the pouch several times. His arm disappeared up to his shoulder as he fished around. With one last thrust, he said, "Got ya." He pulled out a bright golden wisp with a grin.

"It's a super-sunbeam," Ole Grum explained. "Slippery little suckers, if you ask me."

Noah's mouth fell open.

Ole Grum placed the super-sunbeam in his wooden bowl as he chanted a few unrecognizable words. Then he picked up the gnomestool skins and added them to his concoction. Next, he reached inside the bowl and stirred the mixture with his oversized hands. When he was done, the mixture turned into a deep-red liquid, despite the bright glow of the gnomestool skins and the radiant sunbeam that had been added to it.

"Bring that faerie over here to me."

Noah held Neevya out to the gnome.

Ole Grum lifted the wooden bowl and poured the contents over Neevya, all the while saying, "You faeries can't even get yourselves killed properly, gotta draw it out and be all dramatic about it. If you aren't the darnedest and most swollen-headed lot, always wanting to be the center of attention with your wings-this and faerie-dust-that."

Noah thought it was odd how Ole Grum complained, but he didn't dare say a word. If the gnome could heal Neevya, he could say anything he wanted.

The red liquid covered her skin. Had Noah not known the concoction was her cure, he would have thought she was surely dead and bleeding everywhere.

"Blimey!" Ethan whispered. "Look!"

Noah saw it too. As the red liquid soaked into Neevya's skin, the black tendrils receded. Slowly but surely, they wriggled away like writhing snakes crawling along her skin, creeping back into the small wound on her leg. Her pale skin started to slowly gain some color and her wings fluttered weakly.

Neevya shuddered and Noah asked, "Is she okay?"

Ole Grum was still complaining under his breath. "Bloomin' kids don't know when to keep their mouths shut." Then he looked up at

Noah and bellowed, "Of course she's okay! Do you need to have your eyes checked?"

Noah glanced back down at Neevya. The black tendrils were almost completely gone, and her skin was now a pale yellow. It was not quite as yellow as it had been when he'd first met her, but it was definitely a huge improvement.

Neevya inhaled sharply as she stretched and pushed herself into a seated position. She blinked and looked around, as if she were trying to find her bearings. Her eyes were glassy when she looked at Noah, and then to Ethan, and finally to Ole Grum. She shook her head.

"Can I believe my eyes?"

"Believe it, fancy wings," Ole Grum huffed.

She looked back at Ethan and Noah. "You saved me."

"Oi! Have you got petals in your head? I'm the one who saved you, you ungrateful little…" Grum lapsed back into muttering under his breath.

Neevya looked at the gnome, and stepped up to him. He eyed her warily and went silent.

She wrapped her tiny arms around the gnome's chubby neck. "Oh *gratimas*, Grum! *Gratimas*! I didn't know you cared."

Ole Grum's cheeks went pink as he patted her back. "Well, I don't. Not really. But I can't have you going off and leaving the flowers in the lurch, now can I?"

Neevya squeezed him harder.

Noah thought he saw a flash of a smile on Ole Grum's lips, right before he pushed Neevya away. "Well, you look fit enough to me. I'd say it's well time we got you back home." He bent down and picked up her pouch.

Neevya didn't wait for him to hand it to her. She exclaimed with glee, "My pouch! Little acorn! Oh, how I've missed you." She took the pouch and snuggled it close to her chest. Then she peeked inside. "Just how I left you."

She slung it over one shoulder, avoiding her wings, and patted it. Then she craned her neck and said to the pouch, "That's right, little acorn. You've found your perfect home."

Neevya looked up at Ethan, and then to Noah. "Thank you. From the depths of my essence, thank you."

Ole Grum cleaned up his things, stuffing them into his hat. Then he offered Neevya his hand. "Shall we?"

She slipped her hand in his and they walked up to the same large bubble Skye had discovered earlier, but they didn't step into it.

Noah watched as Neevya tentatively reached out. Her fingertips met the surface of the portal, causing the shimmering bubble to ripple in the same way a drop of water strikes the surface of a puddle and sends rings to its very edges. Then, Neevya grabbed a translucent veil and pulled it to the side.

It was as if the very forest had been drawn back like a curtain, and Noah could see straight to the other side. He couldn't believe his eyes. He glanced at Ethan, who was clearly no less surprised. A bright light escaped the portal and washed over Noah. Warm and tingly, the light filled him with a sense of peace and wellbeing. He didn't even mind being temporarily blinded, nor did he mind the white spots in his vision that appeared afterward.

When his vision cleared, he was even more amazed. There he stood, near the entrance to a land that was like nothing he had ever seen, or even dared to imagine.

Wow.

Even though he hadn't stepped through the portal, he could see billowing trees that seemed to breathe in time together, swaying to a rhythm Noah couldn't hear. Bright, vivid colors infused everything; they were breathtaking, and Noah got the impression that they were alive.

The grass looks so much greener! And it's daytime over there!

The sky above the rich forest canopy shimmered in the sunlight that poured from glorious golden beams. Every exquisite flower seemed to emanate beauty more intense than anything Noah knew was possible. They glistened with sparkling dewdrops. The forest was swollen with life and brimming with vitality. Gnomestools spilled from the portal like a psychedelic waterfall, making a short flight of spongy mounds just large enough to allow Ole Grum to use as steps.

Noah slowly walked up to the gnomestools, but Neevya held up a hand, preventing him from coming any closer. That didn't keep the amazing, rich scents that drifted through the entrance from bombarding him. Thick floral perfumes mixed with churned soil should have made him recoil, but they blended together in perfect harmony, creating fragrances that were more lavish and alluring than either of their counterparts alone. He inhaled deeply, wanting to memorize that scent forever.

Large, winged insects the size of mice danced from flower to flower and filled the air with tuneful buzzing. They created an orchestra of harmonious vibrations that flowed into Noah's ears, filling him with instant joy. Gratitude filled his heart and tears welled in his eyes. It was the most beautiful thing he had ever experienced. He would remember this moment forever.

Noah looked down to grab the bottom of his t-shirt so he could dry his eyes, but he paused when Neevya pulled the veil back even further. On the other side of the portal, he would be standing in the middle of a stream. His immediate reaction was to jump to the side, but the water didn't come through the portal. He looked back along the ravine. The human side was still a muddy, empty stream bed. It looked cold, dull, and forlorn. Noah frowned. Now that he'd seen the faerie lands, how could he be happy in this gloomy and mundane world ever again?

"Can you believe this?" Ethan asked, his eyes huge. "This is amazing! And to think, this was here all along and we never knew."

"I wish you could join me." Neevya danced joyfully in the air. "Oh, wouldn't that be wonderful?"

Hearing her words sent an unexpected arrow of devastation straight into Noah's heart. Here he was, standing at the entrance of paradise with a faerie he'd come to love dearly, and he wasn't allowed to join her? "You mean we can't come inside?"

Neevya shook her head apologetically. "I'm so very sorry."

"Of course you can't enter. Humans are prohibited from entering

Faeyelwen. Everyone knows that, or at least they should." Ole Grum looked at Noah as if he were a numbskull. Then he waddled down the gnomestool steps and tugged on Noah's pant leg. "Might as well make yourself useful. A little help here? I need some assistance into that portal. River's too strong for my swimming."

Taken aback, Noah blinked. How was he supposed to help the squat gnome? *He* couldn't enter the portal.

Grum eyed him as if he thought Noah was daft. "You can toss me to the bank on the other side. Otherwise, I'll just get washed right out here again, and you don't want that. Trust me, I'm not pleasant company."

The prospect of hurling a gnome through the air was unexpectedly exciting, and Noah hoped he could do it without hurting the little fellow.

He bent down and reached for Ole Grum.

The gnome slapped his hands. "Careful, that tickles."

Noah tried again, lifting the gnome and placing him in his right hand. He held the fellow as if he were a football. "Are you ready?"

Ole Grum pointed to the bank. "Fire away."

Noah tossed the gnome into the portal, throwing him just far enough to make it to dry ground. Ole Grum rolled several times, picked himself up, dusted his clothes off, and looked back at Noah. Shaking his head, he waved. With that, he turned on his heels and waddled away.

Noah waved and turned to Neevya. "We really can't come in? Not even for a second?" Seeing her world, and coming so close to entering only to be denied was worse than being tortured by Grucker. All he wanted to do was step through for a minute, and it took all his willpower to keep from doing just that.

"As much as I hate to say this, we can't go in there. We need to go after Skye. She might be in real trouble by now." Ethan touched his arm. "The shadow-wolf is still out there. She has no protection. I'm the one with the necklace, remember?"

Noah's dread returned.

"No need to worry. The darkness is gone for now," Neevya assured them.

Ethan cocked his head to the side. "How do you know?"

"I've searched for it in my mind." Neevya's eyes reflected sorrow. "I wish you could join me, I really do. I would love for you to visit, but it's impossible. As Ole Grum said, it's forbidden."

Noah slumped and let Ethan pull him back, feeling unbearably sad. "I understand, I guess." He looked at Neevya, not even trying to hide his tears. "I'm really going to miss you."

Neevya's eyes flooded, and Ethan couldn't hold back his tears, either.

"You'll come back to visit, won't you, now that you're healed?" Ethan asked, unsure. "You can't just bloomin' disappear." He sniffed. "It's not fair."

"Don't you worry, young Ethan." Neevya brushed away his tears. "I'm sure we'll meet again."

Noah saw a flash of uncertainty cross Neevya's face, which was gone as quick as it had come. She fluttered toward Ethan and gave him a small peck on his forehead. Before Noah had time to realize it, she'd done the same to him. Then she reached into her pouch, grabbed something, slipped it into Noah's hand, and coaxed him to close his fingers tightly around it.

She whispered into his ear, "She likes you. Keep her safe. You're her new home now."

"She?" Noah felt the object and couldn't imagine it was anything alive. "What do I do with her…it?"

Neevya answered, "With any luck, she may be our way of finding each other again."

Noah clenched the small, round object in his palm. Fearful he might drop it, he didn't dare open his hand to take a look.

"You two better go. You must look after Skye. Make sure she's all right and give her my love." Neevya backed toward the portal. "I'm safe now; don't worry about me." She pressed her hand to her heart and bowed. "And thank you, my new friends. My love is with you always."

Without another word, Neevya flew into the air, pirouetted in a golden firework of faerie dust, and plunged through the open portal. The boys ran to the entrance and poked their heads inside. They watched as Neevya waved one last time and flew away.

The portal stayed open for a moment longer, but in that short time, Noah saw enough to fill entire volumes. Strange creatures, both small and large, walked between trees of such elaborate proportions it was hard to believe they existed at all. The grass that spread out along the ground moved in odd patterns, as if it were alive and breathing.

Ethan tapped his shoulder and pointed to a wall of brilliant pink flowers. Another faerie buzzed about its petals. Before Noah could get a better look at the new arrival, the veil closed like a sleeping eye, pushing them away.

I can't believe Neevya's gone.

Noah resisted the temptation to pass his hand into the shimmering veil.

"That was…" Noah muttered.

"I know."

"We should…"

"Get Skye," Ethan said.

"Yeah." Noah nodded.

The glow of surrounding gnomestools began to fade and flicker out as some disappeared completely.

As much as they knew they needed to leave, Ethan and Noah stood there for a few more moments. Then Ethan slipped the hood of his jacket over his head.

Noah did the same, zipping the object Neevya had given him safely away in his jacket's inner pocket. "Let's go."

CHAPTER THIRTY
A New Hope

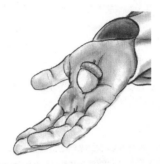

After only two hours of sleep, Noah's alarm blared and he awoke. Noah had arrived home in the wee hours of the morning and snuck into his house. When Madison greeted him with a wagging tail and a loving trill, he had tried to quietly explain to her that Neevya was safe and sound back in her home. But he didn't know if she understood him. Seeing that she'd recovered was the only thing that made Noah glad he hadn't crossed over into Neevya's realm and stayed awhile.

Stretching and yawning, he looked at Madison. "Go outside? Go potty?"

Madison darted off the bed and scratched at his bedroom door.

Noah crawled out from under his covers. His bare feet hit the cold wooden floor, causing his entire body to shiver. "Just a second, Madi. Gotta put these on." He reached into a laundry basket and picked up his favorite pair of thick, cozy socks.

Madison immediately went for the sock in his left hand and tugged.

"No, no, Babygirl. Not this time. I have to get ready for school." He chuckled.

She released the sock, her tail wagging.

Using his desk for balance, he stuffed his feet into the socks as the door flew open.

"I told you he's awake." Noah's father plowed through the doorway. He barely missed stepping on Madison.

"You've been up all night, you're acting irrationally," Mrs. Walters walked in behind him.

Trepidation rising within him, Noah slowly side-stepped and sat on the edge of his bed. Madison jumped into his lap. As much as he knew she needed to go outside, he also knew she wasn't about to leave him to face his father alone.

"You need to calm down." Noah's mother gripped her husband's elbow and pulled. "I'm sure there's a perfectly good explanation."

Mr. Walters grimaced and whirled around to face her. "What kind of excuse could he have for sneaking around and breaking promises?"

The mention of sneaking around almost sent Noah jumping out of his seat, but somehow, he kept himself in check. How could he possibly explain what had happened last night without revealing any secrets?

"Which is exactly why you should calm down and listen. He would never break his word without good reason." His mother stood strong and unwavering.

"Reason? A promise is a promise!" His dad crossed his arms. "Leave us. I need to speak with him, alone."

She stepped between him and Noah. "You've got another thing coming if you think I'm leaving you two alone. You're far too upset."

Noah sat there, dumbfounded.

Mr. Walters stamped his foot. "Of course I'm upset!" He lashed his arm through the air and sharply pointed at Noah. "He's got some explaining to do."

Noah recoiled at the look in his dad's eyes.

"Allen!" Mrs. Walters shouted. "Look at me!"

Noah's dad begrudgingly met her gaze.

She took a slow, steady breath and folded her arms across her chest. "We've discussed this before. He's a sensitive boy. You can't treat him like he's one of your men."

Noah looked up at her, thoughts whirling in his head. *Me? Sensitive? What does she mean by that?*

For the first time since they'd entered the room, it seemed something she said struck a chord with his father. His shoulders fell as he peered around her, studying Noah.

His dad sighed and let his head drop as he gripped her hands. "I'm sorry. You're right, I'll calm down. I promise. I just need to speak with him, man-to-man."

"Why? Why is it so important to speak with him alone?"

His dad closed his eyes and took several deep breaths. The room was quiet. Even Madison sat as still as a statue. Noah's mom peered over her shoulder and gave him a look that said she had Noah's back.

His dad opened his eyes and gently squeezed her hands, bringing her attention back to him. His voice was calm and tender when he said, "I would prefer to keep you with me, honey. But Noah might be tangled in a pretty big mess. There may be some confidential things we need to discuss; things that may involve my work. I need to be free to speak with him without worrying about disclosing national secrets to you."

"National secrets? You're out of the NSA. What're you mixed up in? What's Noah mixed up in?" She seemed as shocked as Noah felt. Was his father finally going to share classified information with *him*?

"That's what I'm trying to figure out. Now please, let me talk to our son in private."

She eyed him warily. "Promise you'll remain calm? Promise you won't do anything you'll regret."

"You have my word."

"Okay, but remember, you're setting an example for the man our son will grow to be."

His father smiled. "You're right." He looked at her thoughtfully. "You're always right."

She turned her attention to Noah and asked in Mandarin, "Will you be okay?"

He considered his options. On the one hand, Noah really wanted his mother to stay. On the other, this was his chance to learn some top secret information. His decision was made. "I'll be fine, Mom. Thanks."

"Back to calling me Mom, huh?" She asked, trying to lighten the mood.

Noah shrugged. He supposed he wasn't quite as British as he'd previously assumed. He'd have to work on it.

She gave his father's hands a squeeze, walked to the door, and called for Madison.

The mini-schnauzer looked to Noah, to his mom, and back to Noah. He nodded, signaling it was okay for her to leave. Madison hopped out of his lap and strolled away, glancing back only once before the door closed behind her.

Mr. Walters ran his fingers through his hair as he paced back and forth, his tension returning. Several mumbles, sighs, and huffs later, he wheeled Noah's computer chair around and took a seat. His jaw was set and stern as he scooted the chair in front of Noah.

"Before we get started, I want to apologize for barging in on you. It doesn't matter how upset I may be; I have no right to disrespect you."

Even though his words seemed calm, his father's crossed arms, furrowed brows, and set jaw revealed ripples of anger just below the surface.

Noah glanced down, not wanting to meet his eyes, unsure how to react.

His dad leaned forward. "Noah, look at me. I need to speak with you about something very important. I need your complete and undivided attention."

Noah tentatively met his gaze, worried his father could see right through him.

Mr. Walters placed his hand on Noah's knee. "Tell me, why did Mr. Solomon recognize you and Ethan at your school's assembly? And why did he say you'd been in that forest when you promised me you'd stay away from that terrible place?"

Noah let out a breath he hadn't realized he'd been holding. As much as he wanted to avoid this conversation, he was relieved he didn't have to explain sneaking out in the middle of the night.

He decided to tell his father the truth; well, mostly. Noah told him about a bully chasing them into the woods, getting lost, running into Mr. Solomon, and how scary it all was. The more he spoke, the more his father's expression softened.

"Seriously, Dad. I didn't mean to break my word. It was the only place we could go. He was going to kill us."

"But that forest is dangerous. You should have never gone in there."

"You don't understand. He would have pulverized us."

"I can teach you to deal with his kind; just don't go in that forest ever again."

"Will you teach me martial arts?"

"We'll talk about it. We have several options."

Noah looked up at him, hopeful. He imagined his expression matched the puppy-dog eyes Madison gave him to get what she wanted.

His father softly cupped Noah's cheek in his palm. "Why didn't you tell me you were being bullied? You know you can always come to me, right?"

"Really?" Noah hadn't known that, actually.

"Really. I'm here for you. I'll always be here for you, whenever you need me."

"But what about your job?"

His father looked him directly in his eyes. "My job means nothing to me compared to you. You're my priority. You hear me? You. Not my job. *You*."

Noah quickly looked down at the floor. He squeezed his eyes shut, fighting to stop the sudden rush of emotions that threatened to surface.

"Oh, my boy." His dad reached out and stroked the back of Noah's head. "I had no idea you were in trouble. You need to tell me things like that." His eyes were glossy. "If anything ever happened to you, I would never forgive myself. I love you so much."

Uncontrollable tears began to run down Noah's cheeks when he saw his father's eyes watering, not out of anger, but out of compassion. His dad gently gathered Noah in his arms.

Noah had never seen his father even come close to crying before; he didn't know what to say or how to react. All he knew was that he was unable to stop his tears from spilling onto his dad's strong shoulder. He cried for his dad, for breaking his promise, for all the missed opportunities to really connect with his father, and because he might never see Neevya or her realm ever again. He cried for the secrets he had to keep and because there was no going back. He was no longer a naïve young boy. He had crossed a threshold and had been changed, forever.

Returning to school just wasn't the same.

Noah managed to avoid the usual bullying from Grucker. He wasn't avoiding the great oaf on purpose; Noah simply drifted through the iron gate in a daze. He found himself inside the main building without being aware that he'd even walked that far. His mind, naturally, was elsewhere. Noah could still *see* that elsewhere—and feel it, smell it, and hear it as if it were right in front of him, coaxing him to pull back the veil and step through the portal.

He looked around the bleak classroom, but found it difficult to pay attention to anything the teacher said and was sucked right back into his spiraling thoughts.

He recalled how Skye had waited for them near Ethan's backyard after escaping Scaretaker. Noah could just imagine what was going through her mind as she waited, not knowing when or *if* they would return. When she saw them approaching, she leapt to her feet and didn't even wait for them to dismount their bikes before squeezing them in a smothering hug.

They told her about Ole Grum, about Neevya's recovery, and about how beautiful her realm was. The look of monumental disappointment that filled Skye's eyes was etched into Noah's memory. She realized he was watching her and tried to hide it, forcing a smile and acting as if everything was okay, but Noah knew better. When they asked about how she had escaped Scaretaker, she overenthusiastically wove a grand tale of luring him into a possible portal and ending up in a field. Then she used her keen wit to slip away.

Noah knew Skye was sad at missing out on seeing Neevya off, even though she assured him she wasn't. She said it was better that Neevya got home safely rather than wait on her for a silly goodbye. Despite her upbeat facade, Noah wished he could do something to make it up to her. Somehow, they had to go back to the portal. The problem was, what would they do when they got there? For all he knew, it was closed forever.

At lunch, Noah met up with Ethan in their regular spot near the wall behind the football pitch. Some of the older kids liked to go there to snog, which was kinda gross when you were trying to eat; but it was quiet today, partially because Skye was nowhere to be seen.

"We're going back. You know that, don't you? We're not chettin' sitting 'round here doing nothin' when we know—*we know*—there's a faerie kingdom just down the chettin' road." Ethan was getting agitated. Crumbs from his lunch sprayed from his mouth as he paraded around, stuffing his face with a sandwich and talking almost without stopping to breathe.

"Keep it down, will you?" Noah checked to see if anyone had heard. "You can't just go around saying stuff like that. We need to keep it quiet."

"As if anyone is going to believe us. Think about it. *I'm* not entirely sure it was real, and I was there. I woke up three times last night and had to remind meself that it actually happened." Ethan frowned and drew closer to Noah. He spoke insistently, "It *was* real, wasn't it? We saw Neevya's realm, didn't we?"

Ethan was not alone in his doubts. Much to his annoyance, Noah's rational mind was already trying to convince him that everything he'd seen could be explained by theories, scientific equations, or at least a good psychologist. He had to keep reminding himself of the bright blue sky, the dew-covered flowers, and the colorful insects.

"Yes. Yes, it happened. We met a faerie. We saw another world through a portal..." Noah trailed off. There wasn't much more to say than that. They had been witness to something no human had seen in hundreds or even thousands of years. Noah struggled to put into words the sense of awe that had gripped him from the minute the portal opened. He knew Ethan was feeling the same—wonder, amazement, and above all, privilege.

Something else preyed on Noah's mind, and it came up to bite him like a feeding goldfish, nibbling at him. "How do you think Skye's holding up?"

Ethan shrugged. "I haven't seen her around. Did she turn up today?"

Noah shook his head. "Don't think so. Haven't even got a text. We should go to her house after school to check on her."

Ethan eyed him mischievously. "Do you have the *thing* with you?"

Noah nodded as he patted the front pocket of his shirt.

"Why wait until school is out? We should go now." Ethan tossed the crust of his mangled sandwich over the boundary wall and swung his bag onto his shoulder.

"In the middle of the day? I'm not sure that's very smart."

"You don't have to be chettin' clever when you're this good-looking." Ethan flashed a cheesy grin.

Ethan didn't have to necessarily make sense to be right.

Skye twirled, gyrated, and twisted to the music's beats. She always felt best when dancing; it took her to a place of inspiration and focus. She had spent half an hour sorting out the perfect playlist—a bit of hip hop, reggae, classic rock, pop. She had to have some good tunes—the right tunes—if she wanted to dance. Sometimes she would put on some of her dad's old nineties' music and crank it up.

The songs had her utterly enthralled. It felt wonderful to let them sweep her into a flow of movement. She got lost in the melodies and beats, transported along crescendos and falling through break-beats. At times like this, she wasn't Skye anymore. She was *a dancer*. And how the dancer moved! Pure energy and grace; bold expression and furious motion; subtle, then funky; serene, and then jarring.

She caught a glimpse of herself in her mirror; she looked good and she knew it. Ever since she was a young girl, Skye knew she was capable of more than others gave her credit for. For as long as she could remember, her one ambition was to become a professional dancer, despite the odds. She had dreams of one day going on a national televised talent show. Then the world would embrace her.

Except, that wasn't enough anymore. There was something else now.

Skye jumped into the air, plopped onto her bed, and used her foot to hit the mute button on the remote.

Dreams of fame and fortune seemed remote and ridiculous now, knowing magic was real. And then of course there was Neevya's homeland, which she swore to see, even if it was the last thing she ever did.

Skye told herself she regretted nothing. She had done something noble—and it wasn't as if she'd gotten into any real trouble. When Scaretaker had caught up to her in the meadow, it was almost as if he didn't know what to do with her, like she was more trouble than she was worth. Which was probably true. As good as she felt about herself for doing the honorable thing, it still left her feeling empty inside. She'd been so close to seeing Neevya's realm, and yet it had been denied to her. She couldn't face seeing Noah and Ethan just yet, not because she wasn't happy for them, but because the one thing she hated more than anything was people feeling sorry for her. That's why she stayed away from school today, feigning an illness. She'd sold it so well that she'd convinced her mother to get Mrs. Gladstone, their neighbor, to come 'round and check on her every couple of hours.

Skye crawled off her bed and decided it was time for lunch, even though she didn't feel like eating. As she absentmindedly prepared a bowl of cereal with chocolate milk—her go-to snack when she was sad—she recalled something the boys said about Scaretaker.

Did he really know about Neevya? And what about the portal?

If he was as familiar with the woods as he claimed, he might be aware of all kinds of strange things sitting in the dried-up stream bed. Holes in the fabric of the universe leading to other realms would be hard to miss. That must have been why he was so keen on keeping them away. But something still wasn't adding up.

Skye's thoughts of the lost opportunity to see Neevya's realm were replaced with a new obsession—*just how much does Scaretaker know?*

Now *that* was a mystery that needed some investigating. Skye was reinvigorated. She busied herself forming a new plan of action as she munched on her cereal. It wouldn't be like before. This time, she would be prepared. A nighttime raid of his lodge, perhaps? Now that they knew how to drive the shadow-wolf away, it might not be so hard. She would do this right. She began making a mental list.

Hmm, what do I need? Olivia's necklace, garlic, wooden stakes, silver bullets—but where to get them? I'll also need rations, a torch, maybe a tent, hiking boots, and one of those big explorer's knives that can hack through weeds.

The doorbell rang, jolting Skye from her planning.

It was too early for Mrs. Gladstone to come over, although the old woman did have an annoying habit of popping in whenever she wanted. As she went to answer the door, she prepared herself to shoo away whoever it was through the letterbox, but when she saw two familiar silhouettes behind the frosted glass, she was unexpectedly overjoyed.

"Are you going to let us in, or do we have to huff and puff and blow the chettin' house down?" came Ethan's unmistakable voice. "Come on, Skye, get a move on. We're on the run, and the longer we're out here the more likely it is we'll get caught."

Skye opened the door and the boys rushed inside. She ushered them into the front room. "I know you didn't come here to see if I was okay. What's up?"

"You're going to bloomin' love this," Ethan said excitedly and pointed to Noah.

"Yeah, just wait to see what we have." Noah slipped something from his shirt pocket.

"What is it?" Skye asked.

Noah produced a small brown acorn. It sat in the middle of his upturned palm and didn't look all that important.

"Is that meant to impress me?" Skye had hoped for a bit more.

Taking it between his thumb and forefinger, Noah held it up to a thin stream of light that beamed through the window.

Now, Skye could see it wasn't just an ordinary acorn. It had a faint, unnatural glow. It was not the kind of glow that would light the darkness. It was as if the object had a shield of undulating, semi-transparent energies that swirled all around it. It reminded her of the bubbles she blew out of dish soap as a kid. It also reminded her of the bubble she'd found in the forest. Skye plucked it from Noah's palm. "Is this some sort of magical acorn?"

Ethan's grin was cheesy and triumphant. "You bet your sweet British bum it is, love!"

"Neevya gave it to me before she left." Noah's eyes were full of expectation and delight. "She said it might help us find her again."

"Find her?" Skye handed it back.

Noah shrugged. "Well, not in so many words, but I think that's what she meant."

Ethan stepped forward. "Just wait till you hear the news."

Skye eyed him distrustfully. "What news?"

Ethan bowed. "Noah, you do the honors."

Noah lifted the acorn as if it were hope itself. His voice carried authority when he announced, "Get your things, we're going to find Neevya."

Skye jumped and clapped her hands together like a giddy little girl. She could have kissed them both.

It was *exactly* what she'd been waiting to hear.

Acknowledgments

I would like to thank my family for offering unending support and encouragement throughout the creation of this book.

I would like to thank my amazing team at Winterwolf Press. Even though my book was dissected and required multiple rewrites, I am confident that all the changes we made were worth the countless hours of editing and revising.

Thanks to Arleen Barreiros—I couldn't have done it without you. You oversaw this project from start to finish; we laughed together, we cried together, and now we are rejoicing together. Thank you for joining me on this magical and inspirational journey.

Thanks to Wendy Scott—Your dedication and willingness to go the extra mile has meant the world to me. Thank you for always being there for me—even in the wee hours of the morning—and for offering comfort and words of inspiration.

Thanks to Teresa Kennedy, John Dixon, and Laura Jones—What an amazing editing team! Your attention to detail and willingness to stop at nothing to make my book the best it could be—even if it meant the possibility of hurting my feelings—has been invaluable. When I turned my book over to you, I knew it was in the right hands. My deepest gratitude.

Thanks to Miranda Spigener-Sapon—Your guidance and creativity never cease to amaze me. I am happy to have you on my team. Thanks for your dedication and hard work.

Thanks to Paul Huxley and Naomi Gibson—Your expertise in everything British helped me bring my story and my characters to life.

Last but not least—Thanks to all my friends who believe in me and have encouraged me along the way; you know who you are.

Laura C. Cantu is a multitalented artist, visionary, and humanitarian. Throughout her life, she has felt an overwhelming desire to explore the mysteries of the unknown and to expand her awareness and experiences. By allowing her perspective to shift and change, Laura has learned to unleash her imagination and use it to guide her through creative processes. She passionately follows her dreams and has achieved high levels of success in her various careers. As a professional dancer, Laura won six national titles and placed fourth in the Professional Argentine Tango World Championships. She also stretched her creative muscles as a visual artist with drawings that toured across the globe. Adding to her diverse accomplishments, Laura earned her master's degree in Oriental

Medicine in 2012, which has afforded her opportunities to assist many along their journeys to realizing wellness.

Despite her already jeweled career, there is another passion Laura delights in—the art of storytelling. Her first young adult fantasy novel, *Xandria Drake: Ancient Rising*, earned rave reviews and a Goodreads book of the month award. Currently working on The Vathylite Realms, Laura is harnessing and focusing her energies to craft engaging stories that are meant to bring joy, inspiration, and awareness to all who read them.

Laura is on a mission to live a life of inspiration, truth, and empowerment. With future books pending release, she continues to dance as a hobby, study energetics and wellness, and explore her imagination. Laura also enjoys drawing and creating 3D art and animations, hiking, meditation, playing guitar, and spending time with her family, friends, and pets.

Social Media handle: LauraCCantu
Website: www.LauraC.Cantu.com

Winterwolf Press

We hope you have enjoyed *Betwixters: Once Upon a Time* by Laura C. Cantu. Would you like to read more titles from our library?

CHECK OUT OTHER INSPIRING NOVELS FROM WINTERWOLF PRESS

What happens after we die? Join Christine and let your inner sleeper awaken with the gentle messages in this empowering novel. Written by Christine Contini

Have you ever wanted a magical sword that could summon dragon fire? Better yet, would you like to learn how to make that sword? Join a young apprentice as he learns about the magical world of blacksmithing.

www.winterwolfpress.com /Social Media Handle: WinterwolfPress

Made in the USA
Lexington, KY
21 June 2018